Glenda James was born in 1955 on a farm outside Swansea where she remained until 1960. She was educated in Mrs Hole's Mirador Crescent and Dumbarton Private Schools before gaining a place to Glanmor High School for Girls. She moved to Exeter, but returned to Cardiff with her husband who became a college lecturer in Gwent. She attended a number of courses on creative writing at the Extramural Dept of Cardiff University, and Coleg Glan Hafren for "A" level English in 1994. She has one son and two grandchildren.

Tracy.

with so many happy memories of your dad.

Glenda

Siblings
ENIGMA

Glenda James

Wild Cherry Press

For Bryan

Prologue

2006

At last I sat down in front of the fire, the sound of the spitting and crackling of the burning logs filling my ears. I love to watch the flames soaring up the long black cavern of the chimney breast, forming rainbows of different colours darting around like dragon's tongues as the logs begin to catch alight. I could now feel the warmth given off by them, while I sat there pensively gazing out through my large bay window which overlooks the garden. It was still snowing heavily outside, and the garden, which had only been tinged with white flakes when I lit the fire earlier in the day, was now covered in a thick blanket of snow. The branches of the tall fir trees surrounding the boundary of the cottage were now laden heavily with white fleecy tufts, clinging tightly to each other. This was the first time I had experienced snow since moving into the cottage. When I first purchased it, there was a large hole in the chimney breast, where its fireplace had once stood. Built in 1900 it was just the property I had always wanted because it reminded me of Aelybryn, another house I knew so well, in the distant past, also built in 1900 but situated some sixty miles away.

I threw another log on the fire and, as I did so, the old

grandfather clock, which had pride of place in my dining room, chimed three o'clock. Its loud booms resounded right through the property, despite the clock's cracked glass face, caused by a stone, which still left its ugly imprint. In front of me on the mantelpiece, were two photographs in brass frames. They were of two spinster sisters, long since passed away. Martha, on the left, was dressed in a self-made crochet V-neck jumper, no jewellery, her long dark curls falling around her shoulders. She had a wicked twinkle in her eyes as she gazed mischievously towards the camera in front of her. She had a round impish face which always seemed to wear a broad smile and, even now, almost looked as if she was laughing at me. Her facial expression reflected her happy-go-lucky character, although her deep blue eyes could not be detected in the now faded sepia photograph.

On the right was Mary. Her fine silk blouse was adorned with a long string of pearls and matching earrings. She managed to wear a half smile, showing her more serious character, with her long hair swept back from her face, giving her an air of sophistication. Her penetrating eyes of hazel brown were not distinguishable, as this photograph too, was now well faded.

I am surrounded by treasures from their home, which mean a great deal to me, bringing back all the happy memories I once shared with the people who lived there. Alongside the photographs were a row of brown, leather-bound books on the bookshelf. These were a complete set of the Works of Charles Dickens belonging to Martha. The old black fire grate and mantelpiece in front of me had been removed from the bedroom Mary and Martha once shared together when they were living. It is fifteen years since the house in which they both grew up and spent the whole of their lives was totally demolished. The old grates were removed and the one from their bedroom was eventually installed in the hole I had in the chimney breast. The fact that the house belonging to these two spinster ladies no longer existed didn't obliterate the memories I had of them.

As I sat down in front of the fire, on my most comfortable old Parker Knoll chair, there was a thud at the window and a bird flew straight at the glass, damaging itself and leaving a nasty splodge of blood. Suddenly my mind went back to Aelybryn. I could so easily remember everything that happened there, together with everything that was told to me many years before. I could still remember quite clearly opening that door, the key of which still hung on the small hook in front of me. It had opened the door to that room. His room. I vividly remember the horror of what I saw, and could still feel that awful rank, unhealthy odour attacking my nostrils as I crept slowly inside. Now, with my head resting on the wing of the chair and the warmth and glow of the fire, I closed my eyes.

Chapter 1

1889

William Thomas lived in a large semi-detached house in a small village on the outskirts of Swansea, a town in South Wales. His home was now shared with his only daughter Ellen since the death of his wife some years previously. Ellen helped him to run the family business which was a smallholding farther up the street at the top of the hill. There was a large shed housing some forty chickens, the eggs from which were sold with the milk which was delivered by horse and trap in well-polished milk churns. Alongside the chicken run were the two cowsheds and the stable, all of which were overlooked by a large dairy and food store. The smallholding comprised of eight cows, a horse, a pony and a dog.

William was a fairly wealthy man, by most standards in those days and was always very sociable. His posture was upright, but with a large stomach and very ruddy complexion. He always wore a smile despite his chagrin at losing his wife so young. He was always well dressed having his clothes handmade by the local tailor and doted on his only child Ellen. Her feelings for her father were reciprocated and she therefore arose very early every morning to prepare his breakfast before going up with him to the cowshed to milk the cows. Once this task was completed, she would help load up the trap ready for the first delivery of milk around the houses in the locality. Ellen was a very pretty girl, with dark eyes and long black hair inherited from her mother. She was tall and slim and obviously admired by all the lads in the village, but she only had eyes for Jacob James who also lived in the same street. Jacob became a market gardener and no one was more delighted than her father when, in 1891, they married and all three lived together in the Thomas household. Their first child was a girl, born in February 1894 and she was named Mary after Ellen's mother. When Mary was two years old, she found she was expecting her second child. They decided they would employ a girl from the village to help Ellen during the last months of pregnancy.

"A maid will be very useful until I can return to doing my usual housework and help you in the dairy," she told Jacob. "Also she will be able to look after Mary for me, as although she is such a good little girl, she is now into everything and needs so much more attention."

One evening, Mary had taken some time to settle, but eventually Ellen was able to send her off to sleep. She crept downstairs quietly to help Daisy the new maid with the last of the washing-up now they had all finished eating supper. As she did so, a sharp pain took her breath away. Perhaps the labour is starting, she thought to herself, although she was only eight months pregnant. Sometimes she felt she had twins inside that large bump of hers: it had been such a heavy weight to carry around this past week. Pain as strong as this was certainly sooner than she had anticipated, but as she didn't want to send for Dr Gilbert before time, she continued to help Daisy with the drying of the dishes. "Hopefully this birth will be slightly easier than when Mary was born," she told Daisy, "and less painful too." Anyway she felt it would all be worth it because she had so wanted to have another baby. Being an only child and doted upon by her father, she had always wished she had a brother or sister, especially after the death of her mother. She had longed to have someone with whom she could share her grief. Somehow it was different for her father. Mothers were very special and she had been so close to hers, but then she had died suddenly and left her. Nothing was ever the same again until she had married Jacob. Now of course he was the love of her life. She still adored her father of course but he was always so busy, and when her mother died he spent more and more time working, trying to do her duties as well as his own. When he and Ellen delivered the milk together, after the funeral, he spent more time talking to the customers about his loss, but she felt she had no one in whom she could confide. She would wait in the trap all alone while her father talked and talked endlessly to his customers. From that time, she was determined that Mary would never be an only child if she could possibly help it. Suddenly there was another sharp pain in her stomach.

"Are you alright, Ellen?" Daisy asked her, looking at her mistress somewhat anxiously.

"Yes, don't worry, just a sharp twinge in my side. I think this baby wants me to know it's time I sat down. I seem to have had a busier day today, even more than usual."

When Jacob came into the house, he noticed Ellen holding her stomach.

"Are you in pain, Ellen?" he asked, but before she could answer, she let out a loud groan.

"Jacob, you'd better go and fetch Dr Gilbert. I feel the baby is coming."

He harnessed the horse and galloped off to the village.

They were back as soon as they could, but by this time Ellen was on the bed upstairs in much greater pain. Daisy was desperately trying to comfort her using a cold cloth to mop the beads of perspiration which covered her forehead. The labour had started and continued to be long and agonising, even more painful than when she had Mary. Dawn came and still Ellen continued to be in labour. Her face now looked as white as the pillow on which her head tossed and turned.

"She is going to be alright, isn't she, Doctor?" Jacob asked anxiously, seeing Ellen looking so deathly white. He hated to watch her writhe with the pain. "Whatever's the problem?"

"It's difficult to say, Jacob. You go downstairs and rest for a while. I'll call you as soon as there is any change."

Jacob left the room as instructed and returned downstairs while Daisy and the doctor remained with Ellen. Soon Mary would be awake. She was the only one who had managed to sleep through the night, unaware of what was going on in the room across the landing.

When dawn came, Ellen gave birth to a strong healthy baby boy. However she looked so old and tired, as if she was fading away. Dr Gilbert was very anxious about the afterbirth; he sent Daisy downstairs to fetch Jacob, who was looking after Mary. Daisy took over from Jacob who immediately went upstairs to Ellen's bedside. He put his arms around her, but her body seemed to be limp and her colour was draining from her already ashen face.

"You'll be soon alright," he whispered, stroking her hair trying to console her and desperately attempting to reassure her while trying not to show her that he was distraught with worry. She looked so ill. She almost looked as if she was dying. She began haemorrhaging heavily, and the room now had an unhealthy smell about it, that of blood and antiseptic. The snow-white sheets on the bed were now crimson.

"I can't do anymore for her," Dr Gilbert whispered sadly. "I can't stem the bleeding."

"But you must," Jacob told him. "You must be able to do something."

But she was slipping away, scarcely breathing, and her voice barely audible. "I love you so much, Jacob. Look after our son," she whispered to him weakly. "Call him John and, and," but her voice trailed away, " tell, tell Mary I…" but her head fell to one side.

With his arms still around her and John lying in the crook of her arm, she closed her eyes and was gone.

Jacob could not believe it. He went downstairs to tell her father the dreadful news. Both were stricken with grief and shock. Daisy witnessed two grown men sobbing pitifully, with their heads in their hands, while she tried to distract little Mary, who was unaware of the tragedy that had taken place. It was a sight Daisy would remember for the rest of her days.

The funeral was a very sad day. Ellen was too young to die and leave two little children motherless. The chapel, where they worshipped as a family on Sundays, was full; some people had to stand outside. There were many milk round customers, neighbours and friends gathered together. Jacob walked slowly behind the coffin on which were displayed bunches of flowers from their garden. The tears streamed down his face while little Mary held his hand very tightly. She had no idea why all these people were gathered together and why she was forbidden even to speak. Daisy carried their new baby in her arms, alongside Jacob. William followed behind, heartbroken, tears dropping on to his cheeks, which he mopped up continually with his handkerchief.

Ellen was laid to rest in the corner of the cemetery behind the chapel, under a weeping willow tree, where her mother had been laid to rest years before. Jacob wondered how they could possibly carry on without her, having a newly born baby. But he had to face the future somehow; there was little choice.

"After the funeral I will be able to move into the house if you wish," Daisy told Jacob. "It will be so much easier for me to look after the children and help run the home."

So Daisy moved into a small boxroom the following week, much to the relief of both Jacob and William.

Mary constantly asked for her mother in the days to follow but, as the weeks went by, she became used to her new routine. She was soon able to attend the church nursery school in the village, which she absolutely loved. She enjoyed the company of the other children, although she was quite a shy child. There had never been time for her to mix with other children before. However she adored playing with the great selection of toys and dolls at the nursery, pouring tea using the numerous sets of teapots and cups, and making little biscuits with cutters. She learned to dance around the room to music, although it took her a little while to participate happily in this activity.

When she came home from school, she loved assisting Daisy with the baby. In fact she was a great help, fetching and carrying items for her. Suddenly she had become much older than her years. She would rock John to sleep and nurse him when he cried.

Within three weeks of the funeral, William Thomas visited his solicitor and made a new will. The previous one had obviously left everything to his daughter Ellen. Now this had to be changed, leaving everything to Mary and John, her beloved children, when they attained the age of eighteen. In the meantime, their father Jacob could manage the business for them, until they were old enough to continue on their own.

William's health deteriorated very rapidly in the months to follow. Somehow he seemed to have lost the will to live and carry on. He omitted to take his medication regularly and became short-tempered with the children, although at times he seemed to adore them. Jacob had the feeling he sometimes resented John being alive when his treasured and beloved daughter Ellen was dead.

Within a year he had joined her. He was laid to rest in the same grave as his adored wife and their daughter, under the weeping willow tree, in the graveyard behind the chapel.

Chapter 2

Mary began to carry out some of the simple tasks around the smallholding, always wanting to be helpful. She loved to collect the eggs in a basket which was almost the same size as herself, but she struggled to ensure that none of the eggs she carried would break before she reached the house. She loved to feed the chickens, throwing them corn which she took out of a large sack in the food store. But Jacob found life very hard. He seemed to have little time to spend with his children, in order to give them any guidance, relying on Daisy to do everything. In fact he seldom found time to play with them during or at the end of his working day.

The following year he met the daughter of a neighbouring farmer, while visiting him to collect corn for the chickens. She offered to help him during the day and assist with his children in order for Daisy to have some long overdue time off.

Margaret was an intelligent, attractive young girl and thoroughly enjoyed working with Jacob and the children. She came in daily, working long hours, being careful not to undermine the authority of Daisy, or to upset her routine in any way. Jacob admired her sensitivity but was always so busy he paid Margaret little attention, allowing her to organise her own work, fully realising her capabilities. He certainly took little notice of her looks or what she wore despite the fact that she was obviously attracted to him, trying very hard to draw some sort of attention to herself. Despite the big age gap, she was drawn to him when he first visited their farm after Ellen had died but he continued to take little notice of her, in the special way she hoped he would as time went on. He was indeed very grateful to her for all that she was doing. Hadn't he told her so many times.

"Margaret, you're doing a great job with the children. They have become so fond of you, I really must give you an increase in your wages," he told her one morning.

"But they are delightful and so obedient. I prefer to be doing something useful and so worthwhile. Often working at home on our own farm, I am not appreciated as much, but naturally taken more for granted," she replied tactfully.

And so the months passed by until one afternoon, after Margaret had gone home, the children said something to their father which certainly made him stop and think.

"Why can't Margaret come to live with us like Daisy does?"

"Because her mother and father need her too, that's why."

Jacob still felt the loss of his beloved Ellen but the children certainly had a point. As time went on, he realized that really he should be thinking about finding himself another wife. Someone who could help him bring up his children. He realised too that they needed to have a mother again, seeing as they were still young. Margaret was a hard-working girl, and being a farmer's daughter, she certainly knew what it was to have little spare time for herself. Why hadn't he thought of it before? Margaret was the obvious choice. She adored his children and did so much with Mary and John while Daisy did the cooking and all the household chores. The children loved having Margaret's attention and she was able to help Mary with her reading and writing from school.

It was no surprise to everyone therefore, that when Mary was six and John was four, Jacob decided to ask Margaret Hopkins to marry him, despite her being ten years his junior. He knew she would make him a good wife and he had become very fond of her. He wasn't sure he was in love with her, not the love he had had for Ellen, but no doubt that would come, given time. In fact he had come to the conclusion he would find it almost impossible now to manage without her.

In 1901, he and Margaret married and she moved into the family home. The children were delighted and welcomed her with open arms. They were so happy to be a family once again.

During that year Jacob decided to build a house on some available ground adjoining the dairy and chicken shed. It was a reasonably sized plot; thus he was able to build the stone detached house which was to be known as Aelybryn. Margaret was from a fairly wealthy family. Her brother and his wife were childless but had been left a number of houses and a shop in a nearby village. Margaret was left money instead, so she was only too delighted when she was able to contribute to the cost of the home she was to share with Jacob.

Aelybryn was completed in 1901. It was the last house at the top of the hill and differed from all the other houses in the street, because it was the only detached property, built of dressed stones, and in its own grounds. A small iron gate led up to the big oak door, which had a large well-polished brass knocker and letterbox. It certainly looked a gentleman's property, although the gentleman living there was working very hard. The property was double fronted, with the parlour and sitting room windows overlooking the street. Upstairs there were five bedrooms and a washroom. The furniture in the house was mostly oak and handmade, some of which came from Margaret's family, while Jacob bought the remainder which was of excellent quality. The toilet and coalhouse were under glass cover outside the back entrance to the house. There was a kitchen at the rear which led out on to a large tiled area, where the children loved to play and watch Daisy do the washing with the dolly tub on Monday mornings. They were always fascinated to see the large mangle in use and would stand and watch her feed the wet sheets through one side, and by just turning the handle, suddenly they would come out as long thin flat planks of white cotton, water spilling from the mangle, completely wetting their shoes and socks. They thought this was great fun and would shriek with laughter.

From Aelybryn, Margaret and Jacob could now quite easily keep an eye on the cattle, horses and chickens and obviously it was far more convenient for milking the cows. Margaret loved her new home and in 1903 she was delighted to give birth to a bonny little girl whom they called Martha. Jacob had dreaded the actual birth as it brought back so many bad memories of the awful tragedy, which befell his first wife Ellen. It was not an easy birth, but Martha was safely delivered into the world, and Margaret coped well, despite all the pain. The new arrival was such a contented baby, who seldom cried and smiled whenever anyone came near. Mary absolutely adored her new sister, and although she was a bright child and loved doing her schoolwork, she wanted to spend all her spare time with Martha. John on the other hand enjoyed helping with the cows and the milking so paid little attention to the new arrival. When Martha was three Margaret found she was expecting her second child.

"I'm so pleased that Martha will now have company nearer her own age," Jacob told Margaret after the birth.

Daniel was born on November 5th, 1906 on Guy Fawkes

Night, amidst the crackling and smoke of bonfires, lighting up the surrounding fields. The two older children were unconcerned whether the new addition to their family was a boy or a girl. They were far more excited about burning an old suit belonging to their father, representing Guy Fawkes. They understood he had been a naughty man, and therefore had taken endless time stuffing him with the straw, which was used as bedding for the cows, delighting in watching his going up in flames. As Margaret cradled Daniel in her arms Jacob then realised how much he had grown to love her. She was a wonderful wife and had given him two more beautiful children. However Margaret had other thoughts going through her mind at that time. She couldn't help wondering whether being born on such a strange night could possibly influence Daniel's character in any way. She hoped not.

During the years that followed, the four children were brought up together, although there was an age gap between Jacob's children from his first wife. However now they had a loving and caring mother who treated them all as her own. The older children worked in the house and in the dairy after they returned home from school and Daisy continued to live with them helping Margaret with the younger children while continuing with her household duties.

Margaret soon became aware that Mary and John were far more placid than her younger two. Martha and Daniel were full of mischief, boisterous by nature, and certainly they seemed to be not quite as bright in school as John and Mary were. No doubt the younger ones were always far too busy talking and playing, instead of listening to what the teacher was telling them, and not the fact that they were any less intelligent. Mary loved to spend time reading and doing arithmetic, when she had finished her dairy chores. John was very interested in the growing of seeds and flowers and took a great interest in horticultural books but seldom expressed what he thought. As time went on, he became more introverted and Margaret worried that, having lost his mother at birth, he had missed out on the attention that a mother would normally give her newborn baby. Perhaps that had been missing in John's life, until she came along and married his father. She had done her best of course, but maybe that was not good enough. She had given birth to Martha, and then Daniel, as well as doing everything else when she could to help Jacob.

"I worry sometimes about John," she told him one day while in the dairy helping. "I never know what he is thinking"

"Ah, he no doubt follows his father in that respect," Jacob told her with a smile.

Yes, she thought, he was always a man of few words, and had he not told her he loved her until after Daniel was born, but she still worried about the fact that John had lost out. Mary had always been involved with the new babies and welcomed them, but girls tended to be more maternal anyway, enjoying playing "mother" to the new baby when it arrived. She wished John would confide in her a little more, and show his feelings. She was so pleased that he seemed close to Mary, and often she would watch them together.

"Come on, John, let's see what you've got in your hand."

"Leave me alone, Mary."

Then John would relent and show her. She would watch them laughing happily together. How good she was for him. Possibly having the same mother, they had a greater bond between them. John had been a very easy child to bring up compared with Daniel who was so demanding. He wanted all her attention and the attention of everyone else, which he usually succeeded in having. Martha was such a happy and contented child and mothered and spoiled her younger brother.

"When can I have a milk round of my own?" she repeatedly asked her father.

"All in good time, now don't pester me any more. Go and help your mother."

The time could not go quickly enough for her to knock on the doors of customers to deliver the milk and eggs and spend time chatting to them. She was a great chatterbox and had been from the day she could talk. When she was twelve years of age, Jacob relented and bought her a small two-quart can.

"Now you can knock on a few doors of the houses down the street and deliver them their milk."

"Oh, can I really go by myself, Dad?"

"Well, just a few houses to begin with."

The customers were greatly amused by their young new milk lady and gradually as the time went on she had more and more customers. Martha simply loved people and was always singing and laughing. She had also begun piano lessons since Mary was doing very well with her music, and it was obvious that Martha was going to be another one in the family who had a musical talent. Daniel was of course still a handful. Both his sisters doted on him and spoiled him, hence he got away with far too much. Being the youngest, even Margaret gave into him just to have some peace, when he had a tantrum, but he was nevertheless a happy-go-lucky lad who loved to be on the go and doing things, never wanting to sit still and do his homework. Margaret was obviously very busy with everything, and rather than argue with him or berate him, he was allowed to do as he pleased and had all his own way.

In the summer of 1914, the assassination took place of

Archduke Franz Ferdinand, heir to the Emperor of Austria-Hungary. This meant absolutely nothing to the likes of Jacob and his family at Aelybryn. But soon Germany gave Austria its full support and the treaty of 1839 guaranteed Belgium neutrality, so Germany delivered the last of its ultimata to Belgium. It demanded the use of its territory in operations against France, and threatened to treat the country as an enemy if she resisted. Once it was learned that France was at war with Germany, it seemed very likely that Great Britain would soon become involved. Every family in every household in the country was terrified. No one wanted a war.

"They achieve nothing, only heartache, worry, anxiety and deaths," Jacob told his family.

"Surely something can and will be done to avert a war?" Margaret responded.

But soon they were to learn that their worst fears had come true.

On Tuesday August 4th 1914 Britain, together with France and Russia, were at war with Germany and the First Great War began. Families were in turmoil because there were appeals in the newspapers for both men and boys to enlist, and posters were to be seen everywhere displaying the photograph of a naval officer wearing a large moustache pointing directly outwards. Underneath were the words "YOUR COUNTRY NEEDS YOU". Because of the nature of the business, John was expected to remain at home as he was needed there. Two famous posters of the war were recruiting appeals which were displayed on every possible free space. One was hoped to play on a father's pride, with the words "Daddy, what did YOU do in the Great War?" and the other was a picture of two women and a child looking through their window, watching soldiers passing by, on their way to war. The caption said "WOMEN OF BRITAIN SAY GO".

"Thank God we don't have the terrible worry that all other parents have throughout Europe, with their sons volunteering for the war," Jacob said to Margaret one evening.

"John has hammer toes and they wouldn't accept him anyway, but also we need him at home to help with the milk rounds and the cows," Margaret replied with a sense of relief. However that relief was very short-lived because within a few months John returned one morning after milking the cows and announced that he wanted to have a word with his mother and father. He had a very serious look on his face. Not that this was unusual for John.

"I know you will be upset by what I am about to tell you both, but I have decided to join the army. I am the only one left in the village my age and all my friends are fighting for their country. I don't want anyone pointing a finger at me and saying that I am a coward, being nice and cosy at home with you all, while their sons are in the war, fighting and risking their lives for us."

Margaret and Jacob looked at each other in disbelief. What could they say to him to dissuade him?

But John could see the expression on their faces and before they said anything more he looked at his father.

"My mind is made up, Dad. There are a few lads in the village who are under age for the war so I'm sure they will be glad of a job here to help you out while I am away."

"But, John, you don't have to go and we need you," Margaret begged, but nothing they said could persuade him to change his mind.

In 1915 John went to fight for his country and was immediately sent to France. His first few letters were that he was happy he was now doing something to help in the war, but the news was bad from the trenches. Christmas came followed by the New Year of 1916 and they had not had another letter from him.

"Martha, I'm so worried about John. He's so far away and I know in such great danger," her sister confided in her tearfully.

"Mary, you must try and not dwell on it, otherwise you'll make yourself ill. I too am worried about him, but I try and think of other things. What's the use of dwelling on things that are beyond our control? Making ourselves ill won't help John."

"Yes, I guess you're right, Martha. I wish I could be more like you."

"Now let's get on with our work. Everything will work out, and John will be safe and he'll come home, and then all the worry will have been unnecessary. I know it's hard, Mary, but you must try. Come on."

There had been no news now for months. Margaret and Jacob were very anxious indeed, but hid their anxiety from the children. Where was John? Had anything happened to him if he was in the trenches? But soon they were to find out. A letter arrived towards the end of May. Jacob opened it, filled with fear and trepidation, as there had been reports of so many bad injuries and many fatalities. Slowly, he read the letter aloud, although his voice was quivering.

Dear all,

I have been sent to the trenches and you have no idea just how terrible things are here. My feet are very bad. I guess it is because of the cold dampness and filth in the trenches with our feet having prolonged exposure to these dreadful conditions. A number of soldiers are in a worse state than us. We are the lucky ones; they have had some of their toes taken off, but I do hope that doesn't happen to me. Even my hammer toes are worth keeping!!! They are calling what we have Trench Foot, but there is now talk of us being issued with waterproof boots so that will help us all a great deal; hopefully they will prevent the skin on our feet from cracking and festering. Sometimes we have to go weeks wearing the same socks, and often wonder if they are completely stuck to our feet. I saw soldiers actually peeling them off and taking the skin off with them. You are physically sick with what you see here.

I think of you all every day hoping everything is O.K. with you all at home. There seems no end in sight.

My love to you all, and God bless,

John

Margaret was very upset after hearing the letter read out, but tried not to show Jacob how distressed she was. When they went to bed that night, they clung to each other, and she couldn't help but say her thoughts aloud.

"Poor John, I can't bear to think of him far away, suffering so much and in great danger." John was now one of her children too, and she felt for him as if he was her very own. She loved him dearly, and she knew what torment Jacob was going through, although he tried not to show her. She put her arms around him comfortingly, saying, "At least when he mentioned his hammer toes he still had a sense of humour, despite the dreadful time he's having in such horrific conditions." They held each other tightly, but sleep did not come easily to either of them.

After that letter, there was no more news again. Time seemed endless despite how busy they were at Aelybryn. In September 1916 Jacob heard soldiers were leaving for the attack at MORVAL and the Battle of the Somme began. There was no word from John. All they knew was that casualties were high. In the news during the first months of the war a

Count Zeppeline had been doing great experimental work on the largest and most successful Fleet airships carrying bombs. By this time they produced a "p" type able to carry a bomb load of 2,500 pounds and these new models produced heavy raids on London. Whole streets were being wiped out and the lives of whole families were lost. So far, their village in South Wales had not been hit. They were safe.

Christmas came and went. It was already 1917. The Thomas family tried to keep up their spirits, but sometimes they could not help but think the worst. They dreaded seeing the telegram boy on his bicycle coming along the street for fear of his coming to the top of the hill, stopping outside their house and propping up his bicycle against their wall. But at last the postman brought a long awaited letter. John had managed to write again.

"He's still alive, thank God," Jacob told them inspecting the writing on the envelope."

Then he opened it, hands shaking again. They all stood around him anxiously to hear what John had written.

The letter read:

Dear All,

This will only be a short letter to tell you that things here have become much worse than when I last wrote to you. We snatch sleep whenever we can, but at least I am sent to the rear lines to fetch rations. Rats infest the trenches and the black and brown ones gorge themselves on corpses until they are the size of cats. The stench is terrible from the rotting carcasses, and we all smell to high heaven. We go days without washing, and often our water bottles are empty so we get so terribly thirsty. Our tongues swell up till they are as big as our cows' tongues, but all we can say is that we are still alive. Snipers' bullets are killing soldiers every day. I have met a soldier from outside London called Rhys, a Welsh name. He comes with me to fetch the rations and we help each other whenever we can. Also last week a great lad from Norfolk came into our trench; a farmer's son who is filled with wit and he keeps our spirits up when we are feeling so low. He is very tall and well built as you can imagine and we talk together about the countryside, trying to take our minds off what is going on all around us. Comradeship is everything in the trenches. You would all like these lads I know and, when this lousy war is over, Rhys says he is going to come and visit us, and I hope to go to Norfolk one day to see Jack's farm. Do you know, Mary, they are both nearly 23, the same age as you.

Keep your fingers crossed for us and pray that we will come home safe when it's all over.

Take care of yourselves,

With much love to everyone and God bless you all,

John

During 1917 Martha begged her father to allow her to leave school and earn her own living. She was still desperate to have a milk round to do herself. Mary had already left and was doing the entire bookkeeping for the business as well as helping in the house, and had a small milk round of her own. She also helped Daisy with the cooking. Tom, the lad from the village who had helped them when John went to the war, had decided to go to fight for his country too, as soon as his age allowed. He had been reported missing, feared dead. The family were all devastated. He had been such a helpful and happy-go-lucky lad, and they had not replaced him after he left them to go to war. By the end of 1917, thousands of British soldiers had been killed or reported missing. A large number had been sent to the Gallipoli front to seize control of the Dardanelles with catastrophic results and enormous loss of lives. There was no news of John.

By September 1918, Jacob heard that the British had begun to use mustard gas. He already knew that the Germans had been using gas as a weapon since 1915, and that the British had tried using chlorine, but it was of no avail because it blew back in their faces. They were then supplied with newly issued gas masks as a result of their suffering from breathing difficulties. John's family dreaded to think what might be happening to their son. They prayed that God would somehow look after him, and bring him home safely.

Chapter 3

Daniel was now twelve. He was a great help to Jacob because it was a long walk to fetch the cows from the rented fields. Daniel was certainly old enough to do that before school in the morning and again in the evening after milking time. The fields were about a mile and a half away up the hill, past a park, which bordered on to the grounds of a large brick building, which had been the old asylum. The latter was quite a long way off the main road and overlooked almost the whole of the area down to the bay. Many of its patients had been inside there from the early days, never to come out again. Daniel so loved being out in the fresh air and walking the cows. He would often look across towards the hospital and think about those unfortunate people locked away inside, not being able to enjoy life and breathe in the fresh air, which he was able to do so freely.

On Sundays they all went to the local chapel to worship. They prayed for the safety of John and for all the other soldiers who were risking their lives for their country. The two sisters would then join their girlfriends to go for a walk after the service, while Daniel returned home to help feed the cows and walk them back to the fields. Some of the boys, who were too young to be called to war, would follow the girls for fun, and although Martha thought this was great, Mary did not appreciate the way the boys teased them, and ran after them, but Martha always managed to persuade her to go with her.

"Come on, Mary, don't be a spoilsport, come with us for a walk. It'll take your mind off the war." So off they would go together, leaving Daniel to return home to Aelybryn. He was not the least bit interested in girls anyway. Having two sisters was enough of a trial, despite the fact he was still completely spoiled by them. They seemed to fuss over him even more since John had gone away. Then, even worse was to come, when they brought their girlfriends back to Aelybryn for supper. They would all go in the parlour, and both Mary and Martha would take it in turns playing the piano while their friends sang. Daniel often got annoyed at the sound of these high-pitched voices of the girls trying to sing "It's a long way to Tipperary" and hearing them intermittently shrieking aloud with laughter. Margaret on the other hand found it was a light relief from the gloom of the news about the war, and she and Jacob always encouraged Martha to bring them all back to their home. They loved having them, filling their house with fun and frivolity during those dark days. At the end of the summer of 1918, there was news that the war could soon be over. But even so, whenever the telegram boy delivered a telegram on his bicycle, Margaret watched him from the bedroom window to see outside which house he propped his bike. The nearer he came, the more frightened she became. If their family didn't receive the dreaded telegram, someone else's did, and their hearts would go out to them, counting their blessings that, yet again, they had not been destroyed as a family with devastating news.

In November, there was an armistice between Germany and the Allies, and at last the postman brought a letter, the writing of which they immediately recognised – John's. When

Margaret opened it with Jacob, they cried for joy. The tears ran down their faces. "John is hoping to be home for Christmas," Margaret blurted through her tears.

"Yippee," shouted the children ecstatically, jumping up and down. Mary and Martha danced around the living room, dragging Daniel around with them. The whole village buzzed with relief and excitement. Was the war really coming to an end at long last? It seemed too good to be true.

On the eleventh hour of the eleventh day of the eleventh month 1918, the Great War ended. Britain had lost over 600,000 men. But their prayers had been answered. John was coming home. Neither Jacob nor Margaret could fully express their excitement at receiving a letter with John's handwriting, giving them news of his homecoming at long last. Jacob tore open the envelope, hands trembling with a mixture of relief and apprehension. It was all too much for him.

"Here, Margaret, you read it to us." So Margaret took the letter and began to read it aloud.

Dear all,

You will, I know, have heard the wonderful news about the ending of the war. I should be crossing from Calais to Dover at the end of this month. If all goes according to plan, I should be home approximately the first week of December. I cannot wait to see you all again. Make sure my bed is ready for me. I also want to let you know that Rhys, my comrade in the trenches about whom I told you, is coming home with me to Aelybryn. I told him there is plenty of room in our house for us both. He only heard last month that a bomb had dropped on his home outside London a while back and his family completely wiped out. His mother, father and sisters all gone. He had no one to go home to, so I said he could share my room, my sisters, and the rest of my family. I know you will get on with him although you will have to be patient with both of us. It has been pretty tough here for so long. I saw my dear friend Jack from Norfolk killed by a German gun, which almost blew his head off. It is something I shall never forget. We have seen so much human suffering here. You cannot possibly imagine exactly what we have been through together, but one day I hope to still go to Norfolk to visit Jack's family and tell them how much he meant to all of us trying to keep up our spirits when we all felt so low.

Rhys has breathing difficulties owing to the gas and, like myself, he too has nightmares. I know you will all understand and am certain you will be very tolerant and very patient with us both, giving him the warmest of welcome into our home.

Not long now before we will meet again. I can hardly wait.

My love to everyone.

John

The two sisters were so excited at the thought of seeing their brother again and that he was coming home at last. They were delighted too that he was bringing his friend and comrade home with him. It would bring some excitement into their lives after the anxiety they had all been through during the war years, and at least they were all about to sacrifice a little towards his rehabilitation, and happy to do so. But Daniel wasn't so sure.

"Before John went away I shared his room, so where will I sleep when this Rhys comes to live with us?" he asked his mother.

"Well, you can go into the little room where at present all the old books and cases, et cetera are kept. We'll have to get it all cleared out before they arrive," his mother told him.

"But you can't swing a cat in there, it's the rubbish room, and there is no space for a wardrobe like I have now. Where will I keep my clothes and stuff?" he complained.

His mother gave him a talking to, lecturing him on being selfish and not thinking of others.

"You were very lucky not to have been bombed out of your home and lost all your family like Rhys. Your brother is such a philanthropist, and you have a great deal to learn from him. Remember what they both have been through while you have been having all home comforts here."

Daniel said nothing, but did feel a sense of guilt. He was so looking forward to seeing his brother again and having him back home. He had missed his company so much. Having three women in the house had been a real trial, and he had longed for his brother to return home safely.

One evening just after they had all finished their supper, Daniel, Margaret and Jacob were up in the dairy while Martha and Mary helped Daisy to clear away the dirty dishes before she went off-duty. She had found it necessary to return home to live because her father was ailing and he could not be left alone during the nights.

Suddenly there was a loud banging on the front door.

"Who on earth is that, using our front door?" Martha shouted, because usually all callers used their side entrance.

"Mary, you go and see who it is." So off she went. When she unbolted the door and opened it, she couldn't believe her eyes. There, standing in front of her was her brother John. He wrapped his arms around her, lifted her off her feet, and hugged her tightly.

"Mary, who is it?" shouted Martha.

"Come and see for yourself," she called back.

Martha went to the front door and, like Mary, she could not believe who was standing in front of her. Was it really John, or someone who looked very much like him? He was unshaven and so much thinner than she had remembered. It seemed such a long time ago since he had gone to the war. As he stepped forward to put his arms around her and hug her, the girls saw the figure of another young man, standing behind him. He was taller than John and, if they were honest, more handsome. He too was unshaven and thin, but he did not speak. Their army overcoats hung loosely over their undernourished bodies, like snakes, ready to shed their outer skins and be rid of them.

"Rhys, meet Martha my younger sister, she's fifteen and the bubbly one. This is Mary. She's the same age as you, Rhys, and I know you will both get on really well."

John looked adoringly at his older sister, obviously his favourite. They both took the stranger's hand in turn, shaking it warmly.

"Why are we standing here in the doorway? Come on in," shouted Martha, jumping up and down with great excitement.

When the others returned from the dairy they heard a great deal of chatter going on in the living room. Obviously there was great jubilation when they saw who had arrived. Everybody was trying to talk at the same time, and before one question was answered, another was asked. John did all the talking while Rhys just listened and nodded his head in agreement with everything John was saying. The chatter went on late into the evening. After supper was over, Jacob stood up and tapped the table to get some attention.

"Come on, these boys must be absolutely exhausted. Up to your old bedroom, John, and take Rhys with you."

He caught around his older son, with tears in his eyes. "It's so grand to have you back safe and sound with us all again. Thought this day would never come."

"Jacob, we shall go up to bed too. You know we will have to

be up very early in the morning," said Margaret, seeing the tears in his eyes, and turning to the two new arrivals, said quickly, "You both will need time to get accustomed to normality again, after all you have been through. Have a really good rest and tomorrow, stay in bed as long as you like. There is no rush for you to both get up."

Soon John and Rhys were alone and in their warm comfortable beds.

"Oh, it's so good to be back home again. Are you still awake, Rhys?"

"Course I am. Can't believe I'm actually here."

"Aren't my sisters great. What do you think of your new family then?"

"John, I was so lucky to have found you in the trenches. No good ever comes out of wars I know, but I'm so grateful I was able to meet you. My whole life will now be changed. Your family are lovely and are so kind. I cannot begin to tell you how much I appreciate them giving me such a warm family welcome home. I'll never be able to repay you for asking me to come home with you when I got that dreadful news. You didn't even have to think about it, did you? You must have had such confidence in your family to know that they would have me."

"Don't talk nonsense. Try and have a good sleep, as we have all day tomorrow to talk, and the next day and the next; well, we now have all the time in the world to decide where we go from here, and what we are going to do."

But deep down John knew what he was going to do. He had had so much time to think in the trenches and his mind had been made up then. All he had to do was to explain to his mother and father his plan. How they would take it was another matter.

Unknown to his parents, John had met a girl, a few years

older than himself, from a neighbouring village, just before going to the war. He had fallen in love with her at first sight, and had written to her a few times during the time he was away. He thought about her a great deal while in the trenches and resolved that if he ever survived this terrible ordeal, he would see her again. Before that though, he was now determined to break away from the business of the dairy and his family. He had inherited money of his own from his grandfather, and now he was of age he could start a business in market gardening.

He was unsure what his father's reaction would be, but whatever it was, he was determined to carry out his plan. Once he progressed with the business, he would see if Jess was still free. If she was, then he would ask her to marry him. So much time had already gone, fighting for his country, but at what cost, and for what purpose in the end? Wars were no answer to anything, as his father had said, only human suffering. He and Rhys had witnessed so much of that.

Neither of his parents was happy in the beginning when John told them what he had in mind, but with the war behind him, John's plan came to fruition. He married Jess and set up a thriving business. They had three children, two girls and a boy, whom they both adored. John was a marvellous father, with Jess proving to be a dedicated, loving mother. They lived so very happily on the outskirts of the village, and were a very close-knit family. That remained until the end of their days. Jess died very suddenly of a heart attack devastating her family, but fortunately their father lived for many years afterwards.

They were both eventually laid to rest in the chapel graveyard near the weeping willow, together with the rest of the family.

Chapter 4

Daniel

After the war ended in 1918 and John had returned with his friend and comrade Rhys, Daniel had certainly not welcomed the idea of having to share his family with a stranger and, even worse, having to give up his bedroom. However as things worked out, it wasn't such a bad idea after all.

John had dropped a bombshell on his return, when he told them all, after being home only a few months, that he wanted the money he had inherited as a child, to start a business of his own. That was not all. He hoped to marry a girl he had met just before the war. His parents were very anxious and apprehensive about these decisions, but they realised there was little point in their objecting, as his mind was obviously made up. Also he was now a grown man and, although the war had obviously changed him, once his mind was made up to do something, he seldom reversed his decision.

As soon as they met Jess, they could all see why he had fallen for her, and especially that she was still free to marry him. She loved helping John in the greenhouses, both working hard together, while she also sold all the produce. They made a very happy and successful couple indeed and Daniel was so pleased for them that John had found true happiness and that their business thrived. Rhys too proved to be quite a useful chap to have around. He certainly had been in the right place at the right time, to come home with John. His breathing had improved tremendously once he was living at Aelybryn and he found he was so relaxed his nightmares grew less and less.

As soon as John left home, Daniel took his place and shared his original bedroom with Rhys. They worked very well together during the day and had plenty to talk about. Rhys had a great deal to learn though. Being a Londoner, he knew nothing of country life. Feeding the cattle was fairly easy, and cleaning out the cowsheds and stable was fine once his strength had been restored. This did not take long with all the nutritious food which the family cooked. But he now had to learn how to milk cows. He thought that was fairly easy until he tried. He tucked his head above the cow's udders, sitting on a three-legged stool and trying to do what Daniel told him. This proved to be no easy task. He was told to take a teat in each hand and gently squeeze and pull at the same time. In between his legs was a bucket, tightly held in place by his knees, which were pressed together firmly to hold it in the correct position. The cow kicked, not liking how it was being squeezed, sending the bucket into the air, with it ending up at the bottom of the cowshed like the clanging of a gong, and spilling the small amount of milk he had managed to obtain onto the cowshed floor.

"Come on, Rhys, try again. Meggy won't kick this time. You probably pinched her udder, and she didn't like it."

So Rhys persevered, and eventually it became easy, just like riding a bicycle.

Daniel soon found Rhys became a strong young man and was good at digging the garden and helping to plant the vegetables. In fact, he didn't waste any of his time, wanting to be as useful as he could. Obviously there was always plenty to do and he seemed happy and eager to learn. Jacob now did less and less. After the war was over, more houses were constructed in and around the village. Their business was expanding, but they had no more room in the cowsheds to accommodate more cows. Thus Jacob went in the horse and milk float, taking with him the brass churns to obtain extra milk from a farm near the coast. It was almost an hour away, so that seemed to occupy quite a chunk of his day. Daniel's mother Margaret, although she was only fifty-one, was not enjoying very good health of late. She had lost a great deal of weight these past six months and constantly complained of chest pains. The doctor saw her regularly, and the children worried about her listlessness whilst continuing to do what was necessary but with far more effort and far less enthusiasm.

Daniel worried that his mother now found everything such a great effort, even the least strenuous of chores. For a few years he had been continually asked to cover more and more for his mother, before school, and on his return. His two sisters continued to give him a great deal of attention, always covering for him when he failed to complete his father's instructions, for fear of his getting into trouble. One afternoon during his holiday from school, Daniel decided to make himself a bow and arrow. He often fancied himself as the Robin Hood of the village, and would ride around on the back of the old pony, pretending to rob the rich to pay the poor. Martha and Mary often smiled at the antics he would get up to, never correcting him when he did wrong. This particular day, he came into the kitchen and brought with him his newly made bow and arrow. "I could easily knock that jug off the hook on the dresser," he boasted to his sisters.

"Don't you dare try," Mary told him, but before she could

turn around, there was a loud crash, and one of the lustre jugs had smashed into pieces on the floor, like an uncompleted jigsaw puzzle. But this puzzle was never going to be put together again. "See, I told you I could hit the target," Daniel boasted yet again, and off he went laughing at his great achievement.

His mother heard the loud crash of china from upstairs, and asked what had been broken.

"Oh, I dropped an old dish," Martha told her, so that Daniel would not have to be punished by his father when he found out.

A few weeks later, when Mary was in the living room, Daniel came in again, but this time with a sling he had made and a small stone in his hand. He stood about ten feet away from the grandfather clock.

"If that was a dartboard, I could easily have a bull's eye. Watch me get that twelve." And before Mary could stop him, the stone hit the glass face of the clock, making a small hole and cracking the surrounding glass.

"Now you will be in trouble with Father," Mary warned him, but Daniel just laughed, walking away believing himself to be so clever, with having such a good shot. That evening when Jacob was winding the grandfather clock, he noticed the face was cracked and there was a small hole in the glass.

"Whatever has happened here?" he enquired crossly.

"Oh dear, yes, a big blackbird flew into the house while the door was open, and in trying to get out, flew against the clock face damaging its beak in the process, poor thing," explained Martha convincingly. It was never mentioned again, nor was it ever repaired.

When Daniel celebrated his fourteenth birthday, he also celebrated his leaving school. For some time he had brought the cows from the fields early morning and returned them again after they had been milked in the evening. This was the best part of his day. He loved going with the dog along the roads and lanes to the rented fields. No matter what the weather, he still enjoyed being with the cattle, out in the fresh air, talking to them as he drove them, whistling his favourite hymns and songs, and passing the time of day with all the other road users, waving to passers-by and stopping to talk to some of them.

It was during this time that he had noticed, when passing a field belonging to another farmer, a young girl sitting on the gate. She looked younger than him, with a very thin body, and long thin arms. She had long fair hair tied back with a ribbon and wore glasses. She didn't look very strong, certainly not like other farmers' daughters he knew. They were all bonny, with rosy cheeks and plump healthy bodies. But this girl always gave him a wave and a smile if she happened to be sitting on the gate when he passed by. She certainly wasn't pretty, but there just was something about her that attracted him, and he wanted to find out a little more about her. Did she actually live there? And why was she on the gate at that time of day?

Often when he passed the gate and she was not there, he realised that he felt somewhat disappointed not to see her. He decided that the next time she was there he would definitely stop by and speak to her.

A few weeks went past, and she was nowhere to be seen. Then one sunny Saturday morning when he was returning the cows mid morning he spotted her on the gate again. Now was his chance. He crossed the road and while the cows slowly walked on, he approached the gate.

"Lovely day it is today. I haven't seen you here for a while. Do you live on this farm?"

"Yes, it is a lovely day, and yes I do live on this farm, but I only work here. My home is in Carmarthen so if I only have a half day off, it's not worth going home. I go for a walk and sit on this gate watching the passers-by. Are these your cows? And why do you walk them back and fore all the time? I've seen you quite often, when I'm here on the gate."

"Well they are sort of my cows. We have a smallholding, my father and mother that is, three miles down the road. I've finished school so I am as good as in charge." He boasted, "My father said I could have his milk round now that I am at home all day. I have two older sisters, not married, also living at home and they too have milk rounds of their own. My brother fought in the war in the trenches in France. There he met a fellow comrade who had no family left to go home to, after the London bombings. He lives with us too. His name is Rhys and is quite a bit older than me, but we all get on very well with him fortunately."

"What's your name?" she asked

"Daniel," he replied. "What's yours?"

"Elizabeth, but everyone calls me Beth. When I was little, I was quite weak and poorly, couldn't go to school very often. Never in the mornings. Then my brother came to work on this farm as a labourer. He said the farmer and his wife were very kind and good to work for, so when they wanted someone to help with the five children, my brother asked if I could have the job when I left school, thinking the fresh air would be good for my health. Also he thought he could keep an eye on me if I lived here with him. If I found anything too much for me, he could give me a helping hand. I have been much better since I've been working here on the farm. The fresh air does suit me, but I don't have much time off. I only get to see my family once a month when I'm free for the whole day. My three sisters are in service too, but we don't always get the same day off. I do miss seeing them a great deal; in fact I sometimes become quite homesick, even though I have my brother near me."

She spoke with a strong Welsh accent and said all her family spoke through the medium of Welsh. None of Daniel's family could speak the language, but before he had time to tell her, she jumped off the gate and shouted, "I have to go. I'm late" and ran off. After that first meeting, Daniel always looked out for Beth, and she would run down to the gate near the roadside when she heard his whistle in the distance as he called his dog. Sometimes he didn't have much time to stop and chat, but one day he managed to call over to her.

"You must come and meet my two sisters one day. Have some tea with us when you have an afternoon off. Mornings are not any good because they are both on their milk rounds, but when you have an afternoon off, I know they would enjoy meeting you, and you'd enjoy their company. They make lovely Welsh cakes and they are great sisters."

"Are you sure they won't mind?"

"Of course I'm sure. I'll arrange it."

With that, she jumped off the gate as before and was soon running up the field towards the farmhouse, arriving there completely breathless, her heart pounding, and her cheeks very red and flushed.

Chapter 5

"Can I bring home a friend I've met, for a cup of tea one afternoon?" Daniel asked his sisters. "It's someone I met while walking the cows to the rented fields."

"Of course you can. I'll make some Welshcakes and Teisen Lap, and Mary will make your favourite, Barabrith, won't you, Mary?"

"Of course I will."

"Great. Then that's settled."

Daniel already knew what their reaction would be before asking. Fair play, they would do anything for him, even if it meant putting themselves out.

"I'll let you know which day later on in the week," Daniel told them gratefully.

His mother seemed to spend a great deal of time in bed these days with the doctor calling now regularly to visit her. But he was sure this was not a problem to invite Beth to meet her and the rest of the family.

"What exactly is wrong with Mother?" he asked the girls.

"Well, we aren't really sure, but you can still bring your friend to tea. It won't affect her as now she seldom comes down for supper anymore, she seems to be so weak these days."

But he was anxious about her. He only hoped it was nothing

life-threatening, but it was obviously very debilitating. She seemed to be getting worse not better, despite the doctor's regular visits and medication, which was very costly. However meeting Beth took his mind off the worries he had about his mother. He and Beth had so much to talk about and she was always eager to listen to what he had to say, unlike his sisters. They were always too busy to stop and chat now their mother needed extra care and looking after. However they always managed to talk to him over supper, to discuss the next day's plan of work.

When a few weeks later Daniel brought Beth to Aelybryn, Mary and Martha had not realised that it was a girl who was coming for a cup of tea, not a boy he had met while taking the cows to graze. But once they had met her they took to her immediately. She was such a polite young girl, and so grateful to the sisters for letting their brother bring her to meet them. She wasn't at all pretty like Jess, and the metal-rimmed glasses she wore didn't help, but she had such a warm smile, one could not help but take a liking to her. They loved to listen to her strong Welsh accent and she was very open and honest about her family which impressed both the sisters. It was obvious that they were fairly poor.

"We don't have the luxury of a washroom and our lavatory is at the bottom of our small backyard," she explained to Mary and Martha. "We live in the end cottage of a row of small ones, called the Rank, which only have two rooms upstairs and two rooms down. As children, all of us girls had to sleep top to tail, four in a bed, while my brother slept on the landing. We don't have hot water in the cottage, only a tap with cold water outside the back door, with no garden at all." She was obviously not ashamed to talk about her upbringing.

"My dad goes around the farms castrating horses, which

48

isn't very well paid, and my mother was in service in the big house up the road. Before she married my father, she had Uncle Ebenezer but he is really a very nice man and calls to see us quite often."

This was what Daniel liked about her, she was so open and honest, and he was sure they would soon become very good friends. He had never had anything much to do with girls, only his sisters, but somehow Beth seemed different, and needless to say, just as he thought, they soon became close, sharing and exchanging what happened to each of them during their working days, and talking about their families together. From that first meeting Beth spent all her half days with the sisters. They would take her off in the pony and trap, and all three would have such fun together, laughing and singing while they went to the bay. They gave her some of their clothes, which she could never have afforded to buy herself, and supplied her with handkerchiefs, soap, and lots of other gifts given to them by their generous customers.

It was less than a year after Beth had been invited to Daniel's home that he arrived at the farm of her employer on his bicycle. Up until then he had always avoided calling on her at her place of work for fear of her getting into trouble.

"You've a visitor, Beth," her employer called.

When she went to the door she realised something serious must have happened by the look of despair on his face.

"What is it, Daniel, what's wrong?"

"It's my mother. She died suddenly this morning. I've just finished my milk round and came to tell you as soon as I could."

How kind her employer was to suggest that she have the rest of the day off to go with him and be of some comfort to him. They walked hand in hand without saying anything to each other, while he pushed his bicycle alongside. Then

Daniel stopped for a moment.

"My sisters of course had to continue with their rounds despite their enormous grief. With a business, life has to carry on even with a death in the family," he told her.

"Don't worry, I'll help the maid to prepare a meal ready for supper tonight."

When the sisters returned from their rounds, tears filled their eyes when they saw Beth. Their father was obviously overwrought and kept taking his handkerchief out of his pocket to wipe his eyes which Beth found quite distressing.

The funeral was a great ordeal too. Beth had not been to one before, except when her baby sister died at childbirth and they had all gone to bury her in the graveyard. But then just her mother, father, sisters and the chapel minister were present and there was no service; only the minister prayed as the tiny coffin, which was carried by her father, was lowered into the earth. Somehow that did not seem anything as distressing as this. She had hated seeing her mother so sad, with tears in her eyes, but they all realised it would have been another mouth to feed, which they really could not afford. The thing she remembered most, which bothered her, was the fact the baby was in the earth, out in the cold and rain, all alone. Now that did not seem anything as distressing as this: seeing Daniel's father Jacob walking behind a much larger coffin, with Mary and Martha on either side of him holding on to his arm, was far worse.

Jacob was once again reminded of all those years ago when he had walked behind the coffin of Ellen, his devoted first wife, with little Mary only two years of age and not knowing what was going on. This time it was very different. It was not only his grief now, but also that of his children. Margaret had been such a hard-working, loving wife and such a devoted mother, even to the children from Ellen. She had never differentiated between them and had always shown them and given them the same amount of loving care. She had truly loved them all.

He witnessed the pain and grief on Mary's face, unlike all those years before, when she didn't understand what was happening. Margaret was the only mother she had remembered and loved. In fact they had seemed just like sisters to each other. Martha too loved her mother very deeply as it was the only kind of love the sisters had experienced. A mother's love is always very special, but especially so when neither of the sisters had experienced any other kind of love.

John and Daniel walked behind them, with Jess in between. Somehow the boys seemed to accept death more as a part of life's great tapestry. Death was a part of life, which could not be avoided whenever the time came; it was something that was out of one's control, could not be planned or avoided. But naturally they both were upset at losing such a kind and devoted mother. However they both had other women in their lives now, to love them and be loved in return. Mary and Martha only had each other. They vowed that day that they would never be separated from each other or leave one another, no matter what happened. They would remain together for the rest of their lives and would always look after each other.

"I mean it, Mary, I will never leave you."

"Nor I, you, Martha."

"Promise?"

"I promise."

Margaret was laid to rest next to his beloved Ellen in the chapel graveyard where they went each Sunday. They had both been such good wives to Jacob. They would all miss her so much.

After the funeral, Margaret's brother Harry called Daniel to have a quiet word with him.

"As you know, Daniel, your aunt and I have not been blessed with any children. Now my dear sister has gone I want you to know that after my days, my houses and the shop will be held in trust for you and Martha. Your Aunt Kate will look after them for her days of course. Then everything will come to you and Martha. I know John and Mary inherited from their own mother, so you and Martha will have my properties. Your Aunt Kate will have all our money to do whatever she pleases with of course, and she will ensure the properties are kept in good repair for you, if I die first."

Daniel longed to own something of his own and was quite excited about this financial prospect, but of course, his uncle and aunt would have to die before he could have his hands on anything. Suddenly his mother's words came flooding back to him, telling him off for his selfish thoughts when Rhys had come to live with them. How he had hated that idea at the time. But what a great help Rhys had proved to be when John had decided to leave home and start out on his own. Now he too longed for a wife and a place of his own.

The next few years flew by, and they were such happy years for Daniel. Beth had almost become one of his family, spending every possible moment with either him or his sisters. When eventually the time came for him to meet Beth's family for the first time, he drove there with the pony and trap. Neighbours from the whole row of cottages all came out and stared at him. They could not believe what they were seeing, such a smart handsome fellow calling on the end cottage where Beth's family lived, and paying so much attention to that once plain sickly child of theirs. They all spoke Welsh of course, so Daniel could not understand what they were saying to each other.

"Where does she get her smart clothes from?" one neighbour asked Beth's mother, in their native language.

"And the boy's not only good-looking, he has money too, we've heard," another remarked to her.

"That's not important, they are happy together. Anyway she is just his sweetheart," Beth's mother told them. "They are just courting at the moment."

When Daniel became twenty-one, everything was to change.

Chapter 6

Daniel had now grown into a tall, dark and very handsome young man. He, like his sister Martha, had a very happy disposition and seldom worried about anything. He was very popular with his customers to whom he delivered daily, and he always had time to have a chat while measuring out their milk which he then carefully tipped into their jugs. He was very polite, and always remembered to close their gate after he had left their house. This was quite important to many of his customers. So often the paperboys left them open, which certainly displeased them because dogs then often entered their gardens. Little wonder that some of his customers took a shine to him.

There was one man in particular who always enjoyed talking to Daniel. His name was Mr Griffiths, who, whenever he saw Daniel at the door, or heard his voice, would ask him all sorts of questions about his family, his interests, and exactly what he would do with his life if he had any choice in the matter.

"Well," replied Daniel, "I really would love to own my own farm. My uncle didn't have any children of his own so when he died he left my sister and I some properties and a shop. My aunt was cross that he had left the properties to us, preventing her from selling them, and having the money for herself, to share out to her family. She has refused to maintain them and keep them in good repair during her lifetime, so I can foresee they will become more of a liability than an asset to us. We cannot afford to renovate them from what we earn from my father, and both my sisters rely on a living from our business. We kept a maid for a number of years, while we were growing up, but now my sisters are at home, we no longer need her. Also my uncle brought home with him a soldier from the army after the war was over. He lives with us too because he lost all his family in the bombings in London, and more or less works for his keep. He has no family at all. So you see, having a place of my own is quite out of the question."

"Well, Daniel, if you ever want to borrow money to buy that farm, I'm your man. I certainly could help you out if you saw anything suitable. I am in the same position as your uncle; I do not have any children. The interest on your loan would be very reasonable and you could pay it back when you were on your feet, so to speak, and felt able to afford the repayments. You remember my offer, my boy."

He often thought about what Mr Griffiths had said but farms for sale were always so far away and cost far too much. They were either much too large in acreage, or a smallholding, similar to what they had.

It was just after Daniel's twenty-first birthday; he was reading the local newspaper one evening when his eye caught sight of an advertisement. A farm was going for auction in three weeks' time at a hotel in the town. It was situated about eight miles away in a small village and was about a mile off the main road. One hundred acres plus the buildings. When he went to bed that night, he mentioned it to Rhys.

"Well, better go and see your man in that big house. Find out how much he can lend you and how much you will be short. You will have to know before the auction how much you can afford to bid. What is the reserve on it?"

"I know you will laugh when I tell you. One thousand, six hundred guineas."

"Yes, you are mad even thinking about it. But, as I said, best you have a talk with that Mr Griffiths first."

With those words, Rhys turned over and fell fast asleep. But Daniel tossed and turned for a long time afterwards, wondering how he could get his hands on enough money to buy that farm. If there was a way of obtaining the money, he would definitely try and buy it. He also knew what he wanted to do next, as soon as he secured a business of his own.

The following week he called on Mr Griffiths one evening on his return from taking the cows to the rented fields.

"The first thing to do, Daniel, is to find out if you can raise any money yourself. I will come to the auction with you and see how the bidding goes. It will all depend on how many are interested in it and how much money they are prepared to spend, in order to purchase it. But first of all we need to visit the farm. We must have a good look around and see what the state of the outbuildings is, and whether there is decent living accommodation. If the farmhouse was a meeting place for worshipping in the last century, which is what is written in the advert, how much has anyone done to the building since then? It may not be habitable. I gather two elderly brothers are selling it. My guess is as good as yours. They may be living like recluses. But we'll see when we visit the farm. I will make an appointment to view it one afternoon this coming week."

"Oh, thank you, Mr Griffiths. I am indeed really grateful to you."

"It's my pleasure, my boy."

That night after supper, Daniel had to tell the family what was in his mind. It had been a great deal easier for John because he had actually been left cash when he was a baby and over the years it had amounted to a reasonable legacy. Jess had her own money too and so between them they could set up their business. But things were very different for him. He had only £20 in the bank: hard-earned savings and all the money he had been given over the years for Christmas from his customers, plus money given to him on his birthdays, which he had saved. Beth of course had no money at all. She didn't earn any money to put in a bank, and her parents could not help either, being fairly poor themselves. When Daniel explained about the farm and the auction, Mary was the first to speak. He could not believe what he was hearing when she announced that he could have everything she had saved.

"I don't need it and it's only lying idle in the bank doing no one any good."

"And you can have mine," piped up Martha. "We are never going to marry, are we, Mary? So we won't be needing it. You can have all of my savings too."

Jacob's eyes filled with tears.

"What wonderfully generous daughters I have. Your mother would be so proud of you if she could hear what you want to do to help your brother."

Daniel was quite overwhelmed by his sisters' generosity. Deep down, he felt a pang of guilt once again.

"It may not come to anything after all," he said quickly, "but I know I can borrow some money from Mr Griffiths, in Danycoed Road."

"Well, Daniel, I am nearing seventy now," said his father. "I cannot do what I used to do. If you go, I suggest that you take the cows with you. At least they will be a start. And you can also take Moira the dog as we shan't need her any more to fetch the cows. We can buy all the milk from Burry Green Farm instead of just the few gallons extra we purchase at present. Mr Jones will deliver it for us, I know. He'll be only too glad of the business. You girls can then just sell it directly to the customers. You can divide Daniel's milk round between you both. Without Daniel, you can't possibly manage the milking even with Rhys to help you. I am doing so much less now, but we can still manage the eggs and the chickens."

"Wait a minute, father, I haven't got the farm yet."

"No, but we have to make some tentative plans in case it all works out for you."

He wished Margaret was still alive to say what she thought about the idea. She had always been such a prudent woman; a person who had wise judgements and someone you could rely on for good advice.

Still, Daniel was of age now. He had to do what he thought best for himself, and the girls were behind him. Jacob had to realise that his last son wanted to be independent.

"Don't forget you are taking a great financial risk, it doesn't bear thinking about, but I will be able to help you with the legal costs and give you a small amount of money to get you on your feet. Then it will be up to you. You realise it will be a great millstone around your neck for a very long time, borrowing all that money, and it will be a very hard life indeed. Farming always is. And there are never any working hours. You'll have to work when the work needs you. Not that you have ever been afraid of work and long hours. I appreciate you have lived with this but on a much smaller scale," his father warned him. "I just hope you realise what you are letting yourself into and you'll be all on your own, remember."

He would be the first to admit that Daniel had always had his own way and a great deal of attention all his life. How would he now cope by himself?

The following week Mr Griffiths picked up Daniel as soon

as he had finished his rounds, and off they set in the horse and trap to view the farm. It had been raining during the night and there were dark clouds hanging low above them. They both hoped it would remain dry to have a good look around. Everything seemed far gloomier in the rain, especially viewing properties.

The farm was nestled in the centre of the small village which only had a few houses, a chapel and a public house. They entered the farm by a large dilapidated white gate which badly needed a coat of paint. They proceeded down the rough track, making the pony constantly stumble, owing to potholes in the ground, for about half a mile. Large purple foxgloves stood upright in the unkempt hedgerows. They then came across what looked like an old disused mineshaft. Leaving the pony and trap at the bottom, they began to climb to the top. There, in the distance, they could see some pink washed buildings covered with rusty corrugated sheets.

"That looks like the farm," shouted Daniel excitedly, running back down to the trap at the bottom. "Come on, Mr Griffiths."

They continued down the winding track for a further half a mile, passing a large pond where geese and ducks were swimming happily despite the fact that it looked quite an unhealthy colour of green. Next to the pond was a large heap of manure, the smell of which almost took their breath away. It was obvious then that some of its contents was spilling into the pond, but the ducks and geese were quite undisturbed by either the colour or the smell of their slimy green swimming area.

Eventually they approached the farmyard in front of the farmhouse, opposite which were quite a few outhouses. All were in a bad state of repair. Daniel glanced at Mr Griffiths who he noticed wore a look of disappointment on his face but made no comment. They knocked on the door of the house and two elderly, scruffy men opened it, unshaven and wearing badly torn trousers and dirty shirts.

"Good afternoon, gentlemen, I'm Mr Griffiths and this is Daniel James. We've come to the view your farm with the prospect of going to the auction to bid for it," Mr Griffiiths told them politely.

"Well, just a moment," said one, closing the door.

Daniel whispered to Mr Griffiths, "They do look scruffy; their clothes are only fit for the rag and bone man" when the door opened again and the two men stepped outside.

"We've just come back from fetching water from the well. We need it, see, for the house and for the animals we got left here. We sold off all our cows at the mart last week." The two men followed the farmers across a yard to the shed where some calves still remained. The shed badly needed cleaning out, and the straw beneath them was hardly visible being saturated with urine and mustard muck from the calves. The smell was not only disgusting but very daunting. There was also a strong smell of pigs. They noticed in the paddock adjoining the yard, two malnourished horses, standing near the gate, waiting in the hope of being given some kind of fodder as there was little grass left in the paddock for them.

When it began to rain, one of the men said to Daniel, "You two better come inside the house, it's raining bad, so we need to fetch some sacks to put over us." Daniel, followed by Mr Griffiths, did as instructed and returned to the house.

When inside, it smelled strongly of damp, and was very dark, due to the very small windows. It was untidy and unkempt. Dirty crockery waiting to be washed filled a large pan, together with other used pots and saucepans nearby on the floor.

"What a mess," commented Mr Griffiths, but soon the two

men returned. They wore sacks which were tied around their bodies with thick yellow cord. When they viewed the outbuildings, they found that they needed re-roofing as they were already letting in water. Everything around seemed to be overrun with weeds. There were some rusty implements lying around on the stoned area outside the barn, all of which were not a very encouraging sight for any prospective purchaser.

The farm extended down to a valley through which ran a stream and wet marshland covered with rushes. Beyond the stream was a wooded area, all part of the farm's hundred acres. A small area had been cleared of trees and a man was sawing the wood into logs with a handsaw, ready for use on the open fire in the farmhouse. Another man was loading the sawn logs into an old cart, which was drawn by an even older looking carthorse. Running alongside the river through the centre of the farm was the London and North Western Railway. A gate crossed the line to the other side where there were more woods and fields. A train passed by and the black coal-faced driver and fireman gave them a wave as it shunted past, grey smoke billowing from its engine. The four men eventually returned to the farmyard, to the outbuildings again, and there they saw some pigs, rolling happily in deep muck. There was a chicken run, where the chickens pecked away happily, and geese hissed loudly as they passed, showing their disapproval at anyone encroaching on their territory. The turkeys gobbled loudly, totally ignoring the men, almost unaware of their presence. From here, they followed the two brothers to view a large orchard containing many apple and pear trees.

"These have eating ones and cookers, and are all laden with fruit during the season," boasted one of the brothers.

Daniel felt Mr Griffiths nudge him with his elbow. "Thank you for giving us your time to show us around the farm," and shaking them both by the hand he and Daniel jumped into the trap and trotted back up the rough track towards the old gate and the main road.

"Well, what do you think, Mr Griffiths?" Daniel asked eagerly.

"If you want my honest opinion, lad," he replied, "best leave it where it is and keep a lookout for something with less repairs and better land. The orchard was the only asset. Anyway, where on earth would you start if you bought it?"

"At the beginning," replied Daniel. "That's where everything has to start."

"You mean you still want to go for it at the auction, despite the fact that you have seen what state it's in?"

"Yes. You see, Mr Griffiths, I've really set my heart on buying it and I know someone who will come with me and help me every step of the way. All I have to do is find enough money to buy it, if it goes for the one thousand six hundred guineas. I know I have enough money for the deposit in cash and for all the legal costs. Will you come with me to the auction next week and lend me the money?"

"Of course I will, lad."

So, that very day, Mr Griffiths gave his word to Daniel that he was prepared to help him with the money for the farm.

"I can see you've set your heart on it so I cannot disappoint you."

The deal was done, and they shook hands on it. Now it would be all down to who would be at the auction on the day, and how many were after it. That was in the lap of the gods. Daniel did not sleep well that night, so much was racing through his mind. He felt like a child again, excited and restless. He could hardly wait for the day of the auction to arrive, and to know what would be its outcome. Then, and only then, would he know exactly where his future lay.

Chapter 7

The auction for the farm took place the following week. Mr Griffiths called for Daniel after he had finished his rounds so that they could arrive at the hotel in the town by 3.00pm, in adequate time to settle down and find a good seat for the auction.

The small room was packed with people and the auctioneer was standing right in the front of the first row of chairs. He was a very large man with a red moustache, smartly dressed in a tweed jacket, with green corduroys. Daniel's heart sank, seeing so many people there, but Mr Griffiths reassured him that a number of the general public sometimes attend these auctions just out of curiosity, with no interest whatsoever in making a bid, let alone a purchase. However he did recognise two of the men, also dressed smartly, in obviously expensive suits. They were fairly wealthy landowners, which wasn't a particularly good sign for Daniel. He was completely overawed by the sight before him. He had heard his father try to bargain with farmers for cows, to buy them cheaper than the asking price, but this was a whole new experience for him. He was glad he had asked Mr Griffiths to come along with him. Not that Daniel lacked confidence; he didn't, in fact he had plenty of it, but this was a completely new venture and he was going into this totally inexperienced. It was the first time in his life he felt his stomach churning with apprehension. He did not feel totally in control, which was unusual for Daniel, but his whole future depended on what happened today, so he was nervous about it. He had never felt like this before in his life. He was so grateful to Mr Griffiths for accompanying him, to advise him and to give him moral support. There were two seats vacant in the centre of the room, so Mr Griffiths led Daniel to them, and they sat down quietly, Daniel giving another quick glance around him and trying to listen to the conversations around him.

The auctioneer began the bidding at nine hundred guineas.

A hand went up from a gentleman behind them.

"One thousand guineas?" the auctioneer shouted.

Daniel quickly nodded.

"One thousand, one hundred guineas?" raising the bidding by another one hundred guineas.

The same man raised his hand.

"One thousand, two hundred guineas?" pushed the auctioneer.

"To the gentleman here," and Daniel realised he was looking at one of the well-dressed landowners sitting in the front row.

Then the bid went to one thousand three hundred guineas. Mr Griffiths nudged Daniel but before he had a chance to raise his hand, the man in the front again shot his high into the air.

Daniel began to fidget in his chair, a feeling of uneasiness crept over him. This was his whole future at stake, and never before had he felt so nervous and apprehensive. Whatever was happening to himself? he wondered. Then he heard the voice of the auctioneer again, reverberating in his ears.

"Who'll give me one thousand, four hundred guineas?"

Mr Griffiths shot up his hand instantly, afraid of Daniel

being too slow.

Daniel wasn't sure what was happening, when Mr Griffiths entered the bidding.

"One thousand, five hundred guineas," shouted the auctioneer.

Again the man in the front lifted his hand quickly. He was obviously determined to buy it at all costs.

"Now who'll give me one thousand, six hundred guineas?" pushing the bid to the reserve.

There was a pause. No one moved. A deathly hush filled the room.

"Come on gentlemen, one thousand, six hundred guineas?"

Again, another pause, and again the auctioneer shouted, "One thousand, six hundred guineas, gentlemen? Who will give me one thousand, six hundred guineas for this farm?"

The room remained still and silent. You could hear a pin drop. Nobody seemed to move a muscle.

Mr Griffiths whispered to Daniel, "Go for it, my boy."

So Daniel shot his hand high into the air.

"One thousand, six hundred guineas I have bid. What about one thousand, seven hundred? Come on, gentlemen, this farm is one hundred acres, with good prospects."

There was silence once again.

"Are there any more bids, gentlemen?"

Again there was silence. Daniel's mouth felt dry, his stomach began to churn over again. Why did he feel like this? He knew he desperately wanted this farm, but another raised hand from one of the other bidders and it would be out of his reach once more.

"Well then it's going to go for one thousand, six hundred guineas. Going once, going twice, going three times."

With that, a loud bang was heard echoing around the room. It was the sound of the auctioneer's hammer crashing down on the bench in front of him.

"Sold to the young man in the centre of the room," pointing directly at Daniel. Was this really happening, or was he dreaming?

"It's yours, lad, it's yours," shouted Mr Griffiths excitedly, a smile beaming from one side of his now ruddy face to the other. Then putting both his arms around him he began to shake him vigorously with excitement.

"Up you go then, lad. Get out your wallet and give the auctioneer your cash deposit."

So Daniel strode up to the front with big steps, feeling all of his six feet four inches tall, hardly believing what had happened to him. Was he really now a landowner owning one hundred acres? Could it be possible that he had actually bought a farm, or would he soon wake up to reality? People began to shake his hand and congratulate him. As he neared the exit one of the gentlemen who had been bidding against him, turned towards him.

"It was never worth that sort of money, my boy. You'll never get your money back on it in a million years. You'll struggle all your life."

He probably wondered how a young man like Daniel could possibly have afforded the money to bid one thousand, six hundred guineas. Mr Griffiths caught Daniel's arm and led him towards the outer door and towards home.

"Take no notice, lad, he is just mad he couldn't afford it himself. Now all we have to do is get an agreement drawn up between us," he said with another big smile.

"So long as you pay me £3 every half year for the interest, I will be quite happy. When you feel able to, you can pay off some of the capital, but concentrate on ploughing your profit back into the farm, because I am in no hurry for the money. I don't need it."

As Daniel approached his home, he could see in the distance Mary and Martha on the road outside the house, waiting for him. They could not remain inside any longer, anxious for his return, and wanting to find out what had happened at the auction. Had he been lucky enough to purchase his dream? Or would he have lost the farm to someone who had a great deal more money?

When he spotted them in the distance, he raised his hand and waved, followed by the thumbs up sign as they came closer and closer. They ran to him as fast as their legs could carry them. They could see by his face it was the good news for which they had hoped and prayed.

"It's mine, it's mine," he shouted, lifting Martha off her feet, much to Mr Griffiths's surprise. His sisters were so overjoyed and happy for him. Of course, his father was delighted too when he heard the news, and so was Rhys.

"You were born under a very lucky star, Daniel. To find a man like Mr Griffiths who had the money and was prepared to lend it to you. Also to have such a generous family, to help and support you. Fancy having two sisters who were happy to give you all that they had in their savings, and lastly of course, to a good auctioneer."

Knowing he was born on Guy Fawkes Night, Daniel looked at Rhys with a big grin on his face.

"I certainly wasn't born under a damp squib. But now I must get back to work and on with the milking, I'm really late as it is. Come on, Rhys, give me a hand. When I take the cows to the fields, I want to call on Beth and tell her the wonderful news. I don't think she will believe what has happened to me today. I can't even believe it myself."

But that was not all he wanted to tell her. When he stopped off at Beth's she was bringing in the washing from the line in front of the farmhouse. Daniel arrived unexpectedly.

"Is everything alright, Daniel?"

"Of course, but I wanted to tell you my good news. Can you walk down to the gate with me? I won't keep you long. I have something I want to ask you."

"Really? Do hurry and tell me."

By the time they reached the gate, Daniel had told her all about seeing the farm in the newspaper and about the auction.

"Why ever didn't you tell me before that you were going?"

"I was afraid to say anything, as the chances were that I was building castles in the air. I really didn't think I would be lucky enough to be successful, but. Beth, I have bought a farm of my own. I want you to come with me. I want you to be my wife."

"What?"

"You heard what I said, Beth, I mean it. Will you marry me?" He caught around her.

Beth felt that although she loved him dearly, and had done so from the first time she had spoken to him on the gate, she could not possibly accept his proposal. They were from such different backgrounds. Daniel had always had everything he wanted and she always had so little. In fact, she had nothing to offer him at all.

"I know if you come to the farm with me, together we can and will make it work. It will be a struggle, but as you have never had a great deal, then you won't find it such a hardship. We will have to live on love, Beth, as that is all we will have between us for a while. Come on, say you'll marry me."

In 1930 Daniel married Beth the day before her twenty-first birthday. Daniel was just twenty-three. Beth felt she was daydreaming.

"I want you to have a day to remember when we get married," Daniel told her.

"But I have no money of my own. My parents can't give me a wedding or even help to pay for anything."

She knew it was usual for the bride's parents to pay but Daniel insisted he would settle all the expenses for it himself. This would be nothing in comparison with what he had paid out in order to buy the farm, albeit from money he had borrowed. But it would be his and Beth's one day. That was all he could think about. What a wonderful future lay ahead for them both.

"I want you to have a very smart frock for the wedding, because I know lots of people will come and see you," Daniel told her. He knew folks would say she was so plain and what did he see in her? Not that he cared a toss what other people thought anymore, but the truth was he always was a person who wanted to impress others. He knew he was quite handsome, everybody told him so for as long as he could remember, and he knew he could have had any girl he wanted. But Beth had come into his life so naturally, and fitted into the family so well. No one knew Beth as well as he did, and looks weren't everything. As far as he was concerned they counted for nothing. Her metal-rimmed glasses perhaps didn't help, and he would try and persuade her to let him pay for better ones for the wedding. She had such a kind face and a genuinely warm smile, as warm as her heart. That was what attracted her to him. Also Daniel fancied her physically too, and often thought what it would be like to make love properly to her. Looks certainly didn't come in to that. He had made up his mind a long time ago that she was the only one for him from the time he saw her on the gate. He knew he had always loved her. She was his only girlfriend, and he was never interested in looking elsewhere.

On the day they married, she looked as beautiful as ever she could have done. Her dress was of white silk covered with seed pearls and nipped in at the waist to show off her slim figure. The hem was scalloped, and she wore white silk shoes to match her dress. Her white hat had a scalloped brim trimmed with orange blossom.

"I want you and Mary to be my bridesmaids," she had told Martha.

"But what about your sisters?"

"You both are my sisters. You mean so much to me."

So Mary and Martha were bridesmaids, and her eldest sister was matron of honour. They were all dressed in floral dresses on a white background with black velour hats shaped in the same style as the hat of the bride. They each carried large bouquets of white carnations, with ferns trailing from them. Beth's brother was the best man, while John and Rhys were groomsmen. The men all looked very handsome in their black morning coats, with black and grey striped trousers.

The wedding took place in the Welsh chapel near Beth's home, because all her family were Welsh speaking. It was full to capacity with lots of families from the poor area where Beth was born, all wanting to see this posh wedding of someone who had very little money, but had done so well for herself. They felt it was like a fairy tale, quite like Cinderella finding her prince. It was certainly talked about as being the wedding of the year. There was no honeymoon, of course. They went straight to the farm, after a reception for just the family in a small hotel near the chapel. They had spent so much time getting the farmhouse habitable, with the help of a local builder friend, which had cost much more than they thought and taken much longer than anticipated.

Daniel had never touched her in all the years they had known each other. Naturally they had kissed and cuddled so much more lately, but he had always behaved like a true gentleman. He had never asked her, or attempted to do anything more. Her married sister had tried to prepare her for her first night sleeping with Daniel, explaining to her that it could be a little painful the first time. Although she loved him dearly, she did not look forward to this new experience to which she was about to be subjected, but she was sure that Daniel would be very patient and gentle with her, alleviating any fears she had. She only hoped she would not be a disappointment to him in any way. That first night Daniel obviously found everything very exciting and passionate and he could hardly wait for the next time. Poor Beth dare not show him that her sister had been quite right in telling her it could be painful. Indeed it was, not only painful but a disappointing experience. She certainly did not enjoy it. The whole episode was over just when she thought she was just starting to feel something. She was sure that the next time was bound to be an improvement and hopefully more enjoyable. Practice makes perfect her employer had always taught her on the farm. But poor Beth always felt so tired after a hard day working, and as time went on, his demands became more and more frequent. He would come into the house, or to the dairy where she would be busy at work with so much to do, put his arms around her and squeeze her, kissing her passionately, almost knocking her over.

"Come to bed with me, Beth," he would say.

"Not now, Daniel, I haven't finished half what I should have done yet."

"Oh, there is plenty of time. You have all day." Then he would lift her off her feet and carry her off into the farmhouse and upstairs to the bedroom. There on the bed he would make passionate love to her. She remembered his words when he had asked her to marry him. "We'll have to live on love as we'll have nothing else."

After that, although she found Daniel's lovemaking very

demanding, she vowed that she would never refuse him, or turn away from him. She would be a good wife in every sense of the word. She also began to enjoy what he did to her.

As soon as they moved to the farm, all the neighbouring farmers offered their machinery and help, completely free. Daniel and Beth could not believe how lucky they were to have the generosity of all the surrounding farmers and their friends. They were very much in love with each other and that was exactly what they had to live on. Every morning they were woken up at five o'clock by the sound of the London and North Western train, getting up steam from the valley below, travelling straight through the farm. So at five o clock every morning, because they were awake, Daniel wanted to make love to her there and then, making, what he felt, a very good start to the day ahead. He ploughed the fields with a horse he had borrowed, because he only had the pony his father had given him. The plough was second-hand, which he bought off one of the local farmers very cheaply. Very soon, seeds had been sown, the fields had been filled with potatoes and food for the cows, and after twelve months, the farm was beginning to take its shape. They both went to bed each night exhausted, but Daniel was never too tired for their lovemaking. He felt that was their reward for all the hard work they had both done during a very full day. Morning lovemaking was the best way to begin what lay ahead, and it finished the day too. They bought a small milk round from a local farmer who found it too time-consuming, so Daniel sold the milk in the village, which took about two hours, but that brought in regular cash. Soon they bought in more cows and increased their customers with Daniel's popularity around the village. Two churns had to be taken daily to the well in the next field to keep cool over night, and then delivered early the following morning. During the summer months, Beth did the morning milking, so that Daniel could get the milk delivered before it became too hot. They would not be paid if it turned sour. That would mean their profit was gone. This of course was unavoidable sometimes during the very hot summer months. It was essential every utensil they used with the milk was well scalded with boiling water to kill all germs, and Daniel was well used to this procedure. But now the water had to be carried from the well and heated over the open fire in the farmhouse. Life was much harder than they had expected but they loved being together, working together, and seeing the fruits of their efforts. It was so gratifying watching the potatoes and vegetables coming up in the spring, watered by carrying buckets from the stream. Then there was the barley, wheat and oats in the fields, all to be harvested, with the help of local farmers. Haymaking was a busy time and even friends came to help, collecting the hay from the fields on the gambo, and taking it to the hayrick ready for food for the cattle in winter. Many farmers would insure the hayrick in case of fire as inside became very hot during the winter months, and fire was always a possibility. But Daniel had always risked things and would never pay the premium, saying it would never happen to him. Many farmers did likewise and were unlucky; the hayrick would be burned to the ground and no food for the cattle all winter. It would prove to be a costly error of judgement not being insured. But Daniel was born under a lucky star. He never insured anything and he never regretted his decision. There was never a fire on his farm.

What he had not bargained for, although he had always taken risks, was that in the spring of 1931, Beth found she was expecting a baby. It was hardly surprising, the amount of times they made love, and Daniel hated the idea of any form of contraception. They had been on the farm just one year.

Their daughter Catherine was born with quite some difficulty in July that year. They employed a girl from the village to help, just before the confinement, and she carried on working with them to look after the baby so that Beth could return to her tasks on the farm as soon as possible.

They bought chickens, pigs and horses of their own, and were soon able to re-roof more of the outbuildings. The farmhouse was renovated and a cowshed adjoining the house was converted into living accommodation. There were two extra bedrooms there now, so Daniel employed two young boys from the village orphanage to work on the farm and live in with them. They were very cheap labour, but the boys loved the life and enjoyed the good food which was plentiful. They did not mind the long hours as they were so well treated and looked after. When eventually they left the farm to earn more money elsewhere, another two boys were employed. Beth enjoyed the extra work cooking and washing, and the boys enjoyed having what they felt was another mother looking after them. She would sometimes get quite attached to these boys and miss them when they left, but they would always be replaced. Some were obviously better than others, and where they could, they tried to employ brothers in order to keep them together.

Just before Catherine was four, Beth gave birth to another girl. She was born the day after April Fool's Day at five minutes past midnight. Daniel had hoped for a boy this time, and when the midwife announced, "It's another girl" he hoped perhaps it was an April Fool's joke. However, another girl it was, so they called her Anne. Beth looked forward so much to seeing Mary and Martha arrive in the pony and trap. The children gave the two aunts a new and exciting interest in life, and Beth adored both her sisters-in-law. They were her best friends, companions and true family. What agreeable girls they were, never arguing or showing any disapproval of anything Daniel or anyone else did. They enjoyed nursing the children and obviously spoiling them, but it was always such a pleasure to have them at the farm. She had three sisters of her own of course. One was married to a butcher and had a shop in the area where they were born. The next eldest married a confectioner, who had his own factory in the town making boiled sweets, and the third was still in service in a large house about three miles from Aelybryn. They all visited her, as often as they could, but they too had busy lives and really it was Mary and Martha whom she saw frequently and whom she loved to see whenever it was possible.

Although Beth suffered four miscarriages, there were no more children. Daniel never had the son he longed for. But something was to happen later, which would change the lives of Mary and Martha forever. Nothing would ever be the same again, for either of them.

Chapter 8

Mary and Martha

When John returned from the war with Rhys in 1918, Mary was twenty-three, but Martha was only fifteen. Both girls worked very hard during the day with their milk rounds, together with helping their mother in the house and concentrating on their piano lessons, both practising daily with great enthusiasm. This was aided by the fact that their parents had managed to buy a piano quite cheaply from one of their customers. It was situated in the parlour and Martha enjoyed playing and practising on it. But Mary preferred the sitting room. In there was an old organ which the chapel had offered to them when they purchased a new one. The piano had candlesticks attached to the front, one on either side, and Martha often lit them to play. She would pretend she was a concert pianist, and Mary often watched her getting up from the piano stool, pretending to bow to an audience again and again for her encores. Mary watched this performing act through the crack in the door, and she would smile to herself, never letting Martha know she had witnessed her imaginative performance. In later years, Martha passed all her exams in music and had the letters L.R.A.M after her name, a qualification that enabled her to give piano lessons to children in the village. She was very proud of this achievement, and would love to have given lessons to Daniel's children, but unfortunately not only did they show little interest but they were always too busy with chores their father gave them to do on the farm. However they loved to hear their two aunts playing tunes they were able to sing to, and the aunts always tried to encourage them.

Martha loved to go out with her chapel friends when everything was done in the home and the dairy. During the summer evenings they would all walk as far as the sea front, through the large park. They would stroll along the promenade and, when the tide was in, the girls tantalised the boys by throwing stones into the water, splashing them. The boys would retaliate by chasing the girls back along the prom. Martha was always full of fun and the boys enjoyed hearing her shriek with laughter when they teased her, or splashed water over her, getting her clothes all wet.

Mary, on the other hand, was quite content to stay at home and read her books. Very often she would spend hours doing the accounts for the business as she was quite clever with figures. They both enjoyed going to what was called "Band of Hope" held in the chapel where they watched glass slides that threw images on the wall. This was what Mary liked doing most of all. Here they were taught the evils of drink and good morals. Each day brought the same routine except for Sundays. They still arose very early for their milk rounds, but in the evening, they would all put on their Sunday best clothes and go to the service in the chapel in the village. On occasions, they would manage to attend Sunday school in the afternoon if they finished the milk rounds in good time. Every week, after the evening service, a singsong took place in the parlour of Aelybryn, with friends from chapel, usually Martha's, and before they could turn around it was the beginning of the week again.

As time went on, Rhys became concerned that Mary was such a lovely girl and not getting out enough and enjoying herself a little more. She always seemed to be busy working.

"Why don't you dress up and go out like Martha. She has a really good time. You spend far too much of yours working alone and you don't appear to have many pleasures at all."

"But I'm quite happy the way things are," she told him. "You needn't be concerned about me, Rhys. I love everything I do. I'm not Martha."

Rhys sometimes felt she was brooding, as she would be often deep in thought when he was talking to her. When Mary had lost her mother, she missed her more than she was prepared to admit. She often thought a great deal about her and how much she missed their long and happy conversations, as well as the time they spent alone together. She was more like an elder sister to her, than her stepmother, and although she did not remember her own mother, she remembered from a very young age that Margaret had come to live with them, bringing great happiness back into their home, especially into her own life. She felt happy and secure again.

The two sisters had totally different personalities of course. Martha missed her mother too, but she seemed to cope by going out more, enjoying herself and filling in the void in a different way. For her, it did not seem enough to be out all the morning on her rounds. During heavy rain, they would get soaked to the skin and would have to bring the pony and trap back home to change into dry clothes. Mary found that delivering the milk to her customers was sufficient so she remained in the house most afternoons and evenings, as there was always plenty to do. She had met a boy in the church school just before leaving to work at home. She and

Tom had been for a walk several times, but once she left school she had no contact with him again. Often she wished she could have kept in touch, as he was such a friendly person, but then she heard he had gone off to the war. It must have been a year later; someone in chapel was heard to report that he had been killed in France. Again she had felt a feeling of loss, but nothing like the loss she had felt when Margaret had died. Maybe it was just as well she had never become close to him after all. The loss could have been much greater. After that she had little interest in the opposite sex. Martha, on the other hand, found boys such good fun. If anything, she preferred their company to girls. She did not seem to have any special boy she preferred, but treated them all likewise, just enjoying their company.

In January 1936, George V died at the age of seventy-one. Both Mary and Martha were always very interested in the royal family, and read with sadness the account in the newspapers.

"Such sad news about the king," said Mary. "I'm sure the country will miss him despite the fact he was known for his gruff manner and loud voice."

"Yes, but he always seemed to carry out his duties with dignity," replied Martha, "and don't forget he encompassed the Great War during his reign. That must have been hard for him. But our new king is so charming, good-looking and energetic. The country will now have a great deal to look forward to in the years to come. Thank goodness his younger brother wasn't born first, as he would then have been king and he is the complete opposite."

Mary did not always agree with her sister's viewpoint, but often she kept her thoughts and opinions to herself. Bertie, the younger brother of the king was indeed quiet, unexciting and unexceptional, but even so, he seemed to be a good family man, married to the very sensible and charming Elizabeth Bowes-Lyon. They had two young daughters, and both Mary and Martha took a keen interest in them. Their father seemed conscientious when duty called, softly spoken, and wrestled with a bad speech impediment with which Mary felt he coped remarkably well and with a great deal of courage.

Unknown to the public, nor even the royal family at this time, when the king was only Prince of Wales, he had met a Mrs Wallis Simpson in 1931. She was thirty-five, American, and had already been married twice. What began then as a flirtatious friendship became a full-blown affair by 1934, and by 1935 the Prince was wholly infatuated. In November 1936, he told his family that he had decided to marry Wallis Simpson who had now divorced for the second time. The king was Supreme Governor of the Church of England, which did not then recognise divorce, but until December the majority of the British public knew nothing of the king's intentions. However his love for Wallis Simpson was not negotiable, and therefore the reign of Edward VIII came to an abrupt end after eleven months and twenty-one days when he broadcast to the country of his abdication. Bertie became King George VI and was nearly forty-one. The country was in turmoil, and the abdication was greatly talked about, especially by Martha and Mary. They both found it all very difficult to understand.

"Surely his duty should have come first," Martha told Mary.

"I cannot believe he has done such a thing. How selfish he is, putting his own feelings before his country. He should never have done that. I know I wouldn't have," Mary retorted.

"Yes, I must agree with you there, Mary, and it will be such a strain on the new king and his family when he hasn't been trained for that position," Martha said angrily, feeling sorry for the whole of the royal family. When Mary and Martha went to bed, they could not stop talking about it. Martha was silent for a while and then told her sister where she had been that day, admitting that she now realised how different the boys were that she met, compared with their brothers and Rhys, who was now just like a brother to them both.

"But I don't feel anything for any of them. I wonder what that sort of love feels like, Mary, like the king's brother feels for Wallis Simpson. Have you ever been in love, Mary?"

"Of course not, silly."

Neither she nor Mary had ever been in love, so found the reason for the abdication difficult to understand. However their conversation soon turned to how much they enjoyed going to the farm to see Beth and the family. That was the important part of their lives. Mary and Martha agreed that they both loved their brother's children, as if they were their own. They loved their brothers too of course, and each other, a sisterly love, but was that the same sort of love as that of loving a man outside the family, they asked themselves. They certainly knew what it felt like to love a mother, and how they missed her, but now they also had Catherine and Ann to whom they could give their love. They were such interesting and entertaining children to be with and were growing up very quickly.

When at the farm, they took great pleasure in taking them to the furthest fields from the farmhouse, carrying tea for Daniel, who would be ploughing there with the two horses.

"Look, Mary, how does Daniel manage to keep those furrows so straight? They are just like railway lines," she would tell her sister adoringly, admiring what she felt was her brother's work of art. The tea would be poured into a jug with a cup on the top, and wrapped in a towel to keep warm, then placed securely in a basket. Also there would be Beth's cake for them all to enjoy when Daniel stopped for his break. He would often continue with his ploughing despite their arrival with his tea, but the sisters knew Daniel only too well, He would stop when it suited him; he made all the decisions, and always had done.

"Had to finish that furrow before having my cuppa," he would tell them, with the usual smile on his face.

The walk to the fields meant going down an overgrown lane, with large deep purple foxgloves standing tall in the hedgerows. They looked like church bells, just about to ring. By the time they reached Daniel, the tea was barely warm, especially when it was a long furrow which had to be completed before he stopped for the break, but he always said cold tea was far more refreshing, and cured the thirst much better in hot weather. They would all sit on the edge of the ploughed field where there was still some unploughed grass, and the sun would be beating down on them, with not a cloud in the sky. It was so peaceful there, with only the sound of birds and the ripple of the stream which meandered through the fields.

Often a train would pass by on the railway, which ran straight through the farm, disturbing the tranquillity, but they would all wave to the people travelling on it. They, in turn, would wave back, which delighted Catherine and Ann. Sometimes on the train there were children waving their spades, obviously going off to the seaside.

"Wish we were going to the seaside," the children would grumble to the aunts. "We never go there." But they would be encouraged by the aunts to make do with taking off their shoes and dipping their feet in the stream, which was so very cold, even on a hot day. Sometimes the flow would be quite fast, and the children would be anxious not to be carried off downstream, but the aunts would hold their hands firmly and they would feel safe and secure again. Then Mary and Martha would dry their feet with the towel in which the tea jug had been wrapped. The children often wondered where those people on the train were going, who they were, strangers to the area on holiday perhaps, but they never saw them again. They would watch as the train gradually disappeared into the distance and eventually completely out of sight, only to hear the faint puffing noise of the engine and see the wisps of grey smoke melting away into the white clouds and blue sky above.

During the summer, on their return journey up the lanes, the children would stop to pick blackberries when they were in season, and fill the tea jug to the top, hands covered in blackberry juice. Aunt Martha would carry the jug carefully so as not to spill the fruit, while the children then picked wild flowers from the hedgerows. Sometimes they would be surrounded by a blaze of colours. There were cornflowers, celandine, cowslips and what Mary called "milk maids" which, when pressed between the fingers, would release a milk-like substance. When the bluebells were out, it seemed as if the fields were surrounded by a blue carpet and the children would pull bunches of bluebells out of the ground, taking with them the half white stems which went into the corms. Wild violets and clumps of wild primroses grew all along the banks of the river and were such a beautiful sight. Mary always thought the country looked like pictures out of a book, and she was right. You would not see these sights living in the town. By this time the children's hands would be hot and clammy, and stained with juice, picking their wild flowers, and by the time they were back at the farmhouse the flowers would often have wilted. However the enjoyment was picking them in the warm sunshine to give as a present to their mother. If the children were stung by nettles, which often entwined the flowers in the hedgerows, Mary would find some dock leaves to rub on the affected area, taking away the sting and soothing them. They had such fun when their aunts were with them. If they wanted to know the time, Mary would pick a dandelion head, which had gone to seed. The bright yellow flower, abundant in meadows and waste ground, would be succeeded by a globular head of pappose seeds, forming what many imagined was a clock. This was the dandelion head of parachute-like fruits.

"Come on, children, see how many times you have to blow on this before the fruits are all blown away, only leaving the stem. That will tell us the time."

They often wished the aunts could come to live with them forever because they knew so many interesting things about nature.

Always on their return from the farm, Mary continued to listen to Martha's endless chatter while they were lying in their bed at night. Martha would jump from one topic of conversation to another, and by the time she had finished, they would both be ready to fall asleep. All Mary had done was listen and nod sleepily in agreement with her sister. She was very good at listening but then she had had very good practice, once Martha had arrived into the world. She had always been a chatterbox ever since she began to talk as a little girl.

"Do you know what happened today on my round?" Martha asked Mary.

"Let's try and go to sleep. It's getting very late."

"I'll just tell you quickly then. I went around to the back door of number 17 Dillwyn Road as usual, and the two elderly men who live there alone had gone out and left their jug on the doorstep, but they forgot to cover it with a saucer, and when I picked it up there were two slugs inside."

"You didn't put the milk in, I hope, Martha."

"Well no, not straightaway. I tried to tip them out but they were stuck and I had to get my pencil out of my book to scrape them off. Then I put the milk in."

"You should never do that, Martha. It is very unhealthy, it could make those men have a bad stomach."

"Well, I couldn't possibly leave them without any milk, could I? Do you think I'll have killed them?"

"No, don't be silly. Now let's get off to sleep."

That was what Mary missed most after losing her mother. She had always found time to listen to what Mary had to say and interested in her opinions. Perhaps Margaret had felt sorry for her, not having her true mother, but she was the only mother she ever remembered and she had loved her dearly. She still missed her so much. But life was soon to change at Aelybryn. Their father suffered a stroke. They had all been concerned for some time about his quite ruddy complexion, in case his blood pressure was getting too high. Fortunately the stroke was a mild one, but they felt they should inform his younger brother who had emigrated to Durban, South Africa years before when he was in his twenties. He had married an English girl out there but was unable to have any children. Evan had never returned to this country in all the years he had been there, so when he received the letter telling him of his brother's stroke he decided to book a passage home and stay for three months.

There was great excitement when the uncle eventually arrived and Jacob was delighted to see his brother again after so many years.

Just when the three months were up, Jacob suffered another stroke. He lost the use of the left side of his body. Evan wired his wife to say he was extending his vacation for yet another three months, but it was during this time he made up his mind that he wanted to settle back at home in Wales, so he wrote to his wife, asking her to join him. The cooler weather suited him much better, and he could see the need for his help at Aelybryn. He asked his wife to sell the house and join him in Wales.

"My brother has asked us to make our home here at Aelybryn. They need me to help out, and my two nieces are very happy for us to live with them. There is plenty of room in this large house."

But when he received his wife's reply, it said in no uncertain terms that she had no intention of leaving South Africa and giving up her life there. They divorced the following year and he never heard from her again.

When Evan had been at Aelybryn for about three years, Jacob had a massive heart attack and died. From that day onwards, Evan rose at five o'clock every morning and in fact his nieces could not have managed without him. He would lift the heavy churns onto the float ready for the delivery, then potter around the dairy until the girls returned. Every afternoon he would scald all the cans and measures with boiling water, ready for the next morning. He wanted no payment so long as he had his food and accommodation free.

"When my money runs out you can give me a wage, but I enjoy listening to the wireless and reading. I enjoy the occasional pint at the local pub, but I need very little money to live on."

Rhys on the other hand enjoyed walking and a visit to the cinema each week which had recently opened in the village, and when Jacob died and Evan decided to remain in Aelybryn, Rhys made a decision. He had thought for some time that he should look for a job. He had seen an advertisement in the local newspaper for an assistant in the draper's shop in the town, so he made up his mind to apply for it. After a successful interview he began working there the following month. This meant he was out of the house six days out of seven, but enjoyed the independence it gave him, whilst earning his own living with a proper salary at last, small though it was. Evan took over the garden and Rhys helped when he had his day off. Things were working out very well indeed. As Evan was always around, customers began to call at the house for the odd pint of milk if they ran out, or sometimes needed extra. From time to time, quite an amount of milk was sold at the door even to non-customers. The eggs were also sold from the house, and Evan found he thoroughly enjoyed the chat with the callers and counting the money he had collected by his answering the door to people.

"I really feel I am making myself useful to you both," he told his nieces.

"But we love having you around, and you are such a great help to us."

If the sisters were in the parlour playing the piano or reading, and the doorbell rang loudly, he would shout to them, "Stay where you are, I'm here. I'll answer it."

This gave them far more freedom. After they had done their rounds and seen to the household needs as well as food for them all in the evenings, they were glad to relax, sit and put up their feet.

One evening Evan was later than usual returning from the local pub. Martha looked at the clock and Mary knew exactly what was going through her mind.

"Yes, I was thinking the same, where has Evan got to?"

With that the door opened and Evan was home, smiling as usual. "You're later than usual, Evan," Martha said quizzically.

"Oh, the pub was full tonight, and I got chatting to a lady sitting in the corner on her own. Anyway, have you had any callers tonight? Who have I missed?" he answered, completely changing the subject. In the weeks to follow, the sisters noticed that Evan seemed to take a little more care dressing to go out to the pub, and began to use grease on his hair.

"Evan is quite smart when he makes the effort," Martha remarked to Mary.

"Yes, do you think he has met someone in the pub? It's a funny life for him having been married and just living and doing everything now for us, year in year out. He must surely find it tedious at times, confined to the house all day as well as six evenings in the week," Mary told her.

"Wouldn't it be exciting if Evan met someone and fell in love again."

But although Evan continued to visit the pub weekly, he made no comment about whom he had seen or talked to and they did not want to pry into his private life. It would of course change their lives now completely if Evan did meet someone, and what if he married her? They certainly would miss all his help. In fact they wondered how they could manage without him since their father had gone. Evan was a godsend.

Often Martha could go out shopping or meet her friends in the town, while Mary would be in the parlour seeing to the bookkeeping or doing the accounts ready for the collection of money on a Saturday. However Rhys would spend more and more time going in to see her on his days off and chatting to her.

"I have told you before, Mary, your life is passing you by. You are thirty-seven now and you should be enjoying yourself with your friends, not working all the time and being stuck in here alone, reading."

"Well, Rhys, you are a fine one to talk. You haven't made any friends all the time you have lived with us. I am quite happy doing what I am doing. I'm out every morning so I see people on my rounds and do all the talking I need to with them. It's enough for me, believe me."

Rhys began to talk to her about the war years and the time in the trenches, when they never thought they would survive.

"I was so fortunate to meet John. He always had the faith that he would come home safely. I could never believe that God would look after us. What had my parents and sisters done to be blown to shreds? I saw too much suffering to believe there was a God. If you had seen all your comrades shot to pieces, was that God's will too? It was just fate that brought me to Aelybryn. I'm so glad I took up John's offer to come home with him, and live here in a lovely home with so much loving care from your family."

He did not mention any personal details of what had happened to his, and Mary never asked him about them. Instead they would have long discussions on religion and books they enjoyed reading. Charles Dickens was a favourite of Rhys, and quite recently he had seen in the newspaper an advertisement offering one of his books, delivered each month, and paid for monthly until the whole works were completed.

"I prefer reading books by Jane Austen," Mary told him.

"But you must read Great Expectations, Mary. You would enjoy it. As soon as it arrives I'll lend it to you so that you can read it."

Often Rhys would try to persuade her to go for a walk with him to the park, about a mile away. Again it was springtime. Such a beautiful season.

"All the azaleas and rhododendrons are in full bloom. You should see them, Mary. The colours are so beautiful, it's so picturesque, they hardly seem real. Will you come with me tomorrow on my half-day if it's fine? We will only be an hour there and back home."

Mary relented and went with him the following week, as it was such a bright sunny day, and before all the flowers would be past their best.

"I hate to admit it, Rhys, but what a change it is from walking around the roads delivering the milk to customers. You were quite right. I'm so glad I made the effort, the flowers are a sight to behold, such beautiful blooms."

After that, they went every week on his day off, in the afternoons, walking around the lake in the park and chatting. She had not chatted like this since her mother was alive.

Rhys would tell her about some of the strange people who came into the shop and how he would show them nearly everything that he had for sale, but they would leave without buying anything. He found this very frustrating.

"At least with you, Mary, you sell to every customer you have and every time you go out."

"Yes, but it is so important to do the books and collect in the money on a Saturday, otherwise we would not make anything. Often on Saturdays, as you know, Martha and I come home late in the afternoon. We've delivered the milk in the morning and knocked on all the doors for the money. But often there's no answer. The jug is left out on the doorstep and a saucer over it, with a note to ask for the required amount of milk. We then have to return again later to see if the customer has returned home. This sometimes necessitates calling on the same house twice or three times, to be paid the money owing. It's not quite as simple and straightforward as you imagine."

Soon Mary began to look forward to the walks with him, even before her round was completed. She could not ever remember looking forward to anything as much. Thus began the very innocent but close relationship between Rhys and Mary. The first time she changed her clothing to go out to the park, Martha had quickly noticed this unusual occurrence.

"Why ever are you changing your clothes at this time of the day? Where are you going now?"

"Oh, just keeping Rhys company again. He seems to go walking so much on his own, and never made any friends since he came back to live here from the war. He really only has us, and it is such a pleasant walk through the park. I really quite enjoy it."

But when it became a habit, her sister walking out in the park with Rhys on her own, Martha was not so happy about it. It wasn't that she was at all jealous. That was not in her nature. It was just that Mary had always been happy to stay in and now she seemed so happy to be going out.

"I'm only thinking of you, Mary. People's tongues wag so much as we are so well known around the village. Mrs Jones down the road said to me only yesterday that she had seen you a few times in the park on your own with Rhys, and were you both in love?"

"Don't be ridiculous, Martha, Rhys is like our brother. He's part of our family and will never be anything more to me than that. You tell Mrs Jones the next time you see her and she says anything to you, not that it is any of her business, of course, but as she is one of our good customers we cannot say that to her. Just tell her nicely that he is part of our family, and it is the same as walking in the park with one of my brothers."

Martha told Mrs Jones very politely what her sister had said when she mentioned the fact again. Martha felt just the same way as Mary did. From the day Rhys arrived at their home with John, he had been accepted as one of their family and that was how it would remain, always. He could never mean anything else to either of them. He was just like a brother to them both.

Chapter 9

Christmas was such a lovely time for Mary and Martha. They were always expected at the farm for Christmas lunch. Daniel had now bought an old second-hand car, so he was able to bring his sisters to the farm as soon as they had finished their milk delivery. They loved watching the children opening their presents; it gave them such pleasure seeing the excited look on their faces when they ripped open the Christmas wrapping paper.

"Look, look, Aunt Martha, see what I've had from Father Christmas," said one.

"Yes, just look at this, Aunt Mary, it's what I really wanted," the other said excitedly, unwrapping the next item from the pillowcase. Then the aunts would look across at each other and smile, and turn towards Beth with a look of satisfaction, knowing that they had been able to make most of the payments for them, and seeing the children so happy at receiving almost everything they had asked for from Father Christmas. What else were they to spend their money on anyway? They had everything they needed. Beth too was so grateful to them because Daniel always wanted to spend any extra money they made on implements and other farm necessities. "Can't waste money on luxuries or presents for the family," he had told her so often. "We must plough it all back into the farm."

When all the Christmas parcels had been opened, they would sit together around the large very substantial wooden table in the kitchen, waiting for the enormous stuffed turkey to arrive, reared on the farm and carried proudly by Daniel to the table. Eventually the turkey dinner was followed by an equally large Christmas pudding, made and carried to the table by Beth. Her puddings were all cooked in her household boiler which took all day to boil and had to be continually refilled with water not for the boiler to become dry. Then Beth made three pints of white sauce, but never adding brandy, because Daniel did not agree with drink at the table or in the cooking. All the potatoes and vegetables were obviously grown on the farm, freshly harvested, and tasted so different from those bought in the shops, sometimes days old, before their actual consumption.

"I'll plate up two extra dinners for Evan and Rhys for their Christmas supper," Beth would always tell her sisters-in-law at this festive time.

They were always happy to remain at home to deal with any necessary jobs and answer the door to any callers. It was surprising how many people ran out of milk on Christmas Day, after using their morning's delivery to make the white sauce to pour over the Christmas pudding. The two men would be kept quite busy at home in Aelybryn while the sisters enjoyed having some time off to themselves, and being with their close family. Joining them for lunch would be Beth's brother Dai, who had remained a bachelor and still worked on the same farm on which Beth and he had worked together when she left school. He always welcomed time with his favourite sister. Now Beth's father also joined them. Unfortunately, her mother had died suddenly after being rushed into hospital with gallstones and not having survived the operation. This had upset Beth greatly at the time, it was such a shock, but with so much going on at the farm, she could not allow herself time to grieve. She had even found Daniel's lovemaking abhorrent during those early days after the funeral, but he continued to expect her to fully enjoy his demands, despite her feelings of grief and loss. "I had the best mother in the world," she told her children. She continued to work hard and not show them or Daniel just how upset she was. She had always said she would never turn away from him and refuse him anything, and she was determined to keep this promise, therefore she continued to persevere with the lovemaking, keeping her grief all to herself. She couldn't talk to Mary and Martha about such things, they wouldn't possibly understand, never having married. Her sisters had their own lives to live with enough complications. As time went on, things eventually began to revert back to normal, but she did not show Daniel or the children how sad she really felt deep inside.

Mary and Martha remembered arriving at the farm on one occasion for their Christmas lunch when Daniel rushed into the house. His face was tense and red, and a look of anxiety filled his eyes.

"We'll have to delay Christmas dinner. One of the cows is having her calf but I think it could be twins. I dare not leave her, as she's one of my best cows. I paid a lot for her, so can't afford to lose her."

The family waited and waited while the children became more and more hungry.

"How much longer do we have to wait, Mum?" grumbled Anne. "We are famished."

The turkey was all ready for carving on to the plates, but there was still no sign of Daniel. Dai went out to the cowshed to see what the problem was and if he could be of any assistance.

Then Daniel called Beth to fetch one of the horses from the stable and bring it to the front of the cowshed. Martha and Mary tried to distract the children by playing a game, while Beth's father watched with interest. He could not speak any English, and Mary and Martha couldn't speak Welsh, but they communicated with the gesticulation of arms and hands, together with the small amount of Welsh the children had picked up from Beth who returned ten minutes later.

"They've had to tie a rope to connect the horse to the feet of the half born calf," she said quietly to the grown-up members, almost feeling the pain the poor cow must be endeavouring to cope with, having no medication which women receive to relieve it.

"The two men can't possibly pull hard enough to get it out, and time is limited, we could so easily lose her if we are not careful and quick."

They all waited anxiously for the two men to return. Eventually Daniel came into the kitchen first, followed by Dai. Perspiration was pouring off them, blood was all over their clothes, and they looked completely dishevelled. The look of dismay on their faces said it all. The cow had died but had left two lovely healthy heifer calves. Their profit for that month at least, would have gone, although two bull calves would have been worth less. Sadly Daniel had lost one of his best milk-yielding cows. He hated to be beaten by anything, and this time he had certainly lost a battle he had hoped to win. Mary and Martha tried hard to conceal the sad misfortune from the children. They chatted continually during Christmas dinner and entertained them again afterwards. But Beth and Daniel could eat very little of the meal they had looked forward to so much. Neither could they conceal their perplexity and disappointment at their costly loss. It overshadowed Christmas for them all that year.

Worse news was to follow when in 1939 Daniel went into the living room to listen to the news on the wireless as there was a special bulletin. He called Beth and they both tried to listen but with great difficulty because the batteries needed recharging. Daniel sat with his ears pressed tightly against the speaker while the one o'clock news was being read amidst crackling and screeching. He had forgotten to take the batteries to the local garage earlier that week. "Try turning the other knob," Beth suggested.

"Hush up, Beth, I'm trying to decipher what's going on. All this whining and interference, I can't hear a thing." But soon they heard enough to realise that the country was again at war with Germany. When Mary and Martha heard the news they had no worries this time about John or Rhys being called up, and they knew Daniel was exempt because of the farm, much to their relief. London was once again being heavily bombed, together with other big cities in the country. "I can't believe that I have lived to see yet another war," Rhys told Mary. "It brings back all the old memories of my family and how they died, blown to pieces in the London bombings." From then on, Mary wanted to spend more and more time with him, feeling really sorry for him. He was often quiet and deep in thought. However Martha also realised that Mary was spending more time getting ready for the innocent walks with Rhys in the park. It was perhaps just her fancy, as she was not always at home anyway when Mary was preparing to go out. But that was not all she had noticed. As Mary came downstairs, Martha looked her sister up and down.

"Why have you put on your blouse that you keep for chapel, just to go to the park?" Martha inquired.

"Don't worry, Martha, I am only going with Rhys, but I never know who I'll see down there. We thought today we might go and have an ice cream in the new ice cream parlour on the sea front, see what it's like inside, if we have time. I thought I should make an effort to look respectable, not out walking in my milk round clothes."

But they did not end up going to the ice cream parlour after all. That was the day she would remember for many years to come. She and Rhys had sat down on the wooden seat near the lake, as they had done so many times previously.

"Mary, you really look lovely today," he whispered in her ear, putting his arm around her. She could feel his hand on her shoulder, then felt it moving across her back, affectionately stroking the back of her neck. Although she was somewhat embarrassed at this unusual gesture of his, she neither objected nor moved away from him. They continued to chat again, but suddenly he glanced around as if to see if there was anybody about. There was no one. Suddenly he took her head in his both hands and kissed her tenderly on the mouth. When his mouth left hers and he kissed her cheek, her mouth still felt wet. Before she realised what she was doing, she instinctively wrapped her arms around him tightly. They held each other closely for a moment and then she felt his mouth on hers again. He was trying to part her lips. Whatever was happening to her? She had never had this happen to her before in her life and her legs began to feel weak. She felt almost like fainting, so she held on to him tightly. He looked at her once again and lifted her chin up with one hand, brushing the hair away from her face with the other.

"You must have realised by now how I felt about you, Mary. I have tried and tried to conceal my feelings and not to regard you as anything more than one of my adopted family, but it has become impossible. I have fallen in love with you."

"Oh, Rhys, I too feel something different has happened between us. Something I've never felt before, but you know there's no possible way anything can become of it. Martha and I have promised each other that we will always stay together. I could never leave her with all the business on her own. In any case, it is shared between us equally and it would be very difficult to divide. Impossible in fact, because our home is also divided between us."

"But there must be some way around it. We can't just stop loving each other, especially living under the same roof. We've both spent all these years together, we don't want to waste any more of our lives."

Mary stood up and walked slowly towards the lake, away from him, but he quickly followed her.

He could see there were tears in her eyes. He couldn't bear to see her unhappy. Once again, he put his arm around her shoulder.

"No, Rhys, please don't. Our mistake was to have shown each other how we felt. It has ruined everything for us now. Whatever were we thinking of? We must never let it happen again, promise me?" He didn't know what to say. How could he make a promise that he didn't feel he could keep?

"Alright, for the time being we will try to carry on as before. I will never mention anything about what happened between us today, say how I feel, or come too close to you. As long as we can still have our long chats and walks. They mean so much to me. This war has brought back so many dreadful memories and having you to talk to, someone with whom I can share all my thoughts, mean so much to me."

So Mary did as he asked. On their walks, he talked a great deal to her about his parents. "My father was working in Rhyl, North Wales when he had met my mother. She had become pregnant with me, and my mother was turned out of her home, bringing shame on the family. They went to live outside London with an aunt of my mother, who was sorry for her. When I was born, my mother wanted my name spelt the Welsh way, because of her Welsh connections. It was ironic that I met John in the trenches and eventually came to live in Wales, back to where I had been conceived. When my aunt died, she left the terraced house to them, and later of course my two sisters were born. Both our parents adored us and we loved and respected them in return. They were such kind thoughtful people, always thinking of others." How much he had thought about them in those early years after the war. What a close-knit family they had once been, and how much he had loved them all. It all seemed so long ago now. He had tried to block them out of his mind for so long because it hurt too much to think about them, but at last, with Mary, he felt able to enjoy remembering them and talking about them with affection once again.

"At least you have me to share all this with," she told him, although he felt a tenseness between them.

That week he had received his second book from the Dickens Collection through the post. It was Great Expectations. He gave it to Mary to read, as he knew she would enjoy it. But in the weeks to follow, Rhys continued to find it a strain, living there in the same house, and seeing her every day, wanting her as he did. There seemed to be no real answer to the problem of loving each other. In fact, no way out of this situation. No way out, at all.

Chapter 10

Back at Daniel's farm, Anne, his younger daughter, desperately wanted a pony of her own. Catherine had had a bicycle for her birthday from the aunts, as she was not interested in the animals. In fact she began to resent having to do so much on the farm, and could not wait for the time to come when she could leave school and obtain some other kind of employment, and earn her own living. Maybe she would be able to leave home altogether one day. What a great thought that was. Gradually she began to hate living on a farm, with everything else it entailed. Because Mary and Martha had paid for the bicycle for Catherine and they treated the children with the same generosity, they wanted to pay for a pony for Anne, but Daniel wouldn't hear of it.

"It would be a complete waste of money. This is just a passing whim of hers." The sisters looked at each other but made no comment. Later that week when Daniel was at the mart, looking for another cow, a neighbouring farmer Dai was chatting about his daughter and girls in general. He had two girls older than Daniel's children, but he also had a son working on the farm. He brought up the fact that children soon tire of hobbies and pursuits.

"I bought my younger daughter a pony, because she kept on and on she wanted one. We've had it twelve years and for the last six, she hasn't bothered with it. She hasn't even ridden it once in two years. Now she has so many other things she prefers doing, I suppose she has outgrown the novelty."

"That's exactly what I told my younger daughter when she asked for a horse of her own," Daniel replied. "This fad will be short-lived, I know. All these novelties soon wear off with kids."

"I have tried to get the animal in foal, so that at least I'd make a bit of money out of her," continued the farmer indignantly, not helping Anne's cause at all, "but there has been no such luck. Now she's far too old. Why don't you come up the farm and fetch her. Let your daughter borrow it for as long as she wants. I tell you one thing, although the pony is sixteen, she will last longer than your daughter's phase of wanting to ride one of her own." He went off towards his truck smiling to himself. Then turning back, he called again to Daniel.

"I meant what I said. Come up the farm and fetch it anytime."

When Daniel mentioned all this to Anne, she was ecstatic.

"Please, Daddy, please let's fetch it," she begged. So Daniel agreed to go and fetch the pony, but weeks went by before he could find the time to do so. Nevertheless Anne continued to pester him.

Eventually Daniel took Anne to Heol Uchaf Farm which was about three miles away. The pony was all black, except for a small mark in white on its forehead. She was called Seren which is the Welsh name for Star, because of the white star-like mark on its forehead. Its coat was quite rough as it had been left out all winter, and its hooves turned up like Dutch clogs, the result of it not being shod for quite some time. It was a very docile creature, and because it was old, it was happy to move very slowly. Anne adored it, spending every minute she could with it, brushing it and taking food to the paddock behind the farmhouse where it was kept.

"The first thing we will have to do is get it shod," said Daniel. "You can't ride it on the road until then. We also need to take the carthorse to be shod next week, so, Catherine, you can go to the smithy at the bottom of the road near Aelybryn, and Anne can take Seren. It will only take an hour or so to walk them there and back."

Catherine wasn't at all keen. She wasn't interested in the horses, but often the children had to do things they did not like. If their father told them they were to do something on the farm, they had to do it, and immediately. So the two horses were taken to be shod. Catherine hated it in the blacksmith's shed. Firstly, he would remove the shoes, but of course Seren didn't have any, so he just had to trim the hooves. Then the shoes would go in the fire until they were red-hot, and he would hammer them and bend them to fit, cooling them in a tank of cold water, which would hiss and spit. When the shoe was placed on the hoof, nails were hammered into the small holes in the horseshoe to hold them in place. It did not seem possible that it was a painless process, and anyway they hated the smell in the blacksmith's shed. However neither of the horses flinched or objected at the treatment they were given, so it could not have caused them any pain or discomfort. "Let's go outside and wait, the smell is dreadful," Catherine grumbled, "and we can watch the traffic go by. We may be lucky and see Aunt Mary or Aunt Martha delivering their milk." However the shoes were soon fitted and they were called inside to collect the horses ready to face the long trek home again.

Anne loved having her school friends to the farm to see her new pride and joy. She was very keen to attract the attention of one of the girls in her class, so at the first opportunity she invited her to the farm after school. She really wanted her to become her closest friend, but Rhian was not interested in Anne. Often she was quite aloof with her, not really wanting to bother with her at all. She lived in a very large house in its own grounds, near the park, not far from the aunts. They were a very affluent family spending holidays abroad, unlike Anne and Catherine who had no holidays at all, anywhere. She thought if Rhian came to the farm to see that she owned a pony of her own she would surely be impressed. That was something this girl did not possess.

"But my mother won't let me. She says farmers and their children are rough people and she doesn't want me to visit your house."

Anne was upset at this judgement of her and her family. They were not at all rough.

"I bet she hasn't got two aunts like we have," Anne told Catherine when they went to bed that night.

"No, and I don't know why you want to have her for a friend anyway," Catherine said, trying to dissuade her from wanting to be friendly with such a disagreeable girl. "She and her mother sound horrid people. Who do they think they are? We own much more ground than they do anyway. You'd think she owned the park next door to them, as well as their house, the way she talks."

But Anne was not put off, and she continued to keep in with her and inviting her to the farm. Then one day, Rhian said her mother had said yes. Anne was so excited at this prospect.

Beth tried to be in the farmhouse when the girls came home from school, which was quite rare. Often the children would have to make their own tea while their mother was out helping in the fields. When they had finished tea, the children went out to the paddock behind the house to feed Seren and have a ride on her. "Let's not put a saddle on the pony. We could ride it bareback," Rhian boasted, as if she was an experienced rider.

"That's how they do it at the circus," she insisted. "I've seen them lots of times."

Anne had never been to a circus. Her parents never had the time to take them, but she did not want Rhian riding without the saddle. However, when Rhian continued to insist, Anne relented to her request, eager to please her, and especially as she seemed to know exactly how it was done.

"That's what the girl did in the Big Top, when I went with Mummy and Daddy," she boasted. "It looked great fun. Come on, Anne, you go first. It's easy."

"Yes, I know I can, as I am used to doing it, but I'm not so sure about you trying."

Anne jumped on the pony, held it tightly around its neck, and gave it a tap with her heels, and Seren took off slowly around the paddock. She had often ridden the pony bareback and had also done so with one of the carthorses because they also went quite slowly. The carthorses were obviously not bred for riding and Seren's saddle was far too small to put on a carthorse, but because sometimes two friends wanted to ride together, Anne would use the carthorse and ride it bareback.

"Come on, Anne, hurry up," shouted Rhian. "It's my turn."

Anne helped Rhian to mount the pony and told her to hold on tightly around the neck. Then she gave it a tap on the bottom and off it went around the paddock.

"This is great fun," she shouted to her friend, laughing and waving one hand in the air to show how cleverly she could ride, with only one hand around the pony's neck. Anne was delighted to see that Rhian was doing something she had not done before, and really enjoying herself. This would surely impress her, and her mother too, when she returned home and told them what she had been doing at the farm.

On that particular day, Beth, whose washing line was in the paddock, had done a load of washing, pegged it out on the long line of wire, and dried it, but when she took it into the house, she had omitted to take the wire line down. As usual she had been in a hurry to do some other chores, before the girls arrived home from school.

Rhian decided it would be a good idea to now try her skill at standing on the pony's back, just as the girl had done in the circus. When she tried to put one foot on the pony's back, she did not realise she was heading straight for the washing line, which would catch her across her neck if she came in contact with the wire. It was just the right height. Anne immediately recognised the impending danger and shouted, "Look out" almost hysterically, but it was too late. Rhian, in trying to duck and miss the wire, fell off the pony and landed straight in a bush of brambles and nettles.

There were loud screams to be heard echoing around the farmyard. Beth ran out from feeding the calves to see what had happened. When she arrived at the paddock, to her dismay she could see Rhian in the centre of the bushes and nettles, legs and arms scratched and covered in a red rash from the nasty green monsters.

She was unhurt from the point of view of there being any bones broken, as the pony was going quite slowly, but her legs and arms were stinging and the poor child was howling, rubbing her legs and calling out for her mother.

"Take me home," she cried earnestly.

Aunt Mary and Aunt Martha had recently arrived at the farm, so they both dashed out to see what all the commotion was about. Immediately they cut some dock leaves to rub on the nettle rash, which Aunt Mary had always done when the children had a nettle sting. This, however, was a different kettle of fish altogether. The child had masses of nettle stings, far too many for the dock leaves to soothe. Beth carried her into the kitchen, and tried covering them with a calamine lotion, trying to clean the scratches as best she could. Rhian ran round the room, up and down the stairs, trying to cause a draught to cool her body, while the nettle stings continued to burn. Wearing a pair of shorts had given her even less protection to her legs when she fell.

"If only you had worn long trousers," Anne said in retrospect.

"Oh shut up, it's too late now to tell me that. It's your fault," Rhian said angrily, still crying.

Eventually things calmed down and Rhian was consoled and soothed by all the family's attention which she now seemed to be enjoying. Catherine made a stage on the landing at the top of the stairs where curtains concealed an extra bedroom. The children dressed up in old clothes, playing Cinderella, with Rhian playing the lead of Prince Charming, with the help of the aunts, who were the ugly sisters. They were always so good at that sort of thing. Anne of course was Cinderella in rags, and Rhian soon forgot her fall and scratches and nettle stings, thoroughly enjoying herself again at last.

Fortunately, when the time came for her to go home, the nettle rash had subsided but the scratches were still evident.

"We can take her home safely," volunteered the aunts, looking at Beth, knowing it would save her a journey, as it was not too far out of their way near the park. Time was always so precious on the farm, so Beth was grateful for the offer.

"Serves her right," said Catherine when they had gone.

"Now, Catherine, that's not a very nice thing to say," her mother rebuked, "but that's what happens when you try to be too clever."

Anne was very sorry her friend had fallen off her pony, and no doubt Rhian's mother would be even more sorry that she had allowed her precious daughter to mix with such rough people.

She did not pay the farm another visit, and did not become her favourite friend, until many years later, when they met up once again. They reminisced about that memorable day Rhian had fallen into the bushes at the farm, all those years before, and both had a laugh about it. They became firm friends and remained so well into adulthood and their married lives, often talking about that first disastrous experience they had had together on the farm.

When the pony was twenty-two years old Anne really was too big to ride it any longer. Mary and Martha overheard their brother saying to Beth when they were visiting the farm one day, "It's time we took that pony back to Dai. We don't want it to die here. It's looking so well now, having put on some weight since no one rides her any more. Even her coat is looking better than I've seen it for a long time. There isn't enough grass anyway in the paddock, that's why I had to put her with the other horse and stallion out in the big field, months ago. The old animal really must go back."

When Beth told Anne, she did not want to return it. Although she did not ride Seren any more, she had become very attached to her. She couldn't bear the thought of not having her at the farm any longer.

Both aunts hated to see the children upset.

"It's obvious Anne doesn't want to part with it, and what difference does it make, keeping it? The farmer doesn't want it returned. Sometimes Daniel is so hard with them," commented Mary.

"I know, I feel the same, but we must never interfere about

anything we see or hear, or give our opinions. It's nothing to do with us."

However Daniel was insistent, and Beth usually found it was easier to agree with him than have an argument. He always had his own way in the end, so it wasn't worth making a fuss. He had always had his own way since he was a child, and there was no way he would ever change now. No matter what faults he had, she had been so lucky to meet him all those years ago. He had been a marvellous husband and so good to her, and what was more, he had loved her and continued to show her how much by his continued lovemaking and affection. This however he always reserved for bedtimes only, since the children had arrived.

"There's time and place for everything," he would say, but certainly lost no time when they were alone in bed.

Anne began to cry after her father had gone out to the fields, so Martha gave her a hug.

"Something will come. Don't be upset, Anne. We hate to see you unhappy."

The trouble was that on a farm, all the animals were treated the same and none were treated as pets. The dogs lived outside in the barn and were not allowed in the house, as were the cats which kept the mice at bay. They sometimes wished Beth would side with the children for a change, but they would never say anything. They knew their place, and they realised too that she knew how best to handle these situations. Often they felt she was torn, wanting to take the side of her children, instead of siding with her husband, but as the aunts had neither husband nor children themselves, they felt they were not the best people to judge.

There was another event that took place at the farm which they knew the children hated. It was when the time came to kill a pig. During the war years, farmers were restricted by regulations, as to how many pigs they were allowed to kill. Also every farmer had to have a permit, and the village policeman would have to sign it and visit the farm to check how many pigs were there to commence, and then return again after one had been killed. Every farmer was permitted to slaughter two pigs each year. But the children had often told Mary and Martha how much they dreaded this event. They hated it.

"When Daddy goes to the pigsty with Mr Prichard to get the pig, it squeals and squeals so loudly the noise rings in our ears much louder than a baby screaming into them, or ringing a loud bell, and it goes on and on for so long. They have to tie it securely to a bench and the poor pig doesn't know what is happening to it. It is so frightened."

"Yes," interrupted Anne, "it's dreadful. We keep our hands over our ears, don't we, Cath, but we can still hear the squeals. Then, when we feel we can't bear it any longer and can't wait for it to stop, suddenly there is silence at last. When this happens, you know Mr Prichard has put the knife in its neck and killed it. Everything seems deathly quiet around the farm afterwards."

"Yes and there is blood everywhere as if someone has tipped a big pot of bright red paint over the floor. I feel quite sick now, at the thought of it," said Catherine with a shudder.

"And there is blood all over Mr Prichard and Daddy. Why has a small animal like that got so much blood inside it, Aunt Mary?" asked Anne.

"Well, you've heard the saying. When someone cuts himself or herself and it is difficult to stop it bleeding, they often say they are bleeding like a pig. It probably means pigs lose a great deal of blood when cut, that's all."

The aunts hoped that would be the end of the conversation

about the pig, but Anne continued.

"As soon as the pig is dead, Mum has to make sure that there is plenty of boiling water and the two men carry it to the bench, and pour it over the pig. I'm not sure if it is to sterilise the poor thing or whether all the hair on it comes off more easily when it has been covered in boiling water."

"Yes," continued Catherine, " they use the lids of the milk cans to scrape the hair all off, because they are very sharp around the rim. It leaves the skin of the pig nice and smooth. Then Mum has to boil the lids to sterilise them to put back on the cans."

Anne picked up the story and continued. "Then Mr Prichard hangs the pig up in the barn and cuts it open and lets it hang there till the next day. He returns to the farm and he chops it all up into pieces."

"Yes," agreed Catherine, "and then we have its fresh liver for breakfast, and pork tenderloin for dinner."

"Mind you, it is all really tasty, if only we didn't know it was that poor squealing pig we were eating," said Anne.

"Mum has to boil the pig's head to make brawn, which is lovely in sandwiches, and you like that too, don't you, Aunt Martha."

She wished she could say she didn't, but she did, and she also loved the faggots that Beth always made and shared with them after they had killed a pig. Home-made faggots were delicious.

"We have to cut up all the blocks of salt," grumbled Anne, "and our knuckles really hurt and burn when we have to roll all the lumps out of it with Mum's rolling pin she uses for making pastry."

Mary and Martha knew that all the hams and bacon were salted on slabs in the dairy and remained there where it was cool. After a period of time, they would be hung up on the farmhouse kitchen ceiling with a metal hook, ready for all the cooked breakfasts and suppers. The gammon from the farm tasted so different from that in the shops and Mary and Martha were always well provided for, with produce and everything the farm produced. They always had enough for the whole winter, for Evan and Rhys as well.

But the aunts certainly were not happy when, during the war, the children told them that they had gone with their mother and father to fetch another pig, when it was dark and during the blackout. By law, farmers had to have permits to buy pigs, and as they had used up all the bacon they were allowed, Daniel needed to kill another one. After supper with the farmer and his family, the children told the aunts of their experience.

"Daddy told Anne and I to get into the back of the van and to lie down. The new pig had been given something to make it sleep, so Daddy and Uncle Syd carried the poor animal out and put into the back of the van with us. Then he told Mummy to throw the large blanket over the pig and us, and told us to go to sleep till we got home."

"Yes, it was really scary," Catherine continued with the account of what happened. "Daddy turned around to us, suddenly driving slower, with a sense of urgency in his voice. 'You two in the back there, keep very still and quiet, not a sound. Pretend you are fast asleep.'

"I was just going to ask why, when the van stopped abruptly. It was the police. They had flashed their large torches in the middle of the road, to stop our vehicle. They were checking on the movement of animals by black market, from farm to farm. That's what Daddy was doing, of course."

Daniel realised then what a risk he had taken, but he was fearless and always seemed to enjoy tempting fate, taking these risks, and the aunts knew that, always believing he would never be caught. It looked as if this time his luck had run out. He would be caught this time, red-handed.

"So what happened?" the aunts asked, knowing their brother was a quick thinker and never ran out of excuses when in trouble.

"Daddy wound down the window and was so unperturbed," Anne continued. "He spoke to the policeman in such a calm friendly voice, saying something like, 'Good evening, officer, anything wrong?' Then the policeman who was really nice said, 'No, only stopping to do the usual road check for carrying black market animals. Just like to ask you a few questions. Where have you been? And where are you going?'"

"Yes" Catherine said, "and Daddy replied cool as a cucumber that his children were in the back sleeping under the blanket, nice and warm. That was us two. The worse part was when a strong light from the policeman's torch was shone all over the back of the van and he even shone his torch on to our faces. We kept our eyes tightly shut but were so frightened, we couldn't swallow, could we, Anne?" Anne looked at her sister with that same frightened look on her face, still remembering the event as if it was something that only happened the day before.

"Daddy said we had all been to a party that evening in Pontadulais at the farm of friends and did not realise it was so late, and that he was just getting us home as soon as he could, to get us off to bed."

Then Anne piped up, "Yes, but the officer said it was very late for children to be out and in the blackout. Then he shone the torch on us again and said, 'You'd better be on your way and get to your home before there is another air raid. We've been told to expect one again later on tonight. Get on your way.'"

The children said that their father quickly wound up the window, started up the engine, and the van drove off quickly, with them all feeling a great sense of relief. Their father must have had a smile on his face, because their mother said to him, "I don't know how you can smile after all that" although she had remained silent all the time the police were at the window searching.

"Then Daddy said it had been a very close shave, but we didn't know what shaving had to do with the pig, nor why Daddy thought it funny being stopped by the police, and, even worse still, hiding the pig from them."

Catherine overheard her mother saying to their father, "I do wish you wouldn't take such risks, Daniel, especially when the children are with us."

"That's why I did it. They would never dream that we had a drugged pig in the back, lying down with the children under a blanket. Nobody would do such a thing."

Catherine and Anne told their aunts they always remembered how frightened they had been that night with the police, and they were never happy when a policeman came to the farm to check the pigs, after that episode. In fact they never really liked policemen at all when they were young. They had been so worried in case the pig had moved and their secret would have been discovered.

"We were so afraid of being found out and all of us being sent to jail," the children confessed. Mary and Martha were so often not really happy with what their brother did but it was up to Beth to tell him. Daniel had always been spoiled by them both and had all his own way, and once again had done whatever he wanted. It was too late now to change him.

When the village policemen called some months later to check that they only had one pig hanging in the house, Daniel had shown him the pig in the kitchen, being salted and then ushered him into the parlour. "Beth, make a cup of tea for Sergeant Willis, and give him one of your Welsh cakes you've just made." Then he was given a chair to sit on, immediately in front of the curtained alcove where the second illegal pig was hanging in the dark, like a bat in the belfry. Beth told Mary and Martha she could hardly swallow for being so frightened in case the policeman enquired what was behind the curtain. She understood then how frightened the children had been in the van.

"What lovely Welsh cakes," the sergeant had said, to which Daniel had then offered to give him some more to take home for his wife. The policeman left quite happily with the bonus of some freshly made home-made cakes for his wife and Daniel had got away with it once again. Another pig had been killed, salted and ready to eat.

Yes, the aunts often wished Beth would stand up to him more. Why was he always so fearless, not even afraid of the law? He had always been his own boss and had never had anyone to tell him what to do, but he was very lucky that Beth had gone along with everything he said or did, never arguing with him. Why did he always seem to be amused and happy about doing these wrong things and why did Beth allow him to do it? That must be what loving someone so much was all about. It did seem a bit one-sided in their brother's case, but how could they judge what the love for a husband was all about, anyway?

Visiting the farm a few weeks after Daniel had said the pony was to be returned, it was still there. Beth explained to them that Daniel had been too busy to think about the pony, much to Anne's relief. Just as the aunts were about to leave for Aelybryn, Daniel called his sisters over towards the gate into the nearby field.

"Come and have a look at this before you go. Something seems to have got into the field by mistake. Looks from here as if it's a stray greyhound in poor condition. What d'you think?"

The aunts peered across the field in the direction of the pony. Sure enough, there was something moving quite near to Seren, but she certainly wasn't afraid of it. Beth came out from the farmhouse to say goodbye to Mary and Martha and seeing them standing on the gate looking out towards the field, she too joined them.

"Open the gate and take a closer look. If it's a stray dog it will run away," she told them.

They all went into the field to take a closer look. To their amazement, there next to Seren was a tiny black foal, trying to stand on its thin, long spindly legs. They could not believe what they saw. Where on earth had it come from? Mary, Martha and Beth looked on while Daniel brought the pony and foal from the paddock to the nearby stable.

"Can't believe old Seren has had a foal," Daniel said smiling, but with a surprised look on his face. When they went into the stable, Seren was making a big fuss of her great new achievement, which had difficulty standing on such thin long legs. Soon the foal was sucking away enjoying a drink of milk from its proud mother and surrounded by fresh clean straw.

When the children came home from school, Daniel called over to them.

"Come and see what I found today in the field."

The children rushed into the stable. "Whose is it, Daddy?" Catherine asked.

"Seren's of course."

Both of the children were so excited.

"I thought she couldn't have one," Anne said jumping for joy, hardly able to contain her excitement. "Oh, it's beautiful.

Can I sleep in here tonight to watch over it, just in case anything happens to it?"

"Certainly not," her father told her, but when she went to bed that night she was far too excited to go to sleep. Even Catherine was quite excited at the new arrival and they both tried to think of a name for it. The following morning of course it dawned on them both that the foal didn't belong to them at all, and Seren and the foal would soon have to be returned to its original home for good.

Beth called in at Aelybryn during their milk delivery in the area, with some more unexpected news for the aunts. The pony had collapsed during the night and Daniel had sent for the vet very early that morning before the children were awake. He could see that Seren was very distressed. By the time the vet arrived, it was too late. Her heart had given out. The strain of the birth had been too much, and Seren had died. The children were told when they came down for breakfast. Anne sobbed.

Beth tried to explain to her. "Seren was only on loan, Anne. She would have been returned if there had been time, a week or two ago."

"But we could have visited her and what about the foal? What will happen to it now?"

"Well, we must ring Dai and tell him what has happened and take his foal back. It belongs to him," her father said quite firmly.

"I can't believe it," Dai told him when Daniel rang him to tell Dai the news. It was not possible for a pregnancy, let alone a birth at that age.

"I can't tell you how many times I've tried to get Seren in foal." But Daniel had put the pony in with the stallion, never thinking for one moment anything would happen, especially after what Dai had said about trying for years unsuccessfully, and now it was far too old anyway.

He told Daniel, "To tell you the truth, I've been waiting for a long time now to have a phone call to say that the old pony had died. I can hardly believe what you are telling me. I have no intention of taking the foal from you. Your daughter can keep it. The father was yours anyway. But it will be up to you to ask Mr Thomkins, the hauler of dead animals, to pick up old Seren, and you can pay for her disposal, as there is no point in bringing her back here now she's gone."

Seren was taken away when the children were out of sight so they did not see her again or know she had been incinerated.

Anne kept her foal and it always remained a favourite pet at the farm.

Chapter 11

For Mary and Martha, visiting the farm was the highlight of their week, and this visit was no exception. They returned after a very exciting day. There had been great activity for two weeks previously as at last Daniel was installing mains water on the farm. For years they had had the well water pumped up to the farmyard by a special pump. This was a tremendous saving, but now they had employed a company to install underground pipes from the main road all the way to the farm. Hopefully they could then run water directly into the house and then into the kitchen. Daniel had already installed a boiler next to the fire to heat water for domestic use. They would all bath in front of the fire in the galvanised one that he always insisted on filling, for fear of anyone scalding themselves with the hot water. Now things would be very much easier, but the children were only used to drinking water from the well. It was so clear and pure.

"I am never going to drink that water," said Anne indignantly.

"Nor am I," agreed Catherine. "I don't fancy the water if it's been in those pipes under the ground, they have to be very dirty."

"We'll stick to our well water, won't we?" said Anne.

"Then you both can go down to the well in future to fetch

every drop of drinking water yourselves," their father snapped, feeling they obviously did not appreciate the tremendous cost for this luxury. But when the moment came to switch on to the mains, there was great excitement as the water gushed out of the taps like small fountains.

"It really does seem like magic," Ann shouted excitedly, as she turned the new metal tap on and off several times, watching the water stop and start by just turning this small piece of metal.

"You try it, Aunt Mary."

Mary and Martha obviously were used to mains water, but were so pleased to be part of the excitement and share this with the children who soon forgot about their demands for drinking water from the well.

"I can't believe how clean it is, coming from those pipes, and so easily too," Catherine confessed.

From that day onwards, the animals only used the well from which to drink their water when they were out in the fields.

On their return to Aelybryn the aunts felt quite exhausted with all the excitement.

The siren had sounded in the middle of the previous night so they had had very little sleep. Rhys always accompanied the sisters over to the Anderson shelter across the other side of the road, as soon as they heard the siren warning them of a raid, but Evan never moved from his bed.

"If I am to die," he would say, "I'd rather die in comfort, in my bed."

The aunts did not interfere, or try to persuade him, if that was how he felt. It was his life, and entirely up to him, but they always worried about him, and were genuinely relieved when the all-clear siren sounded, and Aelybryn and Evan were safe. Before going up to his bed he always sorted out everything ready for the morning delivery, and he saw that the chickens were always all fed and locked up securely for the night. The cunning fox was always a threat. What an asset he was, and how glad they were that he had decided to stay with them when his brother had died. He reminded the sisters of their father, especially now he was older. He looked so much like him these latter years. He had the same build, with a rather large stomach, the same mop of hair now showing signs of grey, with the same thinning patch in the centre of his head. He also had the same ruddy complexion. Evan had a far greater sense of humour than that of his brother. His face always bore a broad smile, exposing a set of large brown teeth, tarnished by nicotine, having smoked all the years he was in Africa. He relinquished this habit when he came to Aelybryn because of the milk business involved there, and felt it was unhygienic to continue this dirty habit as he often called it. He did not feel he should smoke when he lived in a household which was involved with a form of food business. When he smiled, which he seemed to continually do, large gaps could be seen in his gums. When his teeth became loose, he could pull them out with his own hands using a set of pincers. In many ways Martha was like her uncle in temperament. She, like Evan, was very happy-go-lucky and easy to please. She enjoyed teasing other people, and was her happiest when it was reciprocated. This they did with each other a great deal and there was always bantering between them, which Mary would often find somewhat irksome.

When they returned from the farm, Mary and Martha described to Evan everything that had happened apologising for being far later than usual. Fortunately Rhys was delayed getting home from work that particular day, so he was not waiting patiently for his supper on their arrival. However, Mary noticed that he was quieter than usual, but Martha soon filled in the conversation with her chatter. Quite a number of times during the meal he and Mary caught each other's eye, but quickly Rhys turned away looking elsewhere. When he eventually arose from the table, he announced very casually what was obviously on his mind.

"Oh, by the way, I've been thinking about having a change from working in the drapers. A few weeks ago I saw an advert wanting someone to train as a buyer in North Wales. I really didn't think I was in with a chance. Then Mr Lewis told me I should apply. I thought and thought about it for days, and then I decided to have a go at it. I've heard today that I've been accepted. I have to admit it was a difficult decision but I'm tired of going to the shop, day in, day out. It's become so boring, doing the same thing all the time. I've been stock keeper for several departments these past few months and Mr Lewis gave me an excellent recommendation for this training job. I know I won't earn much money in the beginning, but it will be very interesting and do me good to get away and stand on my own two feet. You've spoiled me here, all these years."

He looked across at Mary but before she could say anything Martha piped up. "But we thought you were happy here, Rhys. You are one of our family. Why do you need to go away? And Mary will miss you too, won't you, Mary? You love your walks in the park together."

Mary looked quickly across at Rhys, but said nothing, suddenly picking up some dishes and returning them to the kitchen. She was so afraid of giving away anything by the obviously shocked and disappointed expression on her face.

"Oh, I have been so happy here with you all. Don't think I'm not grateful. I am," Rhys continued, while Mary listened to the conversation from the kitchen, out of his view. "But that is just it, you have been so good to me I feel the time has come for me to move on for a while. The years have flown by so quickly, and you have another man in the house now, you really do not need me as much as you did. Evan will never leave here, will you, Evan, and, besides, I shall be back whenever I can. I know this is still my home. I have nowhere else to go, but don't worry. I'll always return whenever I can to see you all."

Evan did not enter the conversation but sat quietly. When Mary returned from the kitchen Rhys mentioned his Dickens books to her.

"Mary, when my books arrive every month, you can open them for me and take your pick to read them." Then turning to Martha he said, "You can borrow them too, whenever you want. I'm sure you would enjoy reading Great Expectations. When Mary has finished it, she can pass it on to you. You may not like reading as much as she does, but I'm sure once you begin to read a good book, you will soon want to find other one."

Within two weeks, Rhys had packed his bags and left.

Mary really did miss him. She hated passing his room, let alone going in to dust and clean. She continued to go to the park for a walk on her own, but wherever she went, she could not help but think about him. She would remember things he had pointed out to her, or shown her, and especially what he had said to her that day when they had kissed each other. Still, she knew nothing would ever have become of their relationship. She had to admit to herself that she had so much enjoyed his passionate kiss on that afternoon, which was something very special in her life. One she would always remember, to the end of her days. She had never had anyone kiss her like that before. But that was life, and there was little gained by dwelling on things. She and Martha were never meant to marry and have children of their own. But they were fortunate to have nieces and a nephew of whom they saw a great deal, and they loved them as if they were their own. They both would have to be satisfied with that, although for the first time she now knew what it was like to have more intimate feelings, mentally and physically. She understood now a little better how Edward and Mrs Simpson felt about each other. But a promise should not be broken under any circumstances. The worst part of it all was that when she and Martha went to bed, Martha would fire her relentlessly with questions.

"Mary, do you miss Rhys? It does seem so strange without him, doesn't it? Funny after all these years, he decided to go off and leave us. Do you really think it was as boring as he made out at the shop? Or could there be another reason, d'you think?"

But Mary ignored the questions and tried to show it didn't bother her one way or another, quickly trying to change the subject of Rhys.

"Why worry about him, Martha? He can do as he pleases. Anyway we have each other, which is all that matters. Let's get off to sleep."

She realised they would always have to put each other's happiness before their own, and keep to that promise they had made years ago. But after Martha had snuggled down next to her and gone to sleep, Mary would lie awake well into the night thinking about Rhys and what it would have been like to have him make love to her. She was sad in a way that it had not gone just a little further, so that she would have been able to at least know what it was like to have a man touch her. She had never felt this strange excited feeling in other parts of her body before, although only their mouths had actually touched each other. She longed to have that same feeling just once again with him, but it would have been wrong to encourage him when it was such an impossible situation. It was best perhaps the way it was, for him to be away from her, yet she certainly did not really want him to go. The decision was his, and no doubt it was for the best for both of them. When he returned, it would all be in the past and forgotten about. She would never sleep with a man, but now she realised he gave her a different kind of pleasure, and the awful thing was she had enjoyed what he had done, little though it was. Funny she had never thought about those sorts of pleasures before. She had only heard or read about such things. However that was how it would remain, for both herself and Martha. They had such busy lives together there really was no place for the complications of a man and the feelings that went with him. She just hoped nothing would happen to Rhys, because bombs were dropping everywhere. One had dropped in the field below the farmhouse leaving a large crater there. She and Martha had been there when the bomb disposal men had arrived to detonate it. "Suddenly the siren sounded, but there was already a distinct sound of the diesel whine of a German plane overhead. We had all gone to bed and were fast asleep. Beth ran into the children earnestly trying to wake them but trying not to frighten them too much," Daniel told the sisters.

"Quickly get up and come downstairs. There's an air raid and we must get outside to the barn," she whispered to them.

They all crossed the farmyard together, with Daniel leading the way where they usually hid underneath the trapdoor at the back of the barn. He thought this was the safest place to hide. As they were approaching the barn door, an aeroplane flew overhead so low the noise was both frightening and deafening. Quickly they ran inside for shelter, and as they did so they heard a loud thud, and the large barn shook. The children began to cry with fright while Daniel felt sure the barn had been hit. Any minute there could be smoke and fire engulfing them, but everything was still. He wondered then was the barn a wise place for shelter? But they sat on the chaff huddled together quietly, waiting and listening without uttering a word to each other. An hour later the raid was over and the "All Clear" siren sounded. It was such a welcome sound bringing great feelings of relief once more. They had survived, although the German aircraft was right on target for the nearby aerodrome, but had dropped the bomb just short.

Beth made a hot milk drink for them all before they returned to their beds. They were so lucky to all be alive. The bomb could so easily have hit the farmhouse before they left or the barn just when they entered.

Yes, Mary hoped Rhys would be safe, after hearing about the bomb at the farm, and that it would not be too long before they saw him again at Aelybryn. At least after he had left, he had sent them a postcard every week, giving them the latest news, telling them briefly where he was and where he had been. He wrote to say that he had been to the picture house to watch a film, and he would describe what his landlady was like. Another postcard said there had been a number of air raids but he was safe and well. He had mentioned too that naturally he missed them all now he was on his own, but the work was very interesting and he was enjoying his new challenge.

Sometimes he went to Liverpool to a larger store for more experience, and when the postman dropped a card through their letterbox, Martha would run and pick it up and call out to Mary that the postman had been. There was a card from Rhys.

"Guess where he is this week," Martha would say to Mary, reading the card with great interest. Mary's heart would feel as if it missed a beat, and her stomach felt as if it had turned right over, but outwardly she would remain cool and calm.

"Don't tell me, Martha, I can read it myself."

Then she would take the card calmly and read it, hands trembling, yet trying to behave as if it meant little to her where in the country Rhys was at the time, but anxious that he was safe and well.

When he had been away for over six months and had not been back to Aelybryn, Daniel had called, as he often did, from his milk round and informed his sisters of the previous night's air raid.

"Beth and I had just got the children out of their beds, crossing to the barn for shelter again, when a piece of shrapnel flew through the air only just missing Anne's head. The German bombers were targeting the aerodrome again which as you know is so close to our fields."

When Mary and Martha heard this they were very worried for the safety of the children. Mary quickly came up with a brilliant suggestion.

"Why don't you have a word with Beth and see if the children can come here to live with us until the end of the war. It cannot go on for much longer. We'll look after them, and you and Beth can come in to see them anytime you want to, during the week and on the weekends. If the raids subside, they can easily return home again. They could go to your old school from here, and walk there by themselves, as long as Evan crosses the road with them while we are out delivering the milk. We'll be here to see them back after school. We really would love to have them, Daniel, wouldn't we, Martha, and they would be far safer here, away from the aerodrome and the threat of bombs."

Deep down Mary thought the children would certainly take her mind off Rhys and fill the gap he had left behind. Martha looked at her sister lovingly.

"No one, only you, Mary, could come up with such a

practical and helpful suggestion. Of course I'd love to have them," Martha told her. Evan too was delighted with the idea.

"We will all do our bit for the children and I will help and do whatever you want."

"That's settled then," Daniel told his sisters, without consulting Beth.

In 1943, when Anne was eight and Catherine was nearly twelve the children went to live with their aunts. They both found it very strange at first, hearing cars passing outside the window when they tried to go to sleep, and seeing people passing by on the road outside the house. They had always dressed themselves while standing in front of their bedroom window looking out across the fields. Now they had to keep the blinds drawn until they had their clothes on. They lived off the main road on the farm, and it was so peaceful and private.

"I'm homesick, Catherine, I want to see Mum," Anne told her sister the first night they went to bed at Aelybryn.

"Don't be so silly, you're not a baby, for goodness sake. How can you possibly be when we have come to live with two of the most lovable aunts? And we won't have to drink that awful brew of Senna Pods tea every Friday. I can't understand why Mum makes us drink it every week before breakfast, when we aren't even constipated. We both go to the toilet every day without any trouble. Anyway from now on we won't have to take it."

But Anne wasn't convinced. "I know it's awful stuff but it only takes a few seconds to drink. We don't know how long we are going to be here, it could be ages."

"Oh, Anne, get to sleep."

But Anne still missed seeing her mother. She would still have preferred to put up with the Senna Pods, but she had to admit it seemed safer at Aelybryn, away from the aerodrome near the farm. It was so terrifying when the German bombers targeted the area.

However very soon all the attention and the spoiling they both received more than compensated for the homesickness and Anne was happy again. When they returned to Aelybryn after school, their tea would be on the table, instead of having to help themselves when their mother would, more often than not, be out working in the fields or feeding the animals.

"Isn't this lovely not having to do all the chores Dad gives us every morning before school, and again after coming home," Anne confessed, and soon they both began to really enjoy their new life in a private house. Beth naturally missed her children a great deal even though she could see them more or less anytime she needed to. But life was so busy she had little time to herself for calling in at Aelybryn when the children were back from school. She really missed them at bedtime, and again in the mornings. Daniel, on the other hand, quite enjoyed the children being with his two sisters. Not only were they much safer there, but also he had Beth all to himself again. This was what it was like when they were on their own before the arrival of the two children. Now he could once again come in from the fields and take her off to bed whenever he wanted to. Beth often thought seeing the animals on heat didn't help her cause. Little wonder he thought of nothing else at times. When they went to bed tired, Daniel would still expect to make love, despite the fact they had been to bed earlier in the day. But she would do anything to please him, even though they were that much older now. She would always satisfy him in any way she could. Often she preferred to get into bed and fall to sleep as soon as her head touched the pillow, she felt so exhausted. But that was never an option as far as Daniel was concerned.

Life for the two aunts completely changed when the children came to live with them. They would get up long before the children, be out on their milk rounds, always leaving the breakfast set all ready for them.

"Evan, don't forget to call the children in good time so that they can prepare themselves for school," Martha would remind her uncle.

"Now you don't have to remind me. I'll see to it. Leave it to me, and I'll see they cross the road safely."

Every day, under their plates, would be some pocket money and points, or coupons, for sweets. Although shops were on rations, and all confectionery was still scarce, they could still obtain some from the tuck shop near the school. They were milk customers of their aunts, so the latter had preferential treatment. Martha would return to the house before school, to plait the girls' hair, and make sure they were dressed properly. Then she would give them both a big hug.

"Be good girls and we'll see you later. When you come home after school, perhaps Aunt Mary will take you to the picture house to see Ginger Rogers and Fred Astaire. We know you love to watch anything with dancing and music."

The children would be so excited at that prospect and could hardly wait. They loved to go and see musical films in colour and had now begun to collect postcards of their favourite actors and actresses. Many of them, for instance, Margaret Lockwood, Stewart Granger, Tyrone Power, Clark Gable and Vivienne Leigh, whose fan club they wrote to, had sent a postcard of themselves with their autograph. The children were delighted to receive these through the post, addressed to them. They had never before received mail of their own. Their parents had never had the time to take them to the picture house, so it was something new to them when they went to Aelybryn. They well remembered going to see a

George Formby film, one of their favourite persons on the screen, with Aunt Mary, but no sooner than they had found their seats, the siren had sounded, and everyone had to leave very quickly in an orderly fashion, and make their way home. By the time they were approaching Aelybryn, German aeroplanes were already flying fairly low overhead, making for the aerodrome again near the farm. The children were so frightened.

"How much further is it?" Anne continually asked, worrying in case their farm would be hit, and their parents hurt. But their aunts would look at each other and try reassuring them, not knowing for sure what might happen in wartime. Life now was so unpredictable. No one knew from one hour to the next. Then to everyone's relief, the "all clear" would sound. They were safely home and it would be a hot milky drink before bed.

Aunt Mary would help them with their scrapbooks into which they would stick cuttings and photographs of the two royal princesses, Elizabeth and Margaret, and everything connected with the Royal Family. When Buckingham Palace was bombed, there were lots of news cuttings to be cut from the newspapers. Aunt Mary would make them some paste out of water and flour with which to stick them. This gave them great enjoyment and it also filled in the evenings during the long dark winter with the blackout, and being away from their parents and home. Anne missed seeing her foal, despite the kindness and love shown to her at Aelybryn. She still longed for the war to be over, but so did everyone.

As they walked to and from school, Catherine would talk about what exciting things they would soon be doing with their aunts. Sometimes they would take a short cut through the graveyard and stop to look at all the graves, to read the inscriptions on the headstones. They would pass a weeping willow tree and see where their grandparents and other members of their family were buried, which fascinated them both.

Not long after the children arrived to live at Aelybryn, Martha bought a small second-hand car, a Morris 8. Now she was able to take Mary and the children for a ride, stopping at the ice cream parlour near the sea front, for North Poles, which were double wafer ice creams, or an ice cream sundae, which contained fruit, ice cream and raspberry sauce, all of which were such a great treat for the children. They did not understand why Aunt Mary was not so keen on going to the ice cream parlour, neither could Martha understand what possibly could be her reason. She had always loved ice cream.

"Come on, Aunt Mary, we know you like it, so why don't you want to go?" shouted the children trying to encourage her. Then she relented, seemingly enjoying it once she was inside. But Martha noticed once or twice when she looked across at her sister, she seemed deep in thought, but she made no comment.

The children adored their two aunts; little wonder when they received so much attention from them. Sometimes they would go to the fish and chip shop down the bottom of the street owned by Mr and Mrs Watson. Mr Watson was a very large jolly-looking man with grey hair and a large grey moustache. He looked like Father Christmas, except that he wore a large snow-white apron, tied around his equally large stomach that he tried to disguise with a large bow made from his apron strings. Mrs Watson was a small neat-looking lady who wore gold-rimmed spectacles on the end of her nose, but with a warm welcoming smile with which she greeted all her customers. The children loved to order their battered sausages and chips over the counter. Fish, of course, was scarce and expensive during wartime, but the children loved the treat of going to the shop and sitting inside at a table to eat what they had bought. They also enjoyed the dried egg mixture in place of fresh eggs during the war. It was a novelty for them because they seldom went without fresh eggs on the farm. They had never been inside a fish and chip shop before this. In fact they seldom did anything when at the farm, only helping their parents. This was a great treat to be at the fish and chip shop and being allowed to help. If it was very busy there, Mrs Watson would ask the children if they would like to earn some money by helping with the washing of the dishes and glasses, when some customers had lemonade to drink with their plates of chips. They would also help to fill up the salt cellars and the vinegar bottles. In return, they could have pocket money and a free portion of chips and lemonade. They had never had money for doing anything on the farm; therefore they thought this was tremendous. Their aunts also allowed them to keep the money they had given to them to buy the chips in the first place. Soon this became a regular duty on a Friday night, and the only duty that they ever had payment for, until they both eventually began to work outside the farm in proper employment.

It was Martha who supervised the bathing and washing of hair, while Mary always put them to bed and either read or told stories to them. They always loved her to say her very special rhyme. "Peter Piper picked a peck of pickled pepper. A peck of pickled pepper, Peter Piper picked. If Peter Piper picked a peck of pickled pepper, where's the peck of pickled pepper Peter Piper picked?"

She would repeat this, over and over again, saying it faster and faster. Then she would ask the children in turn, to see how fast they could say it, during which time they often fell asleep quite exhausted. Mary was the one who taught them to sew, while Martha taught them to knit. Little wonder then, that when Rhys came home for his first weekend after being away for more than six months, the sisters were so busy, they hardly had any time to themselves, let alone time to stop and listen to all his news about his recent new venture. He was surprised to see how much Martha had changed while he had been away. In fact, it was she who seemed to be far more interested in all his news. Mary was wrapped up with the children. Also, he noticed that Martha had now taken her hair back away from her face, changed the style completely, and had suddenly grown into an attractive woman. She wasn't a child any longer. He had never noticed how large and rounded her breasts were compared with Mary, who was very flat chested. Martha's dresses seemed to accentuate this fact, unintentionally he was sure, knowing Martha. That would not have entered her head. Why had he never taken any notice of her before? He had never paid much attention to Martha at all, in all years he had been living with them. Of course she had only been very young when he had arrived at Aelybryn, about fifteen years of age, he seemed to recollect. Mary was almost the same age as he was, and they had far more topics of conversation.

Now things seemed to have changed, and it was Martha who paid him attention and showed an interest in where he had been, and what he was now doing.

"We loved to have your postcards, Rhys, and read what you had been up to and what part of the country you were in."

"But did you have time to read Great Expectations as soon as Mary finished with it?" he enquired with keen interest.

"Yes, I loved it. I was fascinated reading about Pip visiting Miss Haversham's house and the fact that she had never seen the sun or been outside the room where her wedding reception would have taken place, had her lover not let her down on her wedding day. That must have been dreadful, but I had to remind myself that it was only a story, and it never really happened," Martha told Rhys.

"Imagine the wedding cake still there after all those years, with mice running through it, and Miss Haversham still in the same clothes. Nothing had been touched since that awful day years and years before," Martha recalled again to Rhys over supper.

"I loved the chapter where Pip met Estelle for the first time at Miss Haversham's, and he thought how pretty she was, but she paid him no attention in return; in fact, was extremely rude to him." Martha could not bear that sort of behaviour.

"Yes, it is a fascinating story, I must say. Now you really should try to read 'A Tale of Two Cities' next, when you get the chance," Rhys told her.

"Oh, I shan't have time for reading now. Just as well I read Great Expectations before the girls came to live with us or I would never have finished it," she confessed.

"But you can take your time, I don't need them. If you want to read any of the others, just help yourself. Until the war is over and the children go back to the farm, as you said, I can't see you having any time for reading, or any spare time for that matter. They keep you so busy. However I'm glad to hear you both still manage to play the piano."

During the following year, Rhys came home more frequently and seemed to love being back there once again.

"I have almost finished my training for a managerial job in a shop," he had said to everyone on one of his visits. "I may look back here again for a post, if one becomes free. Perhaps I could have my old room back on a more permanent basis?"

he joked. "I should earn more money than when I was last here, so it would make a big difference to me. I can be more independent from now on and pay more for my keep."

"Of course, your room is still as you left it. You did say you would be back and fore, when you could manage it. This is still your home, Rhys, and you will always be part of our family. You must never worry about paying us more money," Martha told him firmly with great delight.

"Isn't that so, Mary?" She looked across at her sister waiting for her to agree. But she did not sound very convincing.

"Of course," she replied tersely.

Martha was obviously very happy at the prospect of Rhys's possible return, but she noticed that Mary seemed to show no enthusiasm whatsoever. Little did Martha know that, deep down, Mary knew her life had been decided for her years before and Rhys would never be part of it, although she was pleased he was safe, but unsure about his return to live with them again. Now they had such a busy life between everything, and she was happy with it just the way it was. She had the children to think about, caring for them, entertaining them, and looking after them, as well as the business. Her days were now so full. What had happened between her and Rhys seemed such a long time ago. A great deal of water had gone under the bridge since then.

Chapter 12

Rhys managed to obtain a position back in the area, as head of the men's department in a large store in the centre of the town. After heavy bombings in 1941 by the Luftwaffe, later known as the "Three Nights' Blitz", Hope Bros, a smart men's tailor, and many other shops in the High Street had been reduced to rubble. He felt he had been very fortunate to be employed, despite the fact he now had a certificate to prove that he had reached the required standard needed for a managerial position. He was pleased too that he could help Evan in the garden, with the "Dig for Victory Campaign". Anyone with a garden was asked to grow vegetables to help supplement the food shortages. Aelybryn of course were never short of food because there were always adequate supplies at Beth and Daniel's farm. They always ensured the family were well catered for. But everyone felt they needed to do their bit for the country and Martha often cooked lava bread for breakfast, which was made from seaweed, grown and collected in abundance along miles of rocky Gower coastline.

Mary and Martha continued to look after the children and were kept very busy organising them, also having to run a business. Both tried to continue making knitted garments for the serving military forces and encouraged the children to do so. Mary continued to devote a large amount of her time doing all the accounts, and was not interested in teaching herself to drive the car; therefore Martha drove wherever they went, when coupons for petrol allowed, taking Mary and the children with her.

Rhys found Martha great company as she was always full of fun and laughter, and they had teased each other constantly since his return. The house always seem so full when she was around and, although the children loved their Aunt Mary, they too had a lot more fun with Aunt Martha. She was so good at acting and playing tricks with them while Mary had always been more serious and, of course, always very sensible. Rhys noticed that while he had been away she was not the woman he had left at Aelybryn. Now he hardly saw her. She devoted a great deal of time seeing to the children, and after her rounds, spent it on the accounts and reading books, which she did alone in the parlour.

"I had hoped we could have had the occasional walk to the park again now I am back," he told her casually.

"Sorry, Rhys, but I really have very little free time now the children are with us and I do like to try and read when I have the chance. We have so much to do nowadays."

She had always been quite a serious person but surely she should be having a little relaxation. She worked so hard and his thoughts went back to when he had persuaded her to go with him to the park, because he felt she spent too much time alone. Martha on the other hand was equally as busy, but was so bubbly and full of life. She loved to relax and have some fun.

It was during the spring of 1945 that Martha planned for them to take the children back to the farm for half of the day.

"The children want to return home today because Daniel is installing electricity. They want to see what this involves as they hate to think they are missing anything."

"Oh, count me out today. I have far too much to do and anyway I need to get these accounts up to date," Mary told Martha.

"But the accounts are not urgent. Come on, come with us. It could be interesting, and the children are quite excited about it."

"No, you carry on," she told her sister, already having started to go with her accounts books into the parlour. Martha looked across at Evan, who just raised his grey bushy eyebrows, but made no comment.

"Come on, girls," Martha called out to the children, "I'm ready" and putting on her hat and coat, marched out through the door.

"What would we do without her?" Evan said smiling to himself as she went.

Daniel had already changed from oil lamps to calor gas downstairs, but so often just when you needed the light, the gas filament would break and there was never a spare one in the cupboard when you needed it. They still used candles upstairs, and the aunts always worried about the children lighting them in the dark mornings using matches alongside the bed, and at night going up the stairs carrying the candles already lit. They often read whilst lying in bed, and then sometimes they fell asleep without blowing them out. This is what the children loved about Aelybryn. That house already had electricity, so they could see clearly to read and sew without straining their eyes all the time. Even in daylight, the farmhouse was quite dark having such small windows. It was so difficult without artificial lighting. Having electricity would open up a new world as far as the family were concerned, and for the cows too. No longer would they be milked by hand. They had ordered new milking machines which meant that they would be fitted on to the cows' udders while the milk automatically pumped its way into a can, having gone through the attached rubber tubing. The electricians had already spent some weeks previously, getting all the wiring done to bring the power to the farm from the main road.

Beth summoned Martha and the children to the cowshed, while Daniel was instructed to operate the large switch and turn it to the "on" position allowing the power to come through. Immediately the cows began to dance. It was as if they were being tickled simultaneously with a feather duster. Everyone roared with laughter except Daniel, who rushed back to the switch in order to turn off the power. The electrician immediately dashed into the shed saying he had found there was a short circuit somewhere, and the cows were having a slight electric shock from the metal chains securing them to the stalls. This was soon rectified, but it could have been far more serious, possibly electrocuting them, had the current been much stronger. Daniel was not amused.

"That was not a laughing matter," he told them with a very serious look on his face. "I could have lost a great deal of money if they had been electrocuted."

He had never, of course, bothered with any form of insurance, believing nothing would ever go wrong. However he was to find out later that this same method of a slight shock would prove very valuable. It became a means of containing the cows wherever needed. This was known as an "electric fence", which gave them the same type of mild electric shock when they touched it; therefore they moved away. It was very useful when the cattle were not required to go to various parts of the fields, which could then be sealed off at any point, by just moving the fence when required.

After this very exciting day, the three returned to Aelybryn. They had so much to tell the others and the children were still laughing about the cows dancing, even when they went to bed. It was while Mary was seeing to the children upstairs that Rhys had gone into the kitchen to see Martha preparing the supper. Evan was still up in the dairy with the milk churns, scalding them ready for the milk round the following day. Martha was chuckling to herself about the episode of the cows and was telling Rhys about it, despite the fact that her brother was not amused. Suddenly Rhys put both his arms around her waist from behind her. She swung around thinking he was going to tickle her, teasing her as usual, but she swung straight into his arms. Before she knew what was happening, their mouths met, albeit briefly. Martha began to laugh aloud, giving him a good push.

"What do you think you are doing, Rhys, getting right in my way like that?" treating it as if it was a complete accident.

"Well it was nice, wasn't it?" he teased. She was about to answer, when the door opened and Evan came in to the kitchen. Just as well he had not entered seconds before, Martha thought to herself. Whatever would he have thought?

"Supper ready then, Martha? Smells good," Evan's cheerful voice asked, feeling even more hungry when the aroma of Martha's cooking filled the kitchen. "Your food is always so tasty. I feel quite ravenous."

"It's almost ready, Evan, but Rhys here is hindering me and getting in my way," Martha told him, laughing and giving Rhys a hard slap on the back, sending him reeling, almost into Evan's arms. They all laughed, while Martha continued as if the kiss hadn't occurred, regarding it as a playful accident. The incident was soon completely forgotten.

That week, Rhys had been to the pictures on his own as usual and on the newsreel he had been quite disturbed by the discovery of Belsen Concentration Camp. The horrific sights he saw on the screen and which later appeared in all the newspapers made him almost physically sick. There were 40,000 bodies buried in mass graves, 10,000 unburied corpses of inmates who died of starvation and disease. He could not believe the Inhumanity of which people were still capable. Had he not seen enough in the last war? And had they learned nothing? When he arrived home, he spoke to Martha about it, obviously still upset.

"Thank God my family were blown to pieces and hopefully felt nothing. I couldn't bear to think of them in a camp like that. I never thought I would see anything so disturbing again in my lifetime, after what I saw in the 1914-1918 war."

Martha tried to change the subject. She could see he was upset and distressed by it, and who wouldn't be? Soon she was able to turn his mind to something more pleasant and he was smiling again. Martha had that quality about her. She tried not to dwell on anything herself and ensured no one else did either. She was so good for him, and suddenly he felt drawn to her once again. So much so that he desperately wanted to put his arms around her as he had done before, and be able to feel her physical closeness. But Martha suddenly announced, "Mary will be down soon, she's nearly finished seeing to the children, then we can all have supper together. It's ready."

The evening passed by again with a certain amount of amusement, with Martha relating some stories of her customer's escapades. Evan and Mary retired to bed while Martha, as usual, checked that the fire was completely out before going upstairs to bed. Suddenly Rhys caught around her again as he had done in the kitchen. She did not push him away and they held each other very closely, not kissing but just holding each other. This time it was different. Martha did not mock him or laugh at him. She felt so sorry for him, it was the least she could do to comfort him after being reminded of his own terrible ordeal years before in the trenches. Seeing Belsen Concentration Camp in the newsreel had obviously bothered and upset him greatly.

"I understand how you must feel, Rhys, but try not to let it upset you so." Then giving him a hug, she turned quickly and went off up the stairs.

But that was the beginning of a flirtatious relationship between Martha and Rhys. Whenever they were alone, the hugs became longer, and the kisses more passionate, both enjoying this harmless affection. Although in the beginning she had felt sorry for him, now she also enjoyed the excitement of it. Often he would squeeze her hand when passing her, or give her a wink and affectionately smack her on the bottom, which they would both smile about, because it went quite unnoticed by anyone else.

By May 1945, the Second World War had ended. Bunting went up everywhere, and there were street parties. There was dancing on the green, and the children were desperate to take part in the celebrations. Trestle tables were organised in the streets for teas and parties and in the village hall. Back at the farm there would be no such celebrations and they would not be involved at all with such fun and activities. So they were allowed to stay for an extended few weeks. However after all the festivities were over, it was time for them to return home and leave Aelybryn behind for good. The children had been so happy there and had had so much fun. Now they were growing up too. They had learned a great deal from living with their aunts and often over the years to come, they would reminisce about the wonderful times they had had at Aelybryn. One experience, of the many they recalled, was the evening Martha had taken out of her pocket a packet of cigarettes, much to Mary's disgust.

"What are you doing with those?" she demanded, trying to

show her facial disapproval, but could not catch Martha's eye.

"Having a go at smoking, of course. I managed to get them today from one of my customers, I won't tell you who."

"Martha, whatever are you thinking about, especially in front of the children? You know we never wanted to smoke; it's such a dirty bad habit. You always agreed it was."

"Oh come on, Mary, it's only a bit of fun."

"Well, I don't call that fun, so I refuse to try it. Neither Evan nor Rhys would like to think of you with a cigarette in your mouth, especially with the children here, and anyway we have a milk business to think of."

"Well, Evan and Rhys can't see me, can they?"

Martha took a cigarette out of the packet, placed it in between her lips, and struck a match, lighting it by inhaling deeply. Suddenly she began to cough and splutter, almost choking with laughter as well as the effect of the smoke.

"Serves you right," her sister told her.

"Ah, I didn't know what to do. I've not tried it before. I'll have another go."

Mary picked up the newspaper in disgust while Martha tried again at puffing the cigarette, this time keeping the smoke in her mouth, and then blowing it out towards the ceiling. The children thought it was great fun seeing Aunt Martha trying to smoke.

"There, that's better. Do you girls want to have a go?" and getting two cigarettes out of the packet, she gave one each to Catherine and Anne, adding, "Don't tell your father, for goodness sake. He'd kill me."

Mary was appalled that her sister would do such a thing, encouraging young children like that to try smoking. The two children thought this was a great idea. They had watched their favourite actors and actresses on the screen all smoking, so copied their aunt's instructions carefully.

But they breathed the smoke in deeply, as she had done, and soon they began to cough and splutter. Not at all as they had witnessed on screen in the cinema. Catherine felt sick and Anne felt likewise. The children decided that night they did not like the taste of smoke, especially when it made them almost choke. They didn't want to try it again. That night had put them off smoking for good. Martha didn't try it again either.

The children were now of the age to change schools; therefore it was a good time for them to return home. It would be good to be with their mother again after all this time. They had never been close to their father as he was always outside working on the farm until after they were in bed. He had never given them a goodnight kiss or cuddled them as the aunts and their mother did. He had not been a demonstrative father, never showing any warm feelings towards them or towards their mother for that matter.

"Don't know how Mum and Dad managed to have us. I can't imagine him doing that sort of thing with Mum, can you, Catherine?"

"Well, that's private and anyway they must have, mustn't they? Otherwise we wouldn't be here."

"We could be adopted."

"Oh don't be so silly, Anne, you do talk such nonsense."

"Maybe all fathers don't kiss their children, but it will be nice to have Mum's affection again anyway."

Well, home they were going, and back to the chores of the farm, and the dreaded Senna Pods brew every Friday: the cure for juvenile constipation from which they had never suffered. They would also have to make tea for themselves once more while their mother was busy on the farm. It would take some getting used to after the spoiling they had received from everyone at Aelybryn. They often said those were years that they would never forget for the rest of their lives. They had learned so much about living and sharing and working together, never hearing any squabbling or bad feelings, any arguing or raised voices. It was such a calm and loving environment. It had been such a wonderful time in their lives. Time that would leave a lasting impression on both of them.

Mary missed the children terribly and seemed so lost without them. Martha missed them too, but she had so many other things on her mind, places to go, people to see, friends to meet, and of course the new interest in her life. What fun she had with Rhys, knowing it was nothing serious. They were just physically attracted to each other and both were enjoying this close contact. It was so good after the gloom of the war years. Yes, it was such good fun. Innocent passion was a great uplift, but the trouble was that Martha never wanted Mary to know about it or to find out. She would be furious with her. This was far worse than smoking; and Mary thought that was bad enough. She knew it was not the sort of thing she should be doing, but why not when they both enjoyed it? And of course it was harmless as they were both single people. Nevertheless, she felt somewhat guilty at times, as if she was almost being an unfaithful wife, with clandestine meetings and snatching an intimate embrace whenever no one was around.

But continue they did, whenever they found themselves alone, or in the outhouses near the dairy. One day he put his hand inside her blouse when they were together and kissed her quite passionately. His mouth was hard on hers and he tried to part her lips with his tongue. She had only read about this in books, and wanted to stop him but just could not do so. She was enjoying it far too much to stop. When eventually their tongues entwined, searching all around each other's mouths, what a wonderful sensation that gave her. This seemed to send strange feelings and emotions to other parts of her body, which excited her so much, she could hardly wait for the next time. Gradually they enjoyed a little more than just the cuddles and kisses with which they had innocently began.

One afternoon Mary decided she would go to the village to do some shopping.

"Martha," she called, "do you need anything from the grocer's shop?"

"Not anything you can carry. Thanks anyway. I'll get what I need when I go out in the car."

"In that case I may call in and see Mrs Winterbottom with her new baby on my way home."

Rhys had the afternoon off and was going to do some gardening which he thoroughly enjoyed because Evan found digging quite arduous. The gooseberries were ready for picking too, so hopefully he would get enough off the bushes for Martha to make jam and some pies. Gooseberries had been his mother's favourite, he remembered. Evan had gone to bed to have a snooze which he often did nowadays in the afternoons. He could not seem to get out of the habit of rising before 5 a.m. ever since returning from South Africa, and by the afternoon he was ready for a quick nap. He needed to be up at five o'clock to help Martha and Mary.

Martha had taken a cup of tea to Rhys in the garden, but it began to rain so he cleaned the shovel and soon returned to the house. Martha was alone, so they began their usual cuddling and kissing, taking full advantage of being alone together. He had now started to fondle her breasts, which Martha loved him to do. They did not worry about tomorrow. This was today, and they were both excited by what they did and enjoying it. They were two grown-up people, she forty-two and he now fifty-one, and they were both free to do as they wished so long as no one found out. They were doing no harm to anyone.

Mary had not taken her mackintosh with her so decided when it began to rain that she would get back home far earlier than expected. She entered the back way as usual, and as she was about to open the door she saw them, through the window. They did not see her, but she felt sick.

How could they do that? What was Martha thinking of, letting Rhys touch her like that? His hand was up her skirt. How disgusting. And what about Rhys? He had said that he had loved her once, a long time ago. She knew that it was an impossible situation, quite impossible. They had only kissed and it was her choice that it had not continued. Now he was with her sister. She hated him. She did not blame Martha at all. Rhys was to blame. He was older and should know better than to tempt Martha. Yes, she despised him for doing this to them.

She quietly and quickly returned to the street still shocked and upset. She must never show she had seen them together, that was certain, but this was going to be so difficult for her. In the past, Martha had always talked about everything when they went to bed. She could never get a word in. How could Martha keep this secret to herself? And just how long had it been going on?

She was probably just doing it to please Rhys, no doubt feeling sorry for him which is what they had both done, ever since he came to live with them after the war. She knew Martha didn't love Rhys, and you only did that sort of thing if you were in love with the person. She was sure Martha never saw men in that light. They had promised each other years ago to stay together and neither of them would ever break that promise. She remembered how much she had wanted to be with Rhys in the park that one time, but she had put their promise to each other and their happiness above everything. Martha was not as strong-willed as she was. After all they did have different mothers. Martha no doubt found this great fun, and a wonderful experience, something they both had only read about in books. But him, well he should know better. He had been away, and no doubt had been with lots of women before, many times, and it meant nothing, otherwise he would have stayed away and married one. He knew he could not have either of them as she had told him so. What did he think he was doing? He had better not hurt Martha, that's all. This could get completely out of hand and Martha would find herself in great trouble. Poor Martha. But she still believed she should keep this discovery to herself. Perhaps in time, Martha would mention it, and she would pretend not to know. But whatever would she say to her if she confided in her?

She dreaded going back to the house, but she had to. There was absolutely no choice in the matter. Now she realised what Rhys had felt like when he obviously wanted to get away, but that was not an option for her; she had to remain. Besides, there was nowhere she could go. When she returned she tried to behave as if nothing was wrong, but she felt awful. Her stomach churned inside, and she still felt sick. Fortunately Rhys had gone to the cinema and would not be back until later. Well, she would make sure she was in bed when he came in. Things would perhaps seem better in the morning.

Martha said she would stay downstairs and wait until Rhys returned. Mary felt sick again with the thought that they may be kissing downstairs as soon as he came in. Evan was already in bed and they would be alone. However Martha soon followed her sister to bed, behaving like her usual self, as if nothing out of the ordinary had happened.

When she began to chat, Mary put off the light.

"If you don't mind, Martha, I feel quite tired. I've done so much walking today. Also we will have to be up early for the round in the morning. It could be raining again."

Getting wet was always more unpleasant and tiring and Martha, taking her sister's advice, soon fell fast asleep, but Mary lay awake for hours wondering how she would manage to hide what she knew. But hide it she would, at all costs. Neither Martha nor Rhys would ever find out what she had witnessed that afternoon.

Chapter 13

During the weeks that followed, Martha noticed such a change in Mary; she did not seem to be herself. In fact, Martha was quite worried about her. She was not sleeping very well at night, tossing and turning and therefore found it difficult to cope in the day. She always seemed tired.

"Take a visit to the doctor," Evan suggested, because he felt when she arose in the mornings she looked as if she had not been to bed the night previously. Reluctantly she eventually took his advice, although Martha too thought it was the best thing to do. The following day she went to visit Dr Gough in the village. Martha had found him excellent when she had an ear infection which was eventually diagnosed as a mastoid and she had ended up in hospital having an operation. It was not only costly, but the operation had left her slightly deaf in her left ear. However it hadn't affected her being able to distinguish sounds in her music which had been her main anxiety. She didn't always catch what was said to her and, on rare occasions, words had to be repeated. But Martha never let it bother her, and often made a joke of it with her customers. Dr Gough had been wonderful during that time, and eventually Mary went to see him. When she returned from the surgery, Martha was full of questions.

"What did he say, Mary? Did he give you any medicine and

did he find out what was causing your problem? We must realise you are now fifty years of age after all and maybe you are going through the crisis of the change of life, which I've heard so much about from my customers. Some women seem to have very nasty symptoms. Did he say it could be that? I know it seems to affect different people different ways."

"Well, he thinks I have a thyroid problem, so I have some tablets to take. He has given me some mild sleeping tablets too which will help me at night for the time being."

"Oh, I'm so glad you've sorted it out, Mary, you've not been yourself for weeks. A few of your customers have noticed you weren't your normal sociable self on the rounds and they were quite concerned about you."

But Martha still felt Mary continued to act very strangely on occasions, as if she had a heavy weight on her shoulders. Sometimes she was slightly short-tempered with Rhys, but still spoke affectionately to Evan, thank goodness, and herself of course. Martha could not work it out at all and was still very concerned although she was relieved that her sister had sought medical advice.

When they were due to go to the farm the following week, Mary had said she had a really bad headache and that she was going to bed for the afternoon to see if that would help it improve.

"Well, that's probably a good idea, Mary, not to overdo things. You rest. I know Beth will understand. I'll see you later then," Martha told her before going off on her own in the car. She was so glad she had made the effort, for two reasons. Daniel had bought his first tractor, a second-hand Fordson, with large cogwheels. This would make a tremendous difference on the farm instead of using the horses for everything. They would still be used to pull the flat cart for spreading lime and manure and to draw the gambo for haymaking during the summer. But while Daniel would be ploughing and using the tractor for other work, the boys who worked and slept on the farm would use the horses for their other work. A new boy had started the previous week because Jim, the older of the two lads, had wanted to move nearer some relations he had found, so the orphanage had sent a replacement. Beth had told Martha she wasn't sorry Jim was leaving as he walked in his sleep. A neighbouring farmer had a boy who often did that and word went around the village that he had even gone into the stable and harnessed a horse before he had woken up out of his sleep. The remedy was to place a pan of water at the bottom of the stairs so that he would step into it and wake up before he went any further. It was thought unwise to wake them up any other way, but Martha, like Beth, was glad Jim was going elsewhere to work.

The new boy George seemed to have settled in quite well and after three days Daniel had sent him down to one of the fields near the railway line with the horse and cart to spread manure over the field, ready for the planting of potatoes. He had given him a long handled fork and told him to use that to spread the manure, which was mixed with straw from the bedding for the animals. On his return, later in the afternoon, Daniel had noticed that Blackie the horse was limping badly.

"What's wrong with Blackie?" Daniel enquired, looking anxiously at his horse.

"I think he stepped on a large stone," suggested George.

"Take him to the stable and give him some water, but before you put him back out in the field. I'd better come and have a closer look at him after I've had a cup of tea with my sister." It was while he was having his cup of tea that Daniel mentioned his uneasiness to Martha and Beth. While the two boys came into the farmhouse for their break, Daniel went to have a look at Blackie's leg and foot to see what was the problem. Sometimes a small stone could get caught in between the shoe and the hoof, and it would be quite painful to walk on. When he lifted the horse's foot, he noticed blood coming from two places. He filled a bucket with warm water and an antiseptic solution, and dipped the horse's foot into it which made it jump. After cleaning the wound, he took it out into the field to graze, intending checking it again the next morning. He certainly gave the impression to Martha that all was not well, and that he was quite worried which was unusual for Daniel. He was not one to make a fuss unnecessarily. Obviously he refrained from sending for Mr Pugh the vet unless it was very urgent. Vet's fees were always very costly when he had to visit the farm.

The following morning when he went into the stable to check on Blackie, the foot seemed to be worse. Now it was swollen and Blackie could hardly put it to the ground. There was nothing for it but to send for Mr Pugh. The horse was obviously in pain so there was no choice and something had to done immediately, although Daniel hated spending money.

"When did this happen?" enquired Mr Pugh.

"Well, only yesterday," replied Daniel.

"And who was handling the horse at the time?"

"One of my new lads from the orphanage."

"And what sort of implement was he using when he noticed there was a problem with the foot?"

"I don't see what that has to do with it, but well, he was using a four-pronged fork."

"Well, I'm sorry to have to tell you but I think two of the prongs went into the horse's foot. Go and fetch the fork for me to inspect it."

Daniel did as the vet instructed and returned immediately with the implement. The holes in the horse's foot were identical with two of the prongs of the fork.

A look of shock spread over Daniel's face which then turned to anger.

He immediately sent for George.

"Explain to me exactly what happened yesterday," he demanded.

"Well, the horse moved on before I told him to, so I picked up the fork to tap him but it slipped out of my hand, and went into his foot."

"You should never be cruel to dumb animals, mine in particular. You finish working here today. Go and pack your bags and I will return you to the orphanage at once."

He was dismissed without notice, despite the fact that Beth wanted to give him a second chance. But Daniel was adamant. He seldom changed his mind once it was made up.

"No use having a boy I cannot trust," Daniel told Beth. The one thing he could not bear was cruelty to animals. From that day onwards, Daniel did not employ any more boys from the orphanage. Besides, he now needed someone with more experience on the farm and someone on whom he could rely. He advertised in the Farmer's Weekly for the post and they were fortunate enough to find an experienced older man, unmarried, from Carmarthenshire, who could also live in the farmhouse with them.

Despite numerous visits from the vet, the horse's wounds became infected and had to be treated for many weeks to follow. Eventually they healed, but Blackie continued to limp for the rest of her days, and it proved to be a very costly business.

The other new arrival at the farm was a large short-horned brown prize bull. Daniel had always wanted to own one, and he was the first in the village to do so. This meant that all the farmers would be able to bring their cows to be serviced by this prime beast, for which they would be charged a profitable sum of money. It would soon pay for itself, and Daniel could also use it whenever his own cows needed servicing, to produce the calves he required.

Martha went into the shed with Daniel to view this special addition to the stock, while Beth stayed with the children. The children were not allowed into the shed, but stood near the door with their mother. Daniel explained that bulls could be very dangerous animals if not handled correctly, and it was best to keep their distance. Martha thought he really looked a ferocious creature, with a large ring in its nose, and two short, thick, pointed horns. Daniel explained that he had a long handle with a hook on the end and this would go through the ring when they needed to exercise the bull. If it were not obedient, the ring would hurt if twisted, so you always had the animal in full control. Martha decided she would not like to meet that animal anywhere on the farm alone and that she would never want to be confronted by a bull. In fact, that very night, she dreamed that one had chased her and it was big, brown and had short thick horns. She hoped that Daniel would always keep it under close supervision, especially as far as the children were concerned.

When she returned to Aelybryn, Mary was feeling much better for her rest. However the following week, she complained of feeling very tired again, and did not feel up to doing her milk round as usual. She struggled on with it, taking much longer to complete the deliveries. It was only then that Martha feared something serious was happening to her. Physically and mentally, she seemed exhausted. She had been taking her tablets regularly for the thyroid complaint, Martha had seen to that. Also she was sleeping better at night too, and did not toss and turn as much, keeping Martha awake as she had done, although Martha had never complained. She kept that to herself. However Mary became very strange while sitting in the chair, sometimes looking as if in a trance and her thoughts far away. But what could anyone do about it? However matters soon came to a head.

Rhys had come home from work this day in particular and had changed his clothes and gone into the garden to do some digging. The raspberry canes needed clearing of weeds and soon they would be picking raspberries in abundance. Martha loved making tarts and jam out of the fresh fruit from their garden and soon she would be able to do this.

Suddenly Mary arose from her chair and went out into the hall. She grabbed hold of the stick which her father had used to help him walk after he had his last stroke. It was always left in the hallstand with the umbrellas and, without saying a word, she strode quickly past Martha and out of the house, into the garden where Rhys was busily digging around the fruit bushes. Martha followed after her, wondering what the urgency was for Mary to suddenly get up and go into the garden. There, to her horror, she witnessed Mary running towards Rhys brandishing her stick trying to hit him on the head. He tried to run away but she followed him and they ran around the garden. Mary continued to chase him, muttering loudly to herself words which neither Rhys nor Martha could distinguish. Now Rhys was almost caught up by Mary and he frantically tried to wrench the stick from her grip while Martha tried to distract her. Evan was up in the dairy and heard Rhys shouting. He ran down to the garden and could not believe what was happening. There he witnessed Rhys, wrestling with Mary, trying to get a stick from her grip. Martha was pulling her by her cardigan sleeve, also trying to retrieve the weapon. Evan could not understand who was chasing whom. Mary had always been so fond of Rhys, and such a docile soul. Now it looked as though she was chasing him, intent on hitting him and hurting him. But why on earth would she want to do that? Nothing like this had ever happened before at Aelybryn. It had always been such a peaceful and pleasant place to live, ever since his arrival from South Africa.

Eventually he managed to force the stick out of Mary's hand, although she still appeared to be physically quite strong, and it fell to the ground. Mary continued to run around the garden as if she was deranged. Although Martha ran after her trying to pacify her, Mary continued to shout and wave her fists at Rhys. Fortunately she eventually collapsed in a heap on the lawn. Martha remained with her, stroking her head and cradling her like a small child, while Rhys ran into the house and sent for Dr Gough. He came immediately from his surgery down in the village.

"She has suffered a complete mental breakdown, I'm afraid," he told them sadly after he saw her, remaining in a daze, as if it was she who had been struck on the head with the stick.

"I will have to admit her into the mental hospital immediately as she could be a danger to herself and others."

They were all stunned. "Poor Mary," sighed Evan, scratching his head as if he was unable to comprehend what was taking place in front of him. He looked across at Martha whose face was as white as if she had seen a ghost. Rhys too was obviously very shaken.

Mary was immediately removed to the mental hospital which was only about two miles away, bordering onto the fields where Daniel had driven their cows many years before.

She was immediately certified, with the prospect of remaining there indefinitely.

Chapter 14

Martha accompanied Mary to the mental hospital in the ambulance because she continued to be in a daze, hardly knowing what was happening to her. They drove through the hospital entrance, following a narrow winding road for about a mile, until they reached the top of the hill. In front of them stood a large red-brick building with what looked like a bell tower, with many single storey buildings filling what seemed like acres and acres of ground, all fully enclosed by a tall metal fence. The windows were either half or fully barred, as one would have expected a prison to be, although Martha had never visited one. She remembered now how her father had spoken about lunatics, or mad people as he referred to them. In those days many people believed they were possessed of the devil or evil spirits. She was very young at the time but she could still remember his words on that day, having returned from taking the cows to the fields near the lunatic asylum.

"Have to be kind and sympathetic with these folk, but the only answer is to lock them away," he had said. "For there is no cure for madness. A straitjacket is the only way to restrain these people when they inflict injury upon themselves and those around them." She wondered if her father had witnessed some kind of incident at the time, but then she had gone out to feed the chickens and into the fresh air. She did not really want to hear any more on this dreaded subject. Little did her father know then, when he had uttered those words, that his beloved daughter Mary would one day be taken into that very same asylum; the place where everyone loathed visiting, and even worse, having to be admitted there.

They entered through a pair of guarded double iron gates, through to the entrance of the main building. There the ambulance driver rang the bell, and Martha noticed a spy hole in the heavy oak double doors. With the sound of grinding keys the door opened and the porter let them inside. There was a booth on their right with a glass front where the porter entered contacting the nursing staff, two of whom immediately came to meet them. Taking hold of Mary gently, one either side, they spoke quietly to her.

"Hello, Mary," one said kindly. "Both of you just come this way with us."

The security seemed unnaturally strict, unlike the general hospital in the town, which Martha had visited frequently when customers were taken into hospital. She hoped Mary would not have another attack of rage, as she had heard customers talk of padded cells in mental hospitals and could not endure the thought of her sister being taken into one of those and locked away. As they went down the long corridors, each door they entered was immediately locked behind them. Suddenly, the sound of women screaming was heard from behind one of the doors. Then another door opened and a nurse came out, revealing a room full of women, some with long scraggy grey hair, flaunting their bare breasts and showing their knickers. They were screeching and shouting at each other, one pulling the hair of others. Near the door a woman was squatting down exposing two large cheeks of her bottom as if she was about to defecate. Quickly the nurse closed the door and locked it again behind her. Mary did not turn her head to see where the noise was coming from, but continued to walk straight ahead with the nurses, like a lamb to the slaughter. That quick glance into that room was never to leave Martha's mind. That image remained with her each night when she went to bed. She remembered reading in the local newspaper years before, that two inmates had fled, still dressed in their night clothing, and were found wandering in the nearby park. One had jumped on a tram in her nightdress during the day, despite the strict security regulations in all the wards and rooms. Since that episode, all patients were continually kept under lock and key by the well-trained staff. However now she realised that little wonder they had wanted to get away. Some inmates were obviously more insane than others, and where would Mary fit in here? But soon they were taken into a reception area, where Mary was immediately led away to a secure wing of the hospital for examination. Martha felt sick. They had never been separated in their entire lives, but now she was helpless. She was shown into a small room, anxiously waiting to find out the prognosis. She looked out of the window and saw the beautiful view before her. The building looked right over the town, and Martha could see in the distance, the bay, and the waves breaking against the rocks below. She could see the promenade, where she and Mary used to walk on Sundays with the boys from chapel, years before. It was such a magnificent view, being built so high up on top of the hill. But Mary would certainly not be able to appreciate it with her frame of mind at present. Martha worried at having to leave her there, as no doubt her dear sister would be distressed at what was happening to her. Neither of them had ever been away from home before, and again she worried how Mary would feel being separated from her, and in this dreadful environment.

Eventually, after what seemed like hours, a very tall, friendly-looking man in a white coat entered the room. He told Martha he was the consultant psychiatrist on duty. When he had taken down all the relevant particulars about her sister, he tried to reassure her explaining some details to her.

"It is usual for some incident or anxiety to cause a breakdown such as your sister has had. At the moment we cannot put it down as being hereditary; there appears to be no family history of insanity. There is a faint possibility that she has an imbalance of hormones, possibly due to the change of life which could be the cause, and of course there is an added complication of an over-active thyroid. Electric treatment has been used for mental illness for a considerable time, and in some cases patients benefit from it. I feel certain it is the only option. It is unpleasant naturally, and she will have to be sedated with narcotics, but it is necessary to try and regain some sort of mental stability. I don't make any promises that it will be successful, or a lasting cure. We are still not sure of the cause. It is possible that during the treatment she will tell us of any problems she was experiencing, or some serious anxiety which was unknown to you, despite your closeness as sisters. You must realise too that it is always a possibility she will have to remain here for good, unless she responds well to the treatment. Unfortunately she will have to be on medication for this form of depression for the rest of her life. This would have to be strictly controlled by you if she was ever allowed to return to her home. It would be a great responsibility for you. If the medication were neglected, she would be back here in no time at all, in a worse condition than before. But of course, at the moment, I really cannot say that she will ever be able to leave here."

"But I can't bear such a daunting thought, Doctor," Martha

told him. "I will do anything to have her back home. We have never been parted before in our lives. Do you think it could be something to do with the fact that her real mother died when she was two and it has only now affected her mentally? I am so distressed by all this, and can hardly endure the thought of leaving her here, although I know I have no choice."

"Well, all I can say is, she seems to have had a very loving and caring family with a very happy upbringing, so I doubt that has any bearing on her breakdown. You and she are obviously devoted to each other, so she has been very fortunate. Some spend their childhood in an orphanage with no family life at all."

Martha felt devastated. They shared everything: their home, their business, even their bed. The only thing she had ever kept from Mary was obviously her relationship with Rhys. It was far kinder to keep that from her as she did not want her to worry that it would ever become a threat to them both. Nothing would become of that relationship with him. She and Mary had promised each other to always remain together, to look after each other, and no one could, or would, ever come between them. That promise still stood. But it did not stop her from having fun with him, and she so much enjoyed this physical pleasure he was able to give her. Yes, they were intimate, and he gave her these wonderful feelings of satisfaction, something she had never before experienced. She had vowed they would never go "all the way", because they would have to marry to do that, and that was never going to happen. Someone they knew, in the village, was unmarried and expecting a baby. What shame she had brought to her family, and the boy had no intention of marrying her. Martha knew she could still become pregnant at her age so she resolved never to let that happen. Anyway Rhys was only interested in going as far as they were able to, without getting into any danger.

Her thoughts were soon back to where she was, there, inside a mental hospital, and it was Mary, her dear sister, about whom the doctor was still speaking.

"I'm afraid your sister will not be allowed any visitors during the first few weeks of treatment. We find this is more beneficial for the patient during the early days. But we will let you know as soon as visitors are permitted, especially yourself."

Martha left the hospital feeling so very sad. She drove the car back home hardly concentrating on the road or the traffic. By the time she arrived at Aelybryn, she again felt sick inside. Her stomach churned over and over. The house was now so empty without Mary. Not only that, she realised she would be alone to cover the milk rounds, possibly on a permanent basis. Evan could not do it and nor could Rhys. When she told Evan the tragic news, he scratched his head and was silent for a moment. Then he came up with a very sensible idea.

"Your best plan is to go to this new company I read about in the local newspaper last week. They take all the milk from the farmers in the area and bottle it all ready for persons such as you to deliver to their customers. They will wash all the bottles for you and will deliver the full ones to our dairy every day. You will need to buy yourself a small open-sided float to have easy access to the bottles in the crates provided. For the time being you could use the boot of your car and keep coming back to the dairy for me to load you up again. You should also let Daniel have all the chickens. We really do not have the time to see to them now Mary is absent. Your profit will be down, naturally, buying the milk bottled already, but it is the only way you can continue on your own. It will mean that no longer will you have to wait for the customers to come to the door with their jugs. If they are out, they will have to leave you a note on the doorstep for you to know how much milk they want. You simply leave what they require. They will rinse the bottles and put them out for collection the following morning. It will halve your time delivering, so you can then cope with doing Mary's milk round as well as your own. I even heard Daniel saying one day he thought to change to bottles to fill at the farm, and deliver milk in this way, except he has more help to wash them all and fill them. Knowing Daniel, he will get the children to do some of the bottle washing, after they come home from school. The bottles are sealed with cardboard tops, to secure the milk and Daniel will no doubt get the children to do that also before they go to school in the mornings. This all takes time and manpower, but you can have it all done ready for you. I really don't see you have any choice, Martha."

The following week the company Evan recommended began their delivery to Aelybryn. The chickens were taken to her brother's farm, and by the end of 1946, Daniel also turned to using milk bottles.

Martha now had a completely new routine to which she soon became accustomed. She bought a second-hand milk float, which ran on petrol, as did the car. It was difficult to have coupons for them both with all the rationing; therefore she kept the use of the car for very special occasions. It was useful to go out to the farm but this had to be curtailed because of the time spent on the rounds, doing Mary's work as well as her own. She still had the house to run and food to make for her and the two men. She missed Mary's mathematical mind too, as she always saw to the books and the accounts, but she asked Rhys to help her out, as he seemed to have a good head on him. She did miss Mary so much. Hopefully, one day she could return home and they would be able to go together in the car once again, just like the good old days. Unknown to Martha at that time, those good old days were never to return. It was just as well she could not foresee what the future held for her; indeed, what the future held for all of them.

Chapter 15

Martha was surprised to find how quickly the next three weeks flew by. She had visions of them dragging until she saw Mary again. She was very anxious to find out if the treatment was having the desired effect, but she had been so busy reorganising the business the time had soon passed. Rhys had been a great help in more ways than one. He spent a great deal of his spare time going through the accounts, and helping her to add up all the amounts of money owing by each customer weekly, ready for her Saturday collections. He also continued to give her a great deal of attention, fondling her whenever they were alone, which was quite often since Mary was no longer around. It helped her to cope with the sadness she felt about her sister. However she had the feeling that Rhys was now finding it more and more difficult to control his feelings and actions when they were alone together.

She missed having Mary in her bed at night and often she would wake up and feel so lonely without her. She had never slept on her own in her life. Now the bed seemed far too big for one. Mary had always been beside her, and they would often turn over together even if only one of them wanted to do so. It was an automatic reflex action. She missed having Mary to put her arm around and chat to before she fell off to sleep. She even tried putting the bolster down the bed so that she could put her arm around it, substituting it for Mary's thin body.

Sometimes she awoke almost halfway through the night, often at two o'clock and failing to get off to sleep again, tossing and turning, moving from one side of the bed to another. On the night in question she tossed and turned but it was no use, she could not return to sleep. She decided to get out of bed and creep along the landing to Rhys's bedroom. Evan was a very heavy sleeper, and didn't get out of his bed even during the war when the bombs were dropping or when there had been an air raid warning. Now he was snoring loudly, so she was quite safe, he would not hear her. She tiptoed past his room and stopped outside the next door. Slowly and quietly she turned the doorknob, as she knew Rhys always kept his door unlocked. He had suffered from agoraphobia when he returned after the 1914-1918 war in the trenches and hated the feeling of being confined; therefore his door always remained unlocked. She quietly tiptoed up to the bed and leaned over him. He was fast asleep. She gently gave him a kiss on his mouth. Poor Rhys almost jumped out of his skin with fright.

"What on earth are you doing in my room at this time of night?" he gasped on seeing her face close to his. "You really gave me such a fright."

"I can't sleep and I feel so lost and lonely without Mary."

"Quickly, get in here under the bedclothes before you catch your death of cold."

He pulled the blankets over them both and wrapped his legs around her, to warm her body. She could feel the hardness of him against her through her nightdress. Just the feeling of closeness to him sent waves of excitement through her body. Soon they were turning over and over in the bed clinging tightly to each other and kissing each other passionately.

"Isn't this such a wonderful feeling being so close together," she whispered, as they had never been in that position of lying down together in bed before.

"Martha, we must stop. We'll be in trouble otherwise."

"Don't be silly, of course we won't."

"You really must go back to your own bed. What if Evan hears us?"

"But he's fast asleep."

"Be sensible, Martha, and get back to your own bed. I'll see you in the morning."

"You are a spoilsport," she said, getting out unwillingly but doing as he had bidden her. She quietly crept across the landing again, returning to her own bedroom. When she climbed into her bed it was already cold, and she tried hard once again to get off to sleep. She thought she could hear Mary's voice in her ears, calling her, and the sound of doors being locked and unlocked, and voices echoing around her. The sound of jingling keys seemed to be filling the bedroom. When she awoke again, it was dawn and time to get up

The following day Rhys suggested that, as Evan was willing to answer the door and look after the house on a Saturday night, it would be better if they went to the cinema down in the village. This became a regular event every Saturday; no matter what the film, they would go off together. When they were seen with each other in the cinema on such a regular basis, friends and customers often wondered just what kind of relationship they had between them, having spent so many years living in the same household, yet behaving as brother and sister. It was obviously platonic, but it was a strange relationship to outsiders.

At last the day arrived when Martha could visit her sister. She had looked forward to it so much but it was a strange feeling because in a way she somehow dreaded it. Would she be disappointed in her sister's progress? Or would she be thrilled with the news that she was already responding well to the treatment?

Alone, she entered the hospital once again through the main entrance. A nurse took her through the various doors and down the same corridors, locking each door behind them as before. She heard the keys making a familiar jingling sound, as they moved to and fro on the nurse's thick black belt. Once again she had this strange feeling, somehow recalling that she had heard those sounds before, more recently and in the darkness. Could they have been in her dreams perhaps?

Eventually she was shown into a small hall where the chairs were situated around the perimeter. Each patient was brought, one by one, into the allocated area, accompanied by two nurses. One woman began to cry as soon as she arrived, while another man shouted very loudly, waving his fists at everyone. Martha could hear him declare in no uncertain terms to his visitor, where he wanted to go immediately. Home.

"I want to come home. I must come home now. Today. D'you hear me? I hate it here. I'm not staying any longer. Take me with you today, do you hear me?" and he threw his both arms around his visitor, almost sending her off balance. A nurse ran forward to restrain him, and he was immediately taken away. Martha was so sorry for the woman who then sat in her chair, wiping away her tears with a handkerchief before she went out again. Some of the inmates had their arms wrapped around their knees, and were rocking themselves backward and forwards, almost as if they were on a rocking horse, but at least they were quiet. She only hoped Mary would not shout or behave badly when she arrived. She wouldn't know what to say to her or how to cope, and after waiting so long to see her again, she would not want her to be taken away immediately. However she need not have worried.

A large bosomed young nurse brought Mary into the room. Mary had always been on the slim side, unlike herself, but Martha noticed, compared with the nurse beside her, she looked so thin and her face looked quite gaunt. Her hair had been cut very short and on the top of her head, there were signs of the old Dinky curlers, indicating that her hair had not been brushed out properly. Mary's hair didn't look anything like the way Martha used to style it for her when she was at home. She also had a strange look about her, but as soon as she saw Martha, she quietly put both her arms around her quite gently but saying nothing. They held each other momentarily until Martha broke the silence.

"I've brought you your favourite apples and your favourite biscuits, Scotch Highland Shortbread. I've also brought you a bottle of lemon squash. Robinson's. Your favourite. What's the food like, Mary?"

Mary replied in a whisper as if afraid she would be overheard. Martha had to lean closely towards her, in order to hear what she was saying ensuring her good ear was next to Mary's pale dry lips.

"I just don't feel hungry, Martha, but they force you to eat food served on stainless steel plates, not like our china ones. I hate the electric treatment they give me, but I suppose if it will make me better then I must tolerate it. I'll tolerate anything, Martha, only to feel more myself again. I do feel very strange at times and I don't seem to remember coming in here. Who brought me, and when was it?"

Martha told her it had been more than three weeks ago and that she had collapsed in the garden. She did not give her a detailed account of how she had tried to hit Rhys with a stick, as Mary obviously did not remember much about what happened. It was best not to remind her of that awful day, thus putting it all behind them.

Martha told her all about the changeover to milk bottles, and that when she was allowed to come home and return to her milk round, it would be so much easier for them both. They would also have more time to themselves, enabling them to see Beth and the children more frequently and do all the things they had so much enjoyed doing together.

But Mary was not listening. She seemed to be unable to concentrate on what was being said, and showed little interest in the new way of delivering the milk, whether it was far easier or not. Then quite suddenly she asked about Daniel's children.

"I would like to see them, if that's possible. When did I see them last?"

Martha said she would ask permission on her way out when visiting time was over, ignoring her last question. Visiting time went so quickly and a bell rang to denote its termination. Mary did not seem too unhappy to be taken away again and to say goodbye. It was as if it was now part of her new routine, which she obviously accepted. This was her new way of life, and she showed no objection, much to Martha's relief. Was that perhaps selfish of her? She hoped not. But she could not bear Mary begging to be taken back home and to leave this awful place in which she was now forced to remain, especially as the situation was now out of her control.

Martha gave her a long hug and Mary was taken back towards the door where she had entered. She turned around just before the nurse unlocked the door to take her away again and they would be gone out of Martha's sight. She gave her a wave, but suddenly Mary and the nurse were now just a blur. Martha's eyes were filled with tears. Tears for the sister she loved and missed so much. When had she shed any tears before this? It would no doubt have been when her dear father had passed away. How their lives had changed since then, and what had Mary done to deserve all this? It was like being shut away from the rest of the world. It really was. Like being in a prison, except that Mary had committed no crime. Life was so very unfair.

She walked past the other visitors, wiping the tears from her eyes, telling herself this was no way to behave. She was soon outside again, returning to the lovely bright sunshine. Although it was cold outside, the sky was blue and cloudless. Poor Mary was stuck inside that gloomy place, which had such small windows, some of which had bars on them, letting in very little light. At the moment she was not allowed to walk in the gardens and feel the sun on her face, or breathe in the fresh air which she had been so used to doing in her business. But Mary seemed resigned to this fact and that, in a way, was a blessing. It made it easier for both of them.

"Do you think I could be permitted to bring my brother's children to visit my sister?" Martha enquired of one of the nurses on the way out. "She would love to see them as they mean so much to her."

"I'm afraid you will have to speak with the doctor who is treating her," came the reply.

When she had seen him before leaving, he said that progress was slow. Mary was sedated and that was why she had shown little emotion or interest in what was being said to her. It was still early days and as yet they were unable to say if the treatment would be successful. Mental illness was always slow and very unpredictable.

"Give it a few more weeks and you can then bring the children in to see her, but they will have to go into a special reception area. That is the only place where the children are allowed, and then it will only be for a very short visit."

Martha was so grateful. She was sure it would mean a great deal to Mary and bring a little normality back into her life, seeing her favourite children again. That seemed so little to ask.

After a few weeks, the children visited their aunt. Beth accompanied them, but they really hated that awful hospital she was in, locking doors and being watched all the time.

"It's as if she is in prison," Catherine had announced after their first visit to see their beloved aunt.

"Yes, only it's worse," Anne retorted, "because she hasn't done anything wrong to deserve to be locked away inside there."

"But your Aunt Mary is sick," Beth explained. "And the only way she will be well again is to stay there for a while enabling the doctors to keep an eye on her and give her special tablets and treatment. She will soon be home again, I'm sure, so don't worry."

The children understood little of what a mental illness entailed, nor its treatment. Neither were they very keen to revisit the hospital. They dreaded it, but did so when their beloved aunt asked to see them, which fortunately was not too often. They would do anything to please her and if she asked to see them, then they would make the effort, no matter how much they hated the idea.

The weeks went into months. Life carried on, with Mary showing little change and the prospect of her ever coming home more remote as the time went by. Christmas came and went. Soon it would be a new year, 1947 already. The children had missed their aunt at that festive time, with one empty chair where she always sat at the table, but no one said too much about her. It hurt them all too much. The less said, the better. However they all had their own thoughts, which they kept to themselves.

Martha had finished her rounds earlier than usual this particular day. She had not slept very well the previous night and was up before Evan.

"Can't you sleep?" he teased her.

"As I was awake early, I thought I might as well get started. There is snow forecast for us in the next few days, so if I finish in good time, I may go to the farm for a few hours before going to the hospital to see Mary. It's only evening visiting today."

Martha went off to the farm as soon as she had finished her milk rounds. It was so refreshing to be there, away from all the traffic and bustle. She loved to wander around the sheds looking in at the pigs and the calves and helping to feed them with Beth. What she liked doing most was to collect the eggs from the shed and place them in her basket. She had always enjoyed doing that when they had their own chickens at Aelybryn. She remembered, when she was a child, she would arrive sometimes when the egg had only just been laid, and it felt so warm in her hand. It had always fascinated her to think that the somewhat large hard eggshell, yet delicate enough to break so easily, could come from such a small opening in the chicken's bottom. Why did it not cause discomfort when it was laid? The chicken was always happy about it because she clucked away blissfully at her great achievement admiring its safe delivery.

The farm was so peaceful except for the sound of the odd train passing by and the sounds of the animals calling for their food. Little wonder that Beth loved the life so much. But Martha needed people too, and although it was a complete change for her at the farm, she would have found the life far too lonely. Evan had been right of course about taking the chickens away from Aelybryn. It had saved her more work; despite the fact she missed not having any farm animals of their own to look after as they had done in the olden days. He was quite a wise old owl, was Evan. He often gave her very helpful and constructive suggestions and she felt so grateful to him. She wished she could have brought Rhys with her for company today since Mary could not be with her. He had never been to the farm in all the years he had lived with them. On his days off, he seemed to enjoy being in the garden at Aelybryn, and helping to cut all the hedges around its perimeter. There was always plenty to do there.

He and Martha still managed to secretly indulge in their petting which they both obviously enjoyed tremendously. Martha did not know whether this was supposed to be what "love" was, or did she just "love" the attention that Rhys gave her and all the lovely feelings that came with it?

"How do people know if they are in love, how can they tell?" she often asked herself. What they did together certainly brought them very close. It was strange that they had lived in the same house all those years and only now had they become intimate with each other. Rhys never asked for more or said he wished things could be different. He obviously accepted the situation, for which she was very grateful, and therefore she had no regrets at all. It was how things had worked out in their lives. She and Mary would always be together and there would never be anyone to interfere with what they had planned and promised. She was so fortunate that she was able to have any kind of relationship with a man and Rhys was the ideal person, living with them. He was no relation, but someone to whom she could give her affection in a different way from what she felt and did with any other men in her life. Rhys gave her excitement and warmth which sometimes sent electric currents through her body. Something she could never have explained to Mary. Doing it this way caused no hurt to anyone. The trouble was that it was imperative no one ever found out. They still had to be very careful. Rhys fortunately did not seem bothered about marriage and any other sort of commitment. It never came up during their conversations or when they were wrapped around each other. Her only regret at the moment was that her sister's health was slow in improving. She just wished Mary would show more signs of getting well enough to come home again. But then she heard Daniel's voice calling her and she quickly came back to reality from daydreaming. Here she was, still at the farm.

"Have you seen the children?" he shouted to her from one of the sheds.

"Oh, they went for a walk across the fields down to the stream, but they said they wouldn't be away long. Why?"

"Well, I wanted Jack to take the bull for his exercise, then I can start on milking the cows."

Martha hated the mention of the bull. She would have preferred Daniel to do that task by himself as she regarded that a very dangerous one. But, as usual, her brother knew best.

Beth and Martha returned to the farmhouse to enjoy a cup of tea together before Martha set out for the hospital visiting time.

The children returned from the fields and were approaching the farm buildings where Jack was out exercising the bull. They hated walking past this animal even though it was on the pole and fairly safe. As they approached, Jack took a handkerchief out of his pocket and began waving it around, in front of the bull's face.

"What are you doing, Jack? Be careful with that bull. You know they can be dangerous."

"I can handle him, don't worry," and with that he began to show off by waving the handkerchief again in front of the bull.

"You didn't know I was once a matador," he joked, but suddenly he dropped the pole accidentally. It slid out of his hand and the bull began shaking its head. Now he was completely loose and was making for the two girls. Jack tried to run in front of it, waving the handkerchief frantically to distract his attention from them, but the bull was now far more interested in them and was hell-bent on catching up with them. The girls started to run but the bull began to go faster, now almost behind them. Anne began to scream while Catherine tried to pull her by the sleeve of her coat, dragging her onwards. Then the bull had part of Anne's coat in its mouth.

"Take it off. Let him have it," shouted Jack. "Then run for it."

As the bull's head shook backwards and forwards, Anne slid off her coat and began screaming while Jack tried to jump on its back, and take hold of the horns to pull the head around, hoping to grab the ring in its nose. But he slipped. Now the girls were running towards the farmhouse screaming, while Jack continued to wrestle with the bull who was obviously becoming more and more angry.

By the time the girls reached the farmhouse, frightened and exhausted, and Beth had found Daniel, he could see that the bull had pinned Jack against the stone wall. He was butting him from one side to the other with his thick sharp horns, catching the sides of his legs each time. His trousers were all torn and blood was coming from the top of each of his legs.

"Help me, boss," cried Jack. "He'll kill me."

Daniel grabbed the pole while the bull continued to

concentrate on butting Jack. Then he managed to twist the hook into the ring until it was horizontal and it drew blood.

"Stay," bellowed Daniel angrily.

Immediately the bull stood still, its nose now bleeding and obviously in pain. He certainly knew who was his master. Beth stood in the distance watching with horror, while Martha consoled and comforted the girls who were indoors still suffering from shock. Daniel walked the bull back to the shed and tethered it safely before returning to Jack, who by this time had collapsed in a heap on the ground.

"Send for an ambulance quickly," Daniel shouted to Beth. "Jack looks in a bad way."

Jack was taken to hospital suffering from severe shock and two badly injured legs. He remained in hospital for a whole week, but was lucky to be alive. The bull could so easily have killed him and the children, and Jack was fortunate to have only been gored.

When he came out of hospital he returned to the orphanage and asked them if they would find him some other form of employment. He did not want to return to the farm or indeed to work on any other. It was an experience he was never to forget.

When the girls told their father what had happened, he was grateful to Jack for distracting the bull away from his children, but was furious with him for playing with the bull.

"They are not the kind of animal to be teased or tormented. They can be very dangerous unless treated with great caution. I should never have let Jack take it out, but he was a strong lad and I thought I could trust him. Let that be a lesson to all of us."

It was the first time Martha had ever seen her brother look pale and shocked. He had lost that healthy colour from his cheeks which he had always had. It was obvious he had been shaken but he always gave the impression he was never out of control. He was the boss and he knew it. He had been fearless from a child and she had to admire him. He could handle anything.

Martha was obviously late arriving at the hospital to see poor Mary who was sitting in a chair in the usual place looking like a lost sheep. She told her that she had been to the farm and there had been a bit of an accident which had delayed her. Mary at least showed an interest in asking what had happened. Martha did not go into too many details but explained that the bull had got free and Daniel had managed to return it to the shed safely. However the farm labourer had been slightly injured. It was great that she showed an interest in what was going on. Maybe she had turned the corner at long last.

When she went outside, it was snowing heavily. By the time she reached Aelybryn, the roads were thickly covered and becoming quite dangerous. Evan and Rhys were so relieved to see Martha home safely.

Chapter 16

Evan was the first to come downstairs as usual on that morning in 1947. He had felt quite cold during the night, and had reached out for an extra blanket to put over him in bed. His body fat usually kept him adequately warm, without any need for extra clothing, but for some reason he had felt quite cold. As soon as he got out of bed, he peered through the window. Then he could see the reason why. The snow was at least six foot deep in the backyard of the house. He would not be able to open the door. When he went downstairs into the front of the house and looked out, he could not see anything. It was as if a dark blanket was covering the window. The snow was ten feet high, covering the parlour and sitting room windows. The blizzard had caused it to drift and there was an eerie silence around him. The temperature in the house had certainly dropped below zero. The sooner he made up the fire and lit it, the better. Martha would be down any minute.

As soon as she came into the kitchen Evan told her, "You may as well go back to bed. There will be no milk delivery for us today, or tomorrow. There will be no traffic on the roads. Rhys and I will have to dig us out of the house. He won't be able to go into work either as everything will be closed. I hope we have enough provisions in the house, Martha. This snow could take at least a week to clear, so long as we don't have another fall during the day. Once the snowploughs can get through, we may be able to have a milk delivery, but in the meantime customers will have to walk here and get the milk from our door. You can't deliver any yourself. Everyone will be walking to the shops for bread and other provisions, until they run out of course. Everything will become very scarce by the end of the week, you mark my words."

"We still have a few crates over from yesterday, but that will soon go," Martha told him.

"Well, as soon as Rhys is up, we'll make a start to dig. A good job I brought the two shovels down from the shed yesterday when I heard on the radio that there was snow forecast and drifting could occur, because they also predicted high winds."

Evan was right. Lorries were unable to deliver the crates of milk that were ordered. There was nothing to be done for Martha but wait. Fortunately, when she returned from the farm the previous day, Beth had given her a supply of bacon, eggs and freshly baked bread so they were well provided for during the next week at least. She had also given her a loaf of boiled cake which they all loved, together with a tin of freshly cooked Welsh cakes. Beth was such a good cook and was so generous towards them. Then Martha began to worry however: would they be managing at the farm, all those animals to cater for, and the farm was so far off the main road. How would they be milking the cows and getting it up to the main road? If it could not be delivered, then there would be a great deal of wastage and some of their profit gone. She knew Beth made her own butter and cheese during the war years so no doubt she would not be idle and waste anything if she could make use of it. Thus Aelybryn had always been well provided for.

Her thoughts then turned to her sister. There was no way of

visiting her and she had not missed one day apart from when she was not allowed visiting for the first three weeks of her treatment. Mary usually had visits from her other nieces and her nephew, but now no one could go and see her. Poor Mary. But at least she would be warm and safe and have adequate food. Hospitals usually stocked up in case of an emergency.

It took days before the snowploughs were out and Martha received another delivery of milk. People continually knocked at their door and Evan was kept very busy attending to all these customers, a number of whom did not belong to Martha. They promised that as soon as the snow cleared, they would change to her for their delivery of milk. Unfortunately there were more falls of snow, and although Martha had skid chains for the wheels of the milk float, she dared not risk going out even if the road was partly cleared. Customers had to walk to Martha, or go without, and this was hard where children and the elderly were concerned. Rhys and Evan carried a few crates down the road enabling Martha to provide milk for some of her older, sick customers living within easy reach. They were so grateful to her for the effort she made for them. But the snow lasted for weeks and weeks. The whole country was in the grip of blizzards and chaos. Plumbers were on call twenty-four hours a day due to burst pipes which were of course made of lead and, when the water froze, they naturally burst, when the ice expanded. Coal was in short supply so fires could not be kept burning all night, and there were power cuts sometimes from seven o'clock in the morning until late afternoon.

"I can't reach the farmyard to feed the animals," Daniel had told her when she telephoned the farm the first day the snow had arrived. "A good job we still have George living in. He and I have managed to dig a path to the other side of the yard where the cows were waiting patiently for fodder. Fortunately we had taken extra hay into the cowshed in preparation for an emergency if the snow was heavy and continued to fall. The automatic feeders for their water were frozen so I had to free the pipes with hot cloths. Usually they only have to push their nose onto the flap of metal and water comes out immediately through into their trough. Now they were all dry, but I rectified that, thank goodness."

"What about the rest of the animals?" Martha enquired anxiously.

"Well, once we got across to the cows, we dug our way to the pigs and then it was easy to reach the horses in the stable, again by digging a pathway. But I left the two old carthorses out in the field as they had been out all winter. Now I can't reach them." Daniel sounded anxious. Hopefully the snow would clear and he would be able to get food to them. But the snow continued to fall.

"We filled the pigs' troughs to overflowing with swill before the snow arrived, but they were soon empty and needing replenishing. Anything put in front of them is being scoffed up immediately; despite the fact I could only lay my hands on household peelings. We can't reach any of the normal pig food and entry to the farm is impossible. The lane which led to the main road is completely blocked. As soon as it began to thaw, another fall of snow came."

Eventually Daniel telephoned Martha with some good news but also some bad.

"Luckily I had brought Blackie and Anne's foal into the stable, not leaving them out in the field, when the snow came. Today I put Blackie in front of the gambo, then loaded two churns on. I travelled across the fields alongside the lane where the drifts were less deep. I tell you, Martha, even a lame horse can do what my tractor failed to do. Horsepower and their hooves still win the day. Now I can travel to the road with the gambo and sell milk and eggs. There was quite a queue for them. When I got back to the farm though, I managed to get to the two carthorses down the field, but I was too late. They had gone to shelter from the snow under the hedge, but the drifts were seven foot deep there, and they were completely covered. They froze to death." There was a pause, and then Daniel began again. "And there's Beth going on about Anne failing scholarship for entry into the grammar school. I ask you, what does that matter, for goodness sake?"

But Martha knew it did matter. All Anne's friends had passed and she had failed. Beth knew how disappointed and sad she was, and naturally her heart bled for her. Also the grammar school was only a stone's throw from Aelybryn and Anne would be able to call on her Aunt Martha from school had she gained a place.

Martha and Beth knew Daniel had taken it quite hard about losing his two carthorses in the snow. "He has refused to talk about it. The night he discovered them, he tossed and turned all night, hardly getting any sleep. He blames himself."

Beth warned the children not to mention anything to their father about it. "He feels he could have saved them, so it's better we put it behind us. Nothing can be done about it now," Beth told Martha sadly. It was then that Martha realised perhaps something could be done about Anne failing the scholarship. That wasn't too late. She knew she delivered milk and eggs to a small private house converted into a school and often chatted to the headmistress. It was only a few miles away in the more affluent area of Swansea, called the Uplands. Mrs Hole who ran it had once mentioned to Martha that the famous poet Dylan Thomas began his formal education there some thirty years before, then obtaining a place at the Boys' Grammar School in Swansea. It was certainly worth a try to see if she could get Anne a place at the school, where she would have expert tuition before resitting the exam the following year. Mrs Hole obviously was fond of Martha who must have used her influence, because Anne began her new term at Mirador House School, previously named Mrs Hole's "Dame School" only a few streets away from Cwmdonkin Crescent where Dylan Thomas was born and brought up.

"What's your new school like?" Martha enquired a few weeks into the term, not showing Anne that it was she who had managed to get her a place and was paying for her.

"Well, if it will get me to the grammar school, I'll put up with it, but there is no playground, it's a private house. We only have two teachers, Mrs Hole and Miss Sadler. There is only one classroom which smells and only ten children around a large table. Every time Mrs Hole speaks, her false teeth drop down onto her bottom lip and she has to keep putting them back in. I sit next to Rhian, the girl who fell off my horse when she came to tea, and she hardly speaks to me." Well, Martha only hoped Anne would pass the following year and it would all have been worthwhile.

During the winter of the heavy snow, the children loved being at home while all the schools were closed but, as the weeks went on, they were forced to work quite hard on the farm. They longed to return to school. All bus services were suspended, and it was reported that bread, some five thousand loaves, had to be brought from Cardiff by rail during this time. No trains went through the farm, and many other lines were totally blocked with snow. Turbo jet engines were mounted on trucks, the exhausts of which partly melted or blew the snow off the lines to clear them. Most children were off school more than two months, partly because the toilets were all frozen. Owing to the power cuts some days the cows had to be milked by hand, and candles too were in very short supply. However fortunately food was always plentiful on the farm, despite the snow.

Some areas were reported as not having had food deliveries for six weeks. The country was of course on rations even after the war was over, so there was a great deal of black marketing in butter, meat, cheese, eggs, bacon and poultry. There were illicit dealings in the sale of cattle, sheep and pigs and malpractices with their slaughter. Petrol was still on ration and often if the garage owner was a friend of the farmer he would exchange various farm commodities like bacon, poultry, etc. in exchange for petrol or coupons. Yes, farmers like Daniel and Beth went without nothing, neither did their families. Farming certainly had its advantages, during wartime and in the snow. The winter of 1947 was to go down in history as the worst on record.

It was also a year to go down in history because of the long-awaited royal wedding. In November 1947, Princess Elizabeth married Prince Philip at Westminster Abbey. The whole country rejoiced and all the newspapers were full of the wedding photographs. Catherine and Anne were busy cutting out everything they saw to fill their scrapbooks, which they had started when they lived with their aunts. They asked if they could visit Aunt Mary again in the hospital. They wanted to show her what they had accomplished; after all it was she who had encouraged them to make scrapbooks when they lived with them. Mary at least took some interest in what the girls showed her, so they were delighted because it made their visit worthwhile. They hated going to that awful hospital, but they did so much want her to see their efforts. The great thing was she seemed to appreciate it.

A few weeks later after returning from the cinema one evening, when Evan was in bed, Rhys and Martha were alone. They put their arms around each other, and Rhys began satisfying their usual physical desires.

"It's very late," Martha managed to say in between the passionate kissing.

"I know," said Rhys. "But we haven't had the chance to be together alone. Evan seems to have been around all the while lately."

Martha did so much enjoy what they did together. He pulled her against him again.

"Martha, I have been thinking a great deal lately about us."

"What is there to think about?" she replied.

"Well, do you know exactly what the prognosis is for Mary? It is nearly two years since she left Aelybryn and went into hospital. Will she ever come home again?"

"That's impossible to answer. No one seems to know, not even the doctors, but what difference does it make?"

"Well, over the last couple of years, we have become very intimate with each other, the result has brought us very close. We get on so well, we love being together, and you are so much fun. I cannot imagine living anywhere without you being there with me. I certainly never intended to love you, that seems to have developed over the years. I have to confess I did fall in love with someone else, but it was a long time ago."

She was tempted to ask him if it was before the First World War or had he met someone when he was away training in North Wales? But she decided that if he chose not to divulge to her who, or where it was, then she did not really want to ask him. He had not married her anyway, for whatever the reason, and he had come back and chosen to live with them ever since. She did not really care who it was, because it made no difference.

He sat her on his lap, with both his arms around her, sliding one hand under her jumper.

"The truth is, Martha, I want you to marry me. What began as flirtatious fun and physical enjoyment for both of us has now changed. Well, it has done for me anyway. It has become something far deeper. Before it's too late, let's make the most of what we have. We can marry and be able to sleep together at last."

"But you know I am not free, I have Mary to think about."

"But you told me she had been certified when she entered the hospital and you know what that means? If she is to remain in hospital because she will never get well, then she will never know whether we are married or not. She won't know any different."

"But I can never know that for sure. I can't possibly make such a decision, and take that risk. She is my life too."

"Sell the business, Martha, and divide it between you. We can find somewhere to live together while Evan remains here in the house to keep it going. Lots of men live alone. If Mary is ever well enough to come out of hospital, then her home is here waiting for her. Her share of the business will pay for the running of the house. Evan cannot live forever, and Mary and you can then decide what is best to do with the family home. I've never smoked or drank in my life, and have saved all the money I've earned. I have been so lucky to live here for so little. Please will you think about it? I do so want us to be alone, and I want to make love to you properly, not taking whatever we can when no one is around to see us."

Martha had to admit to herself that she hated the element of fear that their relationship brought. The great fear of being caught. They were lucky that when anyone was around, they were both able to act as if they had no interest in each other physically. But her decision had been made for her years before. She would never do anything to hurt Mary. She and Rhys would have to live the rest of their lives just as they had done. She would never know what it was like to sleep with him, much as she longed to. Her sister had to come first. She and Rhys would have to be content with what they had, satisfying each other in the way they had been doing, without ever having the full experience of the complete act of love. Her mind went back to 1936, when the King had abdicated, and had put himself and the woman he loved before his duty. Now she had a slightly better understanding of the situation at that time. However she knew exactly where her duty lay, but Martha was never to forget that decision she made in 1947.

Chapter 17

After that hard winter everyone welcomed the springtime, but no one welcomed it more so than Martha. She loved the first signs of a new season and today was such a beautiful day. Here she was, on her way as usual, to see Mary. She noticed already there were newly born lambs in the fields adjoining the hospital, certainly a sign of spring. Seeing new life around her, she was quite convinced that there would be new life too for her sister, and perhaps today she would learn that her health was definitely improving.

Mary was in the usual day room, when she arrived, but the nurse told Martha that today, after visiting time was over, the consultant psychiatrist wanted a word with her. Martha was so nervous at this request and after saying her goodbyes to Mary, with her legs feeling quite weak, she entered the small consulting room. The doctor was sitting behind his desk, surrounded by papers.

"Please take a seat," he said kindly.

She did as he asked feeling grateful for the chair to which he pointed immediately in front of him. Was she prepared for the information he was about to release? Was it going to be the good news she had waited more than two years to hear, or bad news that she so often dreaded?

"I have sent for you today because here at the hospital the

group of doctors who have been treating your sister these past two years felt it was time to discuss her case very carefully with you. They have come to a final conclusion. Over the time she has been in this hospital, she has had many electric shock treatments, together with medication; we have all come to the same decision. We feel that although she has made some small improvement, she will never make a complete recovery. She has never confided in any of us about any specific event or stressful implication in her life, if indeed there ever was one. We do not know of anything that could have contributed to the severity of the nervous breakdown she eventually suffered before being brought here. Keeping her in this hospital indefinitely will now serve no useful purpose. Because of the devotion you obviously feel for each other we feel returning her to your care would be the best option." Martha held his gaze listening intently to every word he was saying.

"We can do no more for her. But we fully understand that this may not be an option as far as you are concerned. You have to realise that she will always need to be on medication and it will all have to be supervised by yourself. She will never be able to resume any business duties as she had done previously, only menial tasks. She will endeavour to do these with your instruction in the beginning, but hopefully they will become routine to her later. She can be left in the home while you are out on your business quite safely as she will not be a threat to anyone. In fact she will have become much more introverted than you remember her, and conversations with her may be often somewhat strained. I believe there is another relative in the house?"

"Yes, our dear old uncle. He has been with us many years and we are both very fond of him."

"Yes, I gathered that. Mary tells me he always preferred to

remain mostly in the house and as you have just said, she seems to have great affection for him. She has told us that she would be happy to remain with him while you are carrying on with the function of delivering milk to all your customers. I do not know how you feel about having this enormous responsibility put upon your shoulders when you have a business and a home to run? Make no mistake, she will need looking after with great care."

He looked across the desk at Martha inquiringly. He was surprised to hear her giving her answer immediately without any hesitation or thought.

"I only want her back home. I will do everything I possibly can to make her happy again, until the end of our days together. She means everything to me."

"In that case, we will get all the necessary papers for your signature, and you will be able to take her home at the end of next week."

In April 1948, Martha went to the psychiatric hospital for the last time to bring Mary home. Back to their home. Their home at Aelybryn. With such happiness in her heart, and her spirit so full of gladness, she drove into the hospital for that last time. As she meandered through the long narrow entrance, on the high banks either side of the road were masses of yellow primroses in large clumps. The day was cloudless, such a bright blue sky for early spring. Had there been any clouds above, Martha felt she could have easily blown them away with the frame of mind she was in. Today, she felt she could move mountains, she was so happy. On her milk round that morning, every customer knew of her glad tidings. It had taken her twice as long, by the time she told each one about Mary coming home at last. Obviously everyone was delighted for them both.

She parked the car at the end of the car park so that when Mary came outside she could see all the daffodils in bloom in the borders. Bright blue and white hyacinths covered some of the larger areas, and with the windows of the car open, she would be able to smell their beautiful fragrance. Now the snow and hard winter of 1947 seemed to pale into insignificance. She felt a new awakening, a fresh beginning once more, for them both. When she looked at her watch, she had arrived far too early at the hospital. Rather than sitting in the waiting area, it was far better to enjoy the sight of all the flowers in front of her. So she sat in the car quietly and rested for a while. Her mind went to Rhys and of how close she had now become to him. This man who now played a great part in her life. Someone she had known for so long, and yet not really known at all until these past few years. How fortunate she had been, to experience all those wonderful feelings, giving her the most thrilling of sensations. So different from the feelings of spring in the air, or the excitement of any other event happening in her life. It was a feeling of satisfaction of a different kind. Rhys could satisfy this aching in her body by just using his hands. It was incredible that a man could do this simple gesture and give so much pleasure to different parts of one's body. As she sat there she could almost feel him stroking her in all the various places. But for all that, she did not have any difficulty in choosing who came first in her life, and she knew she would never have any regrets. She hoped so much that everything between her and Rhys could continue as they had been doing. However she realised that they would certainly have to revert to being very careful with Mary now around the house again, as well as Evan. That was how it was when they had first become intimate with each other. A lot of water had gone under the bridge since then though. However, from now onwards, she must only think of her sister. She must be her first priority. Rhys, with her feelings for him and the physical urges, would have to take second place. She looked at her watch. How quickly the time had gone daydreaming. It was time at last to go into the hospital and bring Mary outside to the car. She walked in through the main doors and passed the reception area as usual.

She enquired at the desk if her sister was now ready to be discharged. The staff nurse said she would ring the ward and let them know Mary's sister had arrived. The time seemed endless before Mary appeared with a nurse carrying her suitcase. They hugged each other and then taking her suitcase she turned again to her sister.

"Isn't this wonderful, Mary? We're going home together at long last. Evan, I know, will already have the kettle boiling for us and I have made you your favourite fishcakes for supper. Rhys will still be in work of course, but the four of us can eat together this evening. Something we have not done for so long. I'm so excited and happy for us all."

Mary smiled but said nothing. As they approached the front door Mary asked, "Where's the car? Do we have to walk very far?"

"No, it's just outside." Then taking her by the arm Martha said lovingly, "Come on, let's get you home."

Martha opened the door of the car, and Mary sat in the front seat alongside her. She looked somewhat bewildered when she gazed around and when Martha started the engine, poor Mary jumped with fright. She had been startled by the noise it made.

"Sorry, Mary, I forgot the engine might startle you. It's been a long time since you were in a car. But you'll soon get used to it."

Then off they drove together, through the main gates, down

194

the winding narrow lane, so familiar now to Martha, yet so unfamiliar to Mary. Soon they were onto the main road again. Traffic seemed to be very busy that day, busier than usual. While trying to concentrate on the road, she glanced at Mary quickly. Again she noticed that look of bewilderment on her face. Of course, she most probably found the traffic passing alongside the car quite alarming when she had not been on a road for more than two years. She was relieved that fifteen minutes later they were at Aelybryn.

Evan greeted them with his usual great smile, showing his big brown teeth and gaps, as well as what he had eaten for lunch. He was so delighted to see Mary back home with them again. Mary looked at him with some surprise, probably being hardly able to recognise him from the Evan she remembered. He had gained so much weight since she had last seen him. She had no idea how long ago that was. He was now about seventeen stone, with very ruddy cheeks and such a broad smile even his eyes crinkled, when he said, "Mary, my girl, great to see you home again. And I've got great news from Beth. Anne has passed into the grammar school."

"What wonderful news," shouted Martha, but Mary of course was unaware of the facts. It meant nothing to her. In the time she had been away Evan's hair had turned whiter and he looked so much like her dear father. Evan certainly demonstrated his great delight at seeing her back at Aelybryn once more. Martha made the tea in their best china teapot, and as they had almost finished the cake Beth had made for them, the sound of the key in the door signified the arrival of Rhys from work.

When he opened the door and saw Mary, he immediately stretched out both his arms to welcome her.

"Welcome home, Mary. Lovely to see you back with us again. We've all missed you so much." Martha noticed Mary's body stiffened and she appeared to be uneasy.

"Thanks," she answered politely, almost as if talking to a stranger, quickly moving away towards the table.

From that day onwards, Mary continued to speak to him politely, but only if and when it was absolutely necessary. They all noticed this distant behaviour, which baffled them somewhat, but even Mary herself was no doubt unable to find any explanation for it. Both Evan and Rhys were shocked by the transformation in Mary's behaviour. She was not the Mary they had once known. Also the fact that she had lost so much weight from when they last saw her. She seemed happy enough in herself, but she showed little emotion, sitting for hours as if she was deep in thought and far away. Martha fussed around her.

"Are you quite comfortable, Mary? You don't feel tired, do you? Are you hungry or ready for bed? Just say the word and I'll see to it straightaway."

Usually Mary would say, "No thanks, Martha, I'm fine," unless she was ready to go to bed, when she would make her feelings known.

"I feel tired now, Martha, so will you take me upstairs?" Martha would accompany her sister to the bathroom and then to the bedroom, supervising the administration of all her tablets, providing her with a warm drink, in order for her to swallow them. She then settled her into bed, pulling the clothes around her as if she was settling down a child at bedtime. It was obvious Mary was going to be totally reliant on her sister for all her needs. She did nothing unaided.

Mary would sleep soundly until quite late in the morning; the result of the sleeping tablets. Then Martha would dash back home each day from her deliveries, to give Mary her breakfast. The latter would manage to clear the dishes from the table, wash them and put them away. But that was all she ever did using her own initiative. She then sat and waited for Martha's return for her next instructions. She would help to lay the table for lunch and supper but did nothing without being told.

During the afternoons, Mary would listen to the radio or play the piano. Often she would be dozing in the chair when Evan came down from the dairy for a break. He would tease her laughingly, but Mary had lost all her sense of humour.

"Don't be so silly, Evan," she would tell him, but he continued to do so, despite having little reaction or response from her. He had ragged and tantalised Daniel's children when they were living with them during the war, trying to ease the gloom that lingered during those awful years of the bombs. Again he tried to ease the gloom he felt.

"It's almost like having a child living here again, but at least I had a reaction from Catherine and Anne when they lived with us. Of course Mary never did have your sense of humour, Martha, but now she just seems to find nothing I say the slightest bit amusing, try though I may. I simply cannot make her laugh."

"But you must bear in mind, Evan, what she has been through, having all that electric treatment and still on medication. She will never be the same Mary that we knew and remember; but at least she is back with us."

But Evan never gave up trying to get her interested in various issues, despite the fact he often felt as if he was talking to himself. Martha followed Evan's example, trying endlessly to interest her in gossip of customers, or news of their own family, but with very little reaction. She seemed unable to appreciate these things and Martha knew she could do nothing else. Mary dusted the house, but it was Martha who used the electric cleaner and did the actual cooking of meals because Mary refused to use any form of electricity.

She seemed afraid of it. In fact Martha did almost everything, even to the point of thinking for her sister. Now her day began at 4.30 a.m. the same time as Evan. It was he who would call her every morning, and together they would go up to the dairy to ensure all the crates were loaded onto the van for her first delivery, after which she would return to the house to Mary. Martha had a completely different routine now that her sister was back in Aelybryn. But although it was arduous, and she had little time for herself, she never complained nor did she seem resentful. She always wore that lovely smile on her face; the smile that said all was well and that she was happy and contented with her lot.

Her one pleasure came after Mary and Evan were in bed. She and Rhys would sit by the fire and talk together about their day. Rhys told her of his concern that Mary's attitude towards him was still strange and that it did upset him somewhat. He still remembered clearly the unfortunate incident in the garden before her breakdown, but never referred to it.

"Just don't take any notice, Rhys. It could be the result of all the electric treatments she has had over a period of time. Evan finds her different and I have had to explain to him too. The doctor warned me that certain events or people could be sometimes obliterated from her memory, and she may not relate very well to them any more. Places would be likewise. She sometimes may also become disorientated, forgetting where she is. We are fortunate to have her back, after the trauma she has been through. Her life for just over two years, let's face it, must have been frightful, spending that length of time with all the restrictions of a mental hospital, let alone the unpleasant electric shocks she was forced to undergo, and the people she mixed with. I only wish they could have found some explanation for her breakdown in the first place.

It was so unfortunate she took it out on you at the time, when you had done nothing to her. I'd have preferred she'd chased me instead."

Rhys was relieved that Martha had an explanation for Mary's behaviour, so he tried to put it out of his mind. Sometimes, but not always, when they sat in front of the fire, they would fondle and kiss each other as they had done before Mary returned. Martha could relax with the knowledge that she was safely sound asleep under the influence of her drugs, and Evan would never move from his bed once he was in it.

"Takes enough effort for him to get into his bed, with all the weight he has gained, let alone get out again," she would tell Rhys if he was anxious. He was so grateful for Martha's continued sense of humour despite all she had to contend with. What an exceptional woman she was.

Thus life continued at Aelybryn with Martha taking Mary down to the farm at Christmas and Bank holidays, while Beth called regularly to see Mary and brought the children on weekends. Martha bought all Mary's clothes from customer's shops, so that she could bring them home on approval for Mary to try on in the comfort of her own home because she had refused to venture into the town. In fact the only places she went were to the chapel on Sundays, to her brother's farm, and to her other nieces, who also lived near them, but Martha always had to accompany her wherever she went.

In 1950 Rhys confessed to Martha that he had applied for another job. This time it was at the General Post Office in the town. He had been offered a position in the sorting office and it would entail his working nights. He did not tell Martha that he had welcomed the new arrangement for his working hours, because seeing Mary and what she had become bothered him greatly. He recognised the fact that, on her return, she preferred not to communicate with him whatever her reason if indeed she was now capable of any reasoning. It was better that he worked during the night and slept during the day, thus hardly coming into contact with her at all. Martha made no attempt to dissuade him, nor did she say she welcomed the idea. The choice was his and his alone. They would naturally see less of each other, but she had made her own decisions in life, and it was now up to him to decide what he felt was best for himself.

Within four weeks Rhys began his new post at the General Post Office in the town.

Chapter 18

Rhys

Rhys could hardly believe he had been in the sorting department for almost twelve months. He found the work somewhat boring because he worked on his own, seldom talking to the other workers on the night shift with him. But he was more than satisfied with the hours; they suited him far better. Life had changed so much since he had arrived all those years ago with John, after the 1914-1918 war. Then Evan had arrived from South Africa. He had welcomed his arrival, being such a jovial character, and a great help after the death of the old man. What a godsend he was now, doing so much to help Martha. But it still upset him to see Mary. How she had changed. She had been such a bright, intelligent girl when he had met her for the first time and eventually fallen in love with her. He was convinced that she would never have ended up as she did if only they could have continued their life and with their feelings for each other, and eventually they could have married all those years ago. He remembered when he had told her how he felt about her in the park, and they had kissed, only that once. But she was devoted to her sister and she was more important to her than he was. He could still see her on the park seat in her skirt and silk blouse, smiling at him and then walking away from him after he had told her how he felt. At least she had a mind of her own then. Now she was like a puppet, with Martha pulling the strings. Poor Martha. What a life she had now, looking after Mary, running the business and little time for herself. He often felt torn between them, wondering for whom he felt the most sorry. They had both turned him down for the sake of each other and he felt neither of them deserved the life they now shared. But what could he possibly do? Just look on from the outside. The trouble was that, in order to save himself the torture of seeing Mary, unable to make even the most simple decisions any more and always awaiting instructions from Martha, he had to forfeit seeing as much of the woman he now loved. Martha, who never complained, grumbled or objected to anything, but was forever smiling, teasing, forgiving and grateful for such small things in life, which seemed to make her happy. How was it possible for a human being to be so forgiving and bear no malice, no grudges, and especially to be so tolerant?

She was a wonderful person and how he loved her, wanted her so much. He found it very hard to control his feelings when they were alone together for a long period. As soon as he began to fondle her and feel her body next to his, he desperately wanted to take her. No one would know or find out once Evan was asleep, because he never got out of bed. Mary, of course, was in a deep sleep from her tablets. Then he realised Martha had thought those same thoughts when she had woken up during the middle of the night and had come to him in his bed. It was while Mary was in hospital and she had said she was lonely. At that time he had tried to be sensible and firm and stop things before they got out of hand. But since then he had thought about it a great deal. How he had longed to make love to her all night in his bed. But where would that get them? There seemed to be no light at the end of this tunnel he was in. He now slept when she was busy, and when she slept he was in the post office. From that first week when he began his new job, Martha had cut sandwiches for him to take to work, carefully packing them in a box with an apple and some cream crackers and cheese. He usually left Aelybryn at 9.15 p.m. to walk up the road to catch the bus which would get him into work by 10 p.m. His shift was until 6 a.m. so he would arrive home by 6.45 a.m., but Martha would already be on the road. Evan would be sitting there having his breakfast.

"Morning, Rhys. Busy night?" but before he replied, the mug of tea would be thrust into his hand with a smile. "Toast on the way."

They would eat breakfast together before he would go up to his room and off to bed. He often found it difficult to get to sleep, listening to Mary moving around in the bathroom next door. Sometimes he would hear Martha's voice happily chatting to her sister while helping her to dress, preparing her ready for the day ahead. At about 4 p.m. he usually put his alarm clock to sound, in order for him to get up again. Then into the bathroom to wash and shave and read in his room until suppertime when Martha would call him to join them. He was now the proud owner of a complete set of the Dickens Collection but had not read the last one, A Tale of Two Cities, which he had now begun to read and was enjoying. There was little point in asking Martha to read it when he had finished it, despite the fact he knew she would have enjoyed it. She had no time now for reading which was sad after being such an avid reader. Mary, of course, read nothing nowadays, only flicked through magazines as if just looking at the pictures. It concerned him greatly to witness this, when once she had enjoyed reading classical books and done all the accounts for the business. Poor Mary. Whatever had got into her to change her so much?

Whatever would they all do now without Martha? She always saw him to the door before he left for work and she would put her arms around him and kiss him as if she was bidding her husband good night. Mary seemed oblivious to this fact and even when she witnessed her sister giving him a kiss on the mouth, she seemed to take no notice, as if Martha was kissing one of her brothers.

Each week he looked forward to his day off, because he could go into the garden and enjoy the fresh air and sunshine. He even enjoyed the rain, because then he could help Evan in the dairy doing such jobs as whitewashing the walls inside to keep them clean. They had acquired a large walk-in refrigerator, which was second-hand, to keep the extra crates of milk over from the previous day. Rhys would scrub out this cold room on his days off. Sometimes the highlight of the week was to go the cinema for the last showing with Martha on a Saturday night. She would get Mary to bed earlier than usual and give her the medication, together with a collection of magazines with which her customers had finished.

"Mary will fall asleep while browsing through them," she told Evan, "and she doesn't mind my going out with Rhys to the cinema. I only wish she would come with me to see a film which I know she would enjoy, but she refuses. She would have loved doing that before her illness. That was something she so enjoyed doing with Daniel's children when they lived with us during the war. Still it doesn't do to look back, does it?"

Evan always encouraged Rhys and Martha to go to the cinema.

"Off you go, you two," he would insist, wanting Martha to

have some leisure time to herself.

"I'll look after Mary while you're out."

"Dear Evan," Martha thought. "What a blessing it is to have him living with us."

So off she and Rhys would go together. There were occasions when she would be too busy or a visitor would call, and he would go alone, but Martha always waited up for him to come home. He was hardly able to contain his feelings at these times when they would sit on the settee together and chat. Then they would begin kissing and end up making passionate love to each other. But Martha always stopped him when she thought they were getting out of control, and in a way he was grateful to her for this. What was the point? However, he felt time was not on their side and it seemed to be passing so quickly. He could not believe he was fifty-six and Martha was now forty-seven and they could not look to the future. There was little to gain because there seemed nothing permanent to look forward to. These thoughts he kept to himself, not letting Martha have any more anxiety than she already had with Mary. He could not understand how she always seemed so happy with what had been dealt her, and with what they shared together. But of course, Martha would have said she had a very full and happy life, and would be grateful that she had the health and strength to do all she needed to do. What a remarkable woman she was.

Chapter 19

Christmas at the farm in 1951 was the family affair as usual. When everyone had finished their Christmas lunch, as was customary, the adults all sat around to listen to the king's speech, which was broadcast at three o'clock in the afternoon. This year was to be different. Martha had been told by her customers, and had also later read in the newspapers, the fact that the king would not be making his usual live speech to his people. Apparently he had always dreaded making it because of his stammer.

"Yes," continued Beth, "owing to his breathing difficulties, it was decided that an engineer would go to Buckingham Palace on December 21st and piece together a ten-minute recording of the speech which took two painstaking hours to prepare. None of us really know what anxiety he must go through, trying to get words to come to him, with his speech impediment. It really must be very frustrating."

Martha picked up the conversation

"I read that he had hoped to travel to Australia and New Zealand in the spring next year, but it seems his health is going to prevent him from doing so after all." Mary sat quietly, seemingly listening, but making no comment, sometimes looking far away.

Thus, on Thursday 31st of January, the king and queen went

to Heathrow Airport to see Elizabeth and Philip off to Kenya on the first leg of their journey to Australia and New Zealand, representing the king and queen. They were due to be away for nearly six months, and the king was seen on the tarmac bidding his beloved daughter and her husband farewell.

"Doesn't the king look gaunt and ill in these newspaper photographs," Martha had remarked to Mary, showing her the paper.

"He looks windswept, lonely and very sad." But Mary had shown little interest, unlike the interest she had always shown in the royal family before her illness. In fact she remembered during the recording of the king's speech after Christmas lunch at the farm that Mary had seemed far away again with her thoughts, and really did not listen to any of it. Now nothing interested her.

On February 5th, 1952, the newspapers recorded that the king had been out on the estate, shooting rabbits and hares. Martha was so pleased to read this. He was obviously looking and feeling much better if he was enjoying this sporting activity. But the next morning they heard the terrible news that the king had gone to bed that night, and had died in his sleep during the early hours of February 6th. Princess Elizabeth did not know for several hours that she was the new Queen of England. She was in a tree house, set in the branches of a giant fig tree, in East Africa, when she became queen in place of her dear father.

"I wonder did he know he did not have long to live, when he was at the airport seeing them off," Martha said sadly to Evan. "He looked so ill and sad."

Evan always showed he was interested, even if he wasn't, but as all this was to do with Africa, he listened with enthusiasm. He was sorry that the sad news had reached her while she was in this beautiful country, and those memories would always haunt her. It was the first time he had looked back to the past, and to his old life. The life he had left behind all those years ago. He wondered if his ex-wife was still living there? Was she still alive? But he had never for one moment regretted leaving. He had been so happy at Aelybryn when he had returned to his roots and to be of help to his family. Suddenly he could hear Martha's voice.

"You haven't answered my question."

"Well, we will never know. He was nearly forty-one when he became king, and now fifteen years later he has gone. I'm sure all the stress he was under as King of England must have contributed to his untimely death. In fact, I think he literally died for this country. He was a very courageous man."

Mary made very little comment during the days to follow, but Martha read all the newspapers about the funeral, and took a keen interest in the photographs of the royal family standing together veiled in mourning, and at the burial of King George VI at St George's Chapel, Windsor. To her, London was still so far away. Probably as far away to her as Africa was to Evan.

Martha would no doubt always remember that year of 1952. Some time after the king's funeral, one of her customers told her that she could no longer look after the six-year-old dog she had inherited from her daughter who had moved to Spain to live. Martha was well used to hearing all sorts of problems her customers experienced, whether it was in their family, friendships of any kind, or even the breakdown of marriages in their family. These she always listened to, with heartfelt interest, and always offered some sort of comfort or advice, if she thought it would be of some help. When Martha was told that the dog would have to be put down unless she could find it a new home, she told Mrs Evans that she would ask around all her other customers to see if there was someone who could help. When, at the end of the week, she still had not been successful in finding anyone to give it a home, she told Evan to remind her to ask Daniel when he called later that afternoon. Perhaps he would be prepared to have yet another dog on the farm. He already had two sheepdogs, but perhaps he would manage to give it a home just for the time being. This dog was a cross between a sheepdog and a black Labrador, and could be useful for him perhaps.

"But why don't we have it here?" suggested Evan. "We always have money in the house with the business, and it would be good to have a guard dog. I'm sure it would be good company for Mary too. While you are out on the rounds, I am up in the dairy and Rhys is in bed so she does spend considerable time alone. A dog would be great company for her. Why don't you ask her what she feels about it?"

Mary never seemed to have an opinion on anything, since she had come out of hospital, so Martha knew what the reply would be. It would be Martha's decision in the end. However Evan always thought things through so well and his ideas were always so constructive.

"Yes, Evan, you are quite right. What a brilliant idea. I didn't give it a thought that we could possibly take it ourselves, and you are right; it would be great company for Mary. Provided she has no objection to having an animal in the house as a pet. All our animals were always kept outside years ago, just as Daniel's animals are kept. I'll ask her."

"Well, I don't mind what you do really. It's up to you, Martha," she had said. But having given it a great deal of thought, Martha decided to heed Evan's advice. She would inform her customer the following morning that they would take the dog. Mrs Evans was over the moon at not having to have the pet put down, and the fact that it would be going to such an excellent home. "Prince" came to live at Aelybryn the following week. He settled in very well and Mary seemed to enjoy his being around the house as far as they could tell. He was not allowed upstairs, but went up to the dairy with Evan every morning, watching him as he loaded up the van for Martha. Then down he would come again when Rhys came home from work. While he and Evan had breakfast together, they made a fuss of him. But the trouble was, when anyone called at the house, the dog barked while Rhys was trying to sleep. However he eventually became used to the barking of the dog and took no notice of it. He would follow him into the garden on his days off and soon he, like the rest of the family, became quite attached to the new arrival.

Mary would pat him, call his name when she fed him, and put water in his bowl, under Martha's instructions of course. It was good to see Prince sitting at Mary's feet when she came home mid-afternoon. It was as if the dog was looking after her, not the other way around. Although Mary never enthused about anything, or showed little preference to anything or anyone, she certainly warmed to the dog. Martha felt he must be giving her some inward feeling of comfort and companionship, although she still failed to express what she really felt or thought about the arrival of a pet.

When Martha went collecting the money, sometimes Prince would follow her, and would run behind the van, sitting on the pavement until she returned from each house. In the beginning, he had returned to his old home, and Mrs Evans had to return him to Aelybryn. However, after a few weeks, he obviously forgot where he had once lived, and Aelybryn was the only home he remembered. Martha too became very attached to the dog.

"Evan, you were right, I'm so glad you suggested our taking the dog. We all appreciate his company, and I do believe that although Mary fails to show much reaction, I'm sure she enjoys having him around. Have you noticed how he runs to her when he comes through the door? Strange when you think she makes so little fuss of him, but she is the one who gives him his food. If she forgets, he soon reminds her, and gets through to her in his own way. Animals sense so much more than we realise. I don't know what we would do without you, Evan. You come up with so many sensible ideas."

"Oh you'd manage as you have always done, Martha. Look what you have done for me over the years. You are all the family I have and all I have to think about. I'm so fortunate to be able to remain with you at Aelybryn, trying my best to make myself as useful as I possibly can until eventually I guess my end must come sometime. I only hope I will never be a burden to you, Martha. You have more than enough to cope with let alone looking after an old uncle like me."

Life in general continued much the same, at Aelybryn. In fact, nothing changed there, week in, week out. Martha took Mary to the farm as often as she could. Daniel's two girls were growing up into very attractive ladies. Catherine had already left home to work in London, much to Daniel's annoyance, as it meant one person less to help on the farm. Anne had left school to work at home on the farm, which she was not very happy about. Her father insisted she was needed there because her sister had left and labour was very short at that time. As Catherine was nearly twenty-one he could not prevent her from leaving. Beth missed her very much, but welcomed having Anne at home every day to help. She also welcomed seeing Martha. It saddened her to think that Mary was so changed from the person she had met when Daniel had taken her to meet them all those years before. She and

Daniel could never understand why she had suffered a mental breakdown and ended up such a completely different character from the one they had known. She certainly seemed to smile more since the dog arrived and Beth was so pleased to think that there was just one thing in life that seemed to get a reaction from her, small though it was.

June 20th 1952 was just like any other day when Evan called Martha as usual, at 4.30 a.m.

"Going to be another hot day, Martha. The sooner you get on the road to deliver the milk before the strong heat of the sun, the better." Rhys came home from work as usual and greeted Prince, patting him on the head, and in return, the dog wagged his tail frantically, before sitting at his feet waiting for the last pieces of toast. The day passed as usual, but Mary seemed very tired and asked Martha if she would take her up to bed as soon as they had finished supper. After doing so, Martha came downstairs and prepared the sandwiches for Rhys to take to work as usual. He followed her into the kitchen.

"On my day off this Saturday, how about going to the coast for a run in the car instead of the cinema, if it's a fine warm evening?"

"Yes, we'll do that, Rhys. Prince and Evan will be here to look after Mary and I'll get back in time to see her into bed. We'll go as soon as I finish my rounds. Make the most of it."

Evan decided to walk down the road for the evening paper, so when Rhys sat down Martha immediately took advantage of their being alone for a short time, and perched herself on his lap. She teased him about not going to have his hair cut the previous week, ruffling it with her hands. Rhys quickly caught them both in his, and bent her across his lap, kissing her with almost harsh brutality. He forced his hand inside her blouse, not with the tenderness he normally showed towards her. It was as if there was little time to do what he wanted. She could feel his teeth, as he took her nipple into his mouth. His breathing was erratic and, panting heavily, he was about to lift up her skirt when Prince barked heralding the return of Evan. Martha jumped up and dashed out into the kitchen to straighten her clothes and compose herself while Rhys picked up a newspaper and began to read as if nothing had happened.

Soon it was time for him to get off to work so the same routine occurred. Martha went to the door, put her arms around him and kissed him the usual warm goodnight kiss on the mouth.

"Can you make sure the dog doesn't follow me, like the other night? He tried to get on the bus with me and I had a devil of a job to send him home," Rhys told Martha. He did not seem amused when Martha burst out laughing trying to imagine Rhys pushing the dog off the bus with the help of the conductor. Evan overheard this conversation between them.

"Don't worry, I'll see to it," Evan told Rhys and, catching around Prince's collar, he pulled him into the kitchen while Martha quickly closed the door. She watched Rhys through the window until he was out of sight, wishing Evan could have stayed out just that much longer, but somewhat concerned that Rhys had, for the first time, treated her with a little roughness. He had always been so gentle and caring towards her, treating her with such tenderness. "No doubt time was short," she said to herself, knowing Evan would soon return, before Rhys could finish what he had started. Never mind, they would have a chance to be alone together next Saturday on his day off. They would stop the car at some secluded spot at the coast and they would spend an hour or so making love which they had not had the chance to do lately.

Evan put the chain on the door and did the locking up as

he always did. He stood in front of the old grandfather clock to wind it before going off to bed. Martha followed him soon afterwards. When she entered the bedroom, she could see that Mary was sound asleep. Martha slid into bed alongside her, but she tossed and turned, unable to relax, still thinking about the outing she and Rhys would have on Saturday. It could not come quickly enough. Where would be the best place to stop the car, in order to be alone? Maybe they would walk along the cliffs, or perhaps they could go to the small village near the sea and walk along the cliff path to the teashop? She had not done that walk since she was a little girl on the Sunday school outing. Yes, she quite fancied that idea, and Rhys always enjoyed walking in the fresh air, especially since his night work at the post office. He loved being outside; possibly it would be a better idea if she packed a few sandwiches and a flask of tea to take with them. When had they last had a picnic? With those exciting thoughts, she turned over and fell soundly asleep.

Chapter 20

Evan came downstairs as usual the following morning at 4.30 a.m. and gave Martha a call. They had their usual cup of tea together before going up to the dairy in order to load the crates into the van ready for the first delivery. Martha was so grateful to Evan for all his help, not only saving her lifting the crates but also saving her so much of her time. When they reached the top of the path, Martha could see a sandwich box on the old wooden table outside the dairy. It looked exactly the same as the one Rhys had bought when he began his work at the post office.

"Look, Evan," she pointed to the box. "Whatever is Rhys's sandwich box doing here?" lifting it off the table. Then they could see that the sandwiches were still inside.

"Looks as if he hasn't eaten them," Evan remarked, trying not to show Martha his concern when he saw the look of anxiety on her face.

"Wherever has he gone?"

"No idea, Martha."

Martha thought if he had gone away somewhere unexpectedly or had been called away from his work perhaps in an emergency, he would have surely taken the sandwiches with him. This really was a mystery, but no doubt there was a simple explanation.

Evan by this time was opening the door to the dairy, ready to unlock the refrigerator, while Martha continued to inspect the contents of the sandwich box. No, they haven't been touched. The box is just as I packed it last night, she thought to herself.

"I don't think he has even opened it," she called to Evan, but suddenly he turned quickly back towards her as she was about to follow him into the dairy. He suddenly put his arm out to prevent her from going any farther.

"Martha, stay where you are, there's been an accident. Quickly run down to the house and phone for the police and an ambulance."

"But..."

"Martha, do as I say, you can't be of any help here."

"But what has...." she did not finish, before Evan shouted, quite sharply to her, with a distressed look on his face.

"Go at once," he demanded. She jumped, startled, as he had never shouted or raised his voice at her in all the years he had been at Aelybryn.

She ran down to the house, trembling like a leaf, her legs feeling quite weak. She immediately telephoned the police and ambulance. "Please come quickly, there's been a accident. It's urgent. I'm not sure but I think someone has been seriously injured in our dairy. It's the detached stone house right at the top of the hill, Claridon Road. Yes, the house name is Aelybryn but no number."

Then Martha rang the police. When they asked for details, she had none, for she knew not what kind of an accident had occurred, or who was involved. When she replaced the receiver, she was shaking uncontrollably, and she felt sick. Evan soon followed her and put his arm around her gently.

"Sit down, Martha, because this will come as a shock to

you. Rhys is dead. He has hung himself with the rope we kept in the dairy to tow the car. I've cut him down, but he has been dead for some time. My guess is that he didn't go to work last night, but went as far as the bus stop, then doubled back to the yard and went into the dairy. He must have had it all planned. That was why he asked us to keep Prince in the house last night, so he would not follow him and deter what he had in mind. The dog could have barked and raised the alarm. He knows I always go into the dairy before you to open the refrigerator; therefore I was bound to find him, and save you from finding him first. His sandwich box acted as a warning to me. I knew when you said the sandwiches were still inside, something terrible must have happened. Poor Rhys, whatever made him do it? He has left you this note," Evan said, handing her a brown envelope. "It was pinned to his jacket."

Martha was devastated. She simply could not grasp what Evan had said. Surely there had to be some mistake. Maybe it wasn't Rhys after all.

"Are you sure you recognised his clothes. Are you certain it is Rhys?"

"Martha, I know it is, beyond any doubt."

"My God," she gasped. "Whatever made him do such a terrible thing?"

Martha took the letter from him, her hands trembling so much she could hardly open it. She recognised his handwriting. Hadn't she seen it often enough on all the postcards he had sent them when he went away. It was definitely written by him and now her stomach began to churn over and over. She had to run out quickly to the back yard where she began vomiting.

When she returned, her face was like death herself. Evan had put the kettle on to make her a strong cup of tea, with a dash of brandy, which was said to be good for shock.

"Drink this, Martha; it will make you feel better."

She did as Evan had instructed and, sitting down in the chair he had provided, she slowly opened the letter, still shaking like a leaf.

My dearest Martha,

I am so sorry to do this to you but it seemed the only way out.

After what you and all your family have done for me, it seems such a selfish thing to do. But you will now be able to get on with your lives, you and Mary. I cannot face death without confessing to you that the only other woman I ever loved was your sister. I never meant to fall in love with either of you, certainly not to end up falling in love with you both. You were such fun when I returned from my training, and such a breath of fresh air, so fall in love with you I did. The trouble was I truly did love you both, but in different ways and at different times. I should have realised long ago that I never could have either of you for myself. You were both so devoted to each other and I was left completely in the middle. I began to worry whether I could have been at all responsible for Mary's breakdown, if she had discovered the truth about us? Did we ever let our guard down at any time? It began eating me inside from the day she returned home from hospital. I could not bear to see what she had become, and did any of the blame rest with me? Could she have seen us together and kept it all to herself? She was so unselfish, just like you, Martha, in that respect; neither of you would ever hurt the other intentionally.

Apart from the guilt I felt, I have found the strain of not being able to show you just how much I loved you too much to bear. I wanted you more than I can write in words, and I cannot help feeling I have done you both such a great injustice. There was no other way out for me but to let you both live your lives together in peace. The love and devotion you share as sisters is unique, and I am thankful that I could not and did not ever come between you both. I often wondered if Mary grew to hate me, seeing me with you, but I doubt now that she would remember that we had once loved each other too. I did genuinely love her all those years ago you know, when I told her how I felt about her. But although she said she felt the same way about me, she loved you more.

What will you do now, my dear Martha? That remarkable woman who always wore a smile, even in adversity. What will you be feeling and thinking when you know what I have done? Well I know in my heart that you will forgive me because it is in your nature to always forgive, no matter what the circumstances. Unlike me, you believe in God, and both you and Mary have always lived up to everything you believed in. If you are correct, and there truly is a God, then he will forgive me too. I only hope he will permit me to join my family, wherever they may be. My dear mother, father and sisters who were blown to pieces all those years ago.

Lastly, I came to your family with nothing and, owing to your generosity, I have managed to set aside some money. My collection of Dickens books, and what money I have in the bank is all yours, Martha. I know you will spend little on yourself, you always have done. However I know you will happily spend it on Mary and your family. I am very happy with that thought.

Please have my body cremated and I want no headstone by which to be remembered. You must think of me as the past, not to be remembered, grieved or spoken about.

However what you must always remember is that so many

people love you so very much, as I did.

Rhys

Martha folded up the letter and put it in her pocket. There was a loud knock on the front door. It was the police and ambulance. What a godsend Evan was because he was able to take them up to the dairy, show them Rhys's body and identify him. That was something she was saved from doing. They removed him immediately and took him away so she did not see him after that dreadful event. The last she remembered of him was happily saying goodnight, handing him his sandwiches, with the thought of going to the coast on Saturday on his day off. She did not have to decide, after all, where they would stop the car and have their picnic.

Mary was still in bed when she went upstairs. "Did you hear the loud knocking on the front door?" Mary nodded, but seemed unconcerned.

"I'm afraid there has been a terrible accident and Rhys is dead," Martha told her, waiting for a reaction, but there was none. Mary immediately slid her legs out of bed and mumbled quietly, "Oh dear" as if to herself. Then she reached over to the chair, picked up her clothes, which Martha had left out as usual ready for her to get dressed with her help. She did not ask how, or where, or when, regarding the accident, but began trying to dress herself, something she had not done since returning home from the mental hospital. Martha then went out on her rounds, as soon as she had informed Daniel and Beth about the tragedy. She had to tell all the customers she saw that Rhys had taken his own life, but there was no explanation for his actions. Everyone was shocked by the news. His name was never mentioned again between her and Mary. There was nothing to say.

"The police asked if there was any suicide note," Evan told

Martha later, "but I said we had not found anything as yet. I am to tell you that you must notify them if you find anything. My advice is the less said the better. Burn it, Martha."

"Whatever would I do without you, Evan? Do you remember when you used to go to the pub every week, and you told us one night when you were home later than usual, that you had been chatting to a lady in the corner. Mary and I often wondered what would we have done if you had wanted to marry her. Were you ever interested, as you used to certainly make an effort to do your hair a special way for a while?"

"Fancy you both noticed. Yes, Florence was a very nice lady. She had lost her husband and had a sister in Durban so that was how we began to chat. We did get on very well, and I met her in the pub every week after that, but it could never have come to anything. You see, Martha, I did not have a proper job. I could not ever marry again. Here was my life, living and helping you both at Aelybryn. Eventually she went away to live, so that was that. I have no regrets. It's the way life turns out for some, and what is to be, will be. I have made a wonderful life and home here with you."

That conversation was never mentioned again, neither was the note from Rhys. She knew the secret was safe with him, she could trust him with her life. Martha went upstairs and locked Rhys's bedroom door, putting the key in the envelope with his note.

The funeral took place the following week. Martha could not let any of his family know of his death, because she knew he had none. This was indeed very sad. She went into the town the following day and bought a grey coat and hat for herself, and Mary wore her navy dress. She always wore anything Martha chose for her, knowing Martha always knew best.

Evan stayed at home to look after Mary on the day of the funeral. She said she did not want to go anywhere that day, she preferred to remain in the house with Evan and Prince. The funeral took place at the nearby crematorium during late afternoon, after Daniel and Beth had finished their milk rounds which Martha also had to complete. The service was very short and private, with only the close family attending. It all seemed quite unreal, and very strange. Afterwards, they all returned to Aelybryn, where Martha had prepared tea and sandwiches. Mary seemed to accept the fact that it was a different day from any other, having afternoon tea with the family, but never asked what was the occasion for the get-together. In fact she asked no questions at all. Life just carried on as before. It was as if Rhys had never lived there.

"You are a very strong and remarkable woman, Martha," Evan told her after the funeral. But from that day onwards, he did not mention Rhys to her ever again.

Some months later, Beth mentioned Rhys to Daniel.

"How strange that Martha never talks about Rhys."

"What's there to say? No one mentions him."

"Well, she always enjoyed going to the cinema with him on his days off and they seemed to derive pleasure from each other's company, I'm sure."

"Now, Beth, have you fed the calves this afternoon?" Daniel asked her briskly, changing the subject, refusing to make any further comment. Beth remained puzzled, because Martha had remarked to her on many occasions over the years what great fun Rhys was and how much they enjoyed each other's company. Strange she did not say she missed him, coming and going into the house, or their outings together. Now it seemed he was never that important to her in her life. In fact, it was as if he had never lived there at all. It was as if he had never existed.

An inquest was held some weeks later where the verdict was given that Rhys Hopkins had taken his own life while the balance of his mind was disturbed. None of the family ever mentioned his name again.

Chapter 21

On June 2nd 1953 the coronation took place at Westminster Abbey. Never before had there been such adulation for a monarch. Everyone was very excited, and all Martha's customers told her she must find time to see the Queen being crowned. Only three of her customers had a television, offering to have her and Mary to their home enabling them to witness such a unique event.

"We really must go and watch some of it on television," Martha told Mary. "We have had three offers to go and watch it." But Mary seemed so disinterested. Nevertheless, as soon as Martha had finished her rounds, she took Mary across the road in time to see the Queen getting into the Gold State Coach, drawn by eight grey horses, escorted by twenty-seven further carriages, twenty-nine bands and thirteen thousand troops. Hundreds of thousands of the Queen's subjects lined the streets cheering and waving.

"Well," said Martha, "we wouldn't have missed this for anything, would we, Mary?"

"Um, no," she replied unenthusiastically, but Martha was full of it. She wondered if she would ever go to London one day, but realised that was impossible with Mary in the state she was. It was enough to get her to go across the road. Never mind, she had loved every minute of the coronation as much as she saw of it.

In 1955 Martha and Mary became great aunts. Daniel and Beth's elder daughter Catherine, living in London, gave birth to a girl. Sadly Mary was still mentally frail and although she was told the great news she seemed to be unable to enthuse over any happy event in their lives. Physically she was still very strong, but unfortunately she could not use her strength to help Martha in any way. The latter however enjoyed everything she did with so much enthusiasm. She was so thrilled and excited to hear this latest good news. She immediately bought the new baby a carry cot, nappies and baby outfits from one of her customers' shops. However she always gave the gifts to Mary to do the actual presenting of them, despite the fact that it was Martha who was the breadwinner and had been for years. She did not ever want her sister to feel left out of anything or not to be a part of the whole process of earning, paying and giving. How thoughtful she was at all times and in everything she did.

Martha was invited to so many weddings in the years to follow. There were the family ones and those of her customers' children whom she had seen growing up daily while on her milk deliveries. Everyone loved her and she just enjoyed life to the full. Mary, on the other hand, still continued to stay at home and sit near the fire alone with her thoughts, which no one else could comprehend. No one could honestly say she was not contented or that she was unhappy. She just seemed to find it impossible to communicate, or express feelings and thoughts, ever since her breakdown. Martha would always try to encourage her, jestingly at times, which would at least make her sister smile. That meant everything to Martha. A glimmer of hope was always there as far as Martha was concerned. She never gave up. She appreciated having Evan around her so that she had someone to tease and make laugh, and he always reciprocated. He was still someone who could be relied upon for good advice, had sound judgement and continued to help her with the business which she greatly appreciated. She could not imagine how life would be without him.

Martha spent a very joyous Christmas in 1957 at the farm with Mary. Anne returned home from Cardiff with her husband, and Catherine brought their daughter, now two years old, whom they all fussed over and nursed especially Martha. The great aunts had bought her a doll, a pram, and many other presents, supposedly from Father Christmas, of course. It was a repetition of what they had done for her mother all those years ago. However the New Year brought with it great anxiety. An outbreak of foot and mouth disease had been reported twenty-five miles away from Daniel's farm, and although a restriction of the movement of animals and other restrictions were imposed within a ten-mile radius, even twenty-five miles was too close for comfort. Foot and mouth disease, often called hoof and mouth disease, is a highly contagious and often fatal viral disease of cattle and pigs. It can infect sheep, rats and hedgehogs, and dogs can also carry the disease. Blisters inside the mouths of the animals lead to excessive secretion of stringy or foamy saliva and drooling. Blisters also appear on the feet which rupture and cause lameness in the animals. Some that are infected do not suffer or show signs of the disease but are carriers and transmit it to others. The virus is sometimes passed on to susceptible animals through direct contact with infected or contaminated vehicles used to transport livestock. Fortunately humans are rarely affected, but the clothes and skin of animal handlers, standing water, uncooked food scraps and feed supplements containing infected animal products can harbour the virus. However the control measures are every farmer's nightmare, together with the disease itself coming to their farm. Apart from quarantine, the destruction of infected livestock is essential, and this has a devastating effect on their livelihood and those involved with it. The animals are killed on the farm and the carcasses then have to be burned on the premises. This is a heartbreaking experience for any farmer when he sees in front of him the whole of his livestock, his hard-earned livelihood, being killed in front of his very eyes and destroyed. The smell of the burning flesh and smoke travels for miles around, and the flames from the enormous fires light up the dark skies at night, warning the other farmers in the locality that it could be their turn next to encounter utter devastation and ruination. The farmers affected can lose huge amounts of money during a foot and mouth epidemic when large numbers of their animals have to be destroyed. The result of this, of course, is the drastic reduction of revenue from milk and meat production.

The fear was always on all farmers' minds in the localities surrounding the outbreak. Little wonder then that, after the new year of 1957, when Daniel went into the pigsty, he found his prize sow lying down in the straw drooling. Pigs were the most likely of animals to contract the disease because of the swill they were fed on. This sow had recently given birth to eight healthy piglets, all of which were still on the sow's milk. Daniel called Beth immediately, both realising what the possible cause could be. Their one dreaded fear at that time. Foot and mouth disease had by 1957 reached its peak with more than 30,000 animals slaughtered, many of them in Wales.

Beth and Daniel looked at each other aghast. Images appeared in front of them both of what could lie ahead for them all. Beth began to shiver. "Oh, Daniel, I'm so afraid," she told him almost in tears. But Daniel, being the strong person he was, acted promptly with grit and telephoned the vet immediately, describing to him their fears. He then telephoned Martha with his suspicions. He followed the vet's instructions and removed all the piglets to another pen even though the contamination may have already been passed to them. There were no signs of foot blisters as far as he could tell, but the sow was certainly very poorly. The vet arrived very quickly and prepared Daniel for the imposed restrictions on limiting entry to the farm, and disinfectant-soaked straw to be placed at the gate near the main road. He then gave the sow a thorough examination. Gravely he looked up at Daniel. "Your pig certainly has some symptoms of foot and mouth, but also there is a possibility that it may have been poisoned."

"What?" said Daniel, puzzled but relieved. Then he realised this indeed was a possibility. "I have been infested with rats on the farm, and I did put rat poison down to catch them. One must have carried the contaminated bread into the pigsty and the sow must have devoured it." Within hours she was dead. Daniel transported the pig to the orchard in a wheelbarrow and dug a large hole in which to bury the poisoned pig. He told them all to tell no one about the unfortunate incident that had occurred on the farm that day. Beth fed the piglets one by one, using infant's milk bottles, filled with cow's milk, and they soon made good progress. The loss of their mother was costly, but nothing in comparison with the loss that might have been incurred had it had proved to be the dreaded foot and mouth disease and all its dreadful consequences.

January 1958 began as quite a cold month. Martha returned to the dairy one grey morning to reload her van as usual, but

Evan's chair was empty. Well, he seemed to feel the cold more lately and, after all, he was getting older. Possibly he had returned to the house to make himself a hot drink in order to get warmth back into his body. He had done this on occasions before especially in the snow and frosty weather. When she went down to the house, Evan was lying on the sofa. Mary was just sitting down sipping her morning tea, quite unconcerned, as if Evan always lay down on the sofa at that time of the morning. He looked very poorly indeed and found difficulty in getting out his words. He kept muttering something, trying to point to Mary. His speech had obviously been affected.

"Don't worry, Evan, everything will be fine, try not to talk. I'll send for the doctor, straightaway."

An ambulance was called and he was taken immediately to the General Hospital, where he was admitted with a suspected seizure. By the time they reached the hospital he was already unconscious. Martha went each day to visit him after she finished her work in the dairy and the home, but there was no change. She was torn between leaving Mary alone in the evenings, or sitting with her beloved uncle, just in case he came around. She wanted to be there for him, if indeed he ever regained consciousness, despite the doctor in charge not giving them any hope of a recovery. If only he could improve slightly, she could have him back at Aelybryn and find help to look after him. One of her customers was a retired nurse and had volunteered her services once before, when Mary was discharged from hospital.

Because he was still alive after a whole week, Martha felt this must surely be a good sign. But Evan never regained consciousness. He died peacefully in his sleep ten days later, at the age of seventy-eight. Martha was grateful that he did not suffer but went silently to sleep. Within five years, she had lost the two men to whom she was so close. When everyone offered her words of comfort or sympathy after Evan passed away, she would tell them, "We were fortunate to have him at all, and even more grateful that he gave so much of his life to us, helping, advising and bringing laughter into our home. We must not be full of grief, but thankful for having the privilege of having and knowing such a wonderful uncle, returning from South Africa when he did to live with us and help us. He could so easily have wanted to move on, but he remained with us and continued to be a tower of strength to me until the end of his days. Yes, we will all miss him very much. He was blessed with such a cheerful disposition, a happy smiling face, his wicked tantalizing nature and especially his kindness and generosity, all of which we will remember with gratitude. We must not be sad though. That he most certainly would never have wanted."

She had to admit to herself that the house now seemed very empty without him, and no longer could she go out and leave Evan in charge, relying on him as she used to. But she would cope as she always had done. Smile and the world smiles with you, cry and you cry alone. That was her motto. So smile she did through it all. Life began again in Aelybryn, bringing with it a somewhat different routine yet again. She continued to get up early, now doing everything alone, but she loved her life and tried to encourage Mary to enjoy it with her when she was free to do so.

Soon they became great aunts again. Catherine gave birth to another girl, and Anne gave birth to a boy, much to Daniel's delight.

"Too late of course to be any use to me on the farm," he had commented, but nevertheless, Beth was sure he was very thrilled about his new grandson. He just had a strange way of showing it. Beth adored them all, and loved to have them

230

with her at the farm whenever they could come, especially over the Christmas period. Martha and Mary continued to go there over this festive time, enjoying spoiling yet another generation.

The years were flying by so quickly, it was already 1975. Martha was still working very hard and enjoying what few pleasures she could manage, together with her never failing devoted care for her sister. One hot July morning, she went upstairs with Mary's breakfast tray as usual after doing her early morning milk round. Usually Mary stirred when she opened the door, but on this occasion there was no movement. She thought at first she was still fast asleep, but when she tried to wake her there seemed to be no response whatsoever. She was breathing heavily and obviously the situation looked serious. She immediately rang the ambulance service, exactly as she had done for Evan some seventeen years before. Could it really have been all that length of time had passed since he had left them alone in the house together? The time had flown by so quickly.

Mary was taken to the same hospital as Evan. Martha went every evening to sit with her sister, again desperately hoping that she would soon improve and not fade away from her life as Evan had done. But sadly she lived for two weeks without ever regaining consciousness. She died at the age of eighty-one. She had spent twenty-seven years just with her thoughts after suffering from her mental breakdown. Physically she had been capable of doing a hard day's work, but mentally she had remained so very weak. Martha never pressurised her into doing anything during all those years, being patient and understanding and grateful to have her back in their family home, just to be together. Life may have been very different had Mary been forced to remain in the mental hospital for the rest of her days. But Martha never speculated on what might have been. It was never her way of thinking. She was so grateful to those doctors for being prepared to release Mary to her care, all those years ago, and she had done her best to keep her word to them. Fortunately Mary had always seemed to be happy, continuing to take pleasure in playing the piano, never forgetting the notes of her favourite hymns, despite her mental state of mind. It surely must have passed many hours for her whilst being alone in the house. But who could know or tell what Mary really thought because she had never expressed any views. She had also continued to go with Martha to chapel, which she always seemed to enjoy, listening quietly to the sermon, but never actually joining in with the singing of the hymns. She would hum quietly to herself, standing when the congregation stood, looking straight ahead of her while everyone else sang with great enthusiasm, and sat down when everyone else did so. It was there, in that same graveyard, behind the chapel where she worshipped, that Mary was buried with the rest of her family.

Martha must have missed her sister greatly around the house, seeing to her every need, day in, day out, but she never disclosed the fact to anyone. She was often heard to say she was greatly relieved that Mary had never known she had left Aelybryn, and like Evan, she had not suffered any physical pain. After the funeral, Martha hoped and prayed that she was now at peace with herself and had found happiness at last. Possibly the kind of happiness that differed from that in her earthly life.

Martha's mind then went to the earthly life of Daniel and Beth on the farm. Over the past years, farming had deteriorated. In 1967 there had been another major epidemic of foot and mouth disease. The government brought in improved hygiene and animal health standards, at great cost to the farming industry. Many farmers were put under immense strain trying to comply with the new regulations, making many farmers bankrupt.

Although Daniel and Beth's children were both married, the farm was not making a good living for them. Profit from milk was now significantly less and many farmers turned to breeding beef cattle, getting rid of their milking cows. Daniel was no exception. However the cost of buying and rearing steers was far greater than he expected and profit margins were small. More farmers became bankrupt, some committing suicide unable to face the future. Now that all the milking cows had gone and he had sold his milk rounds, Daniel did not have to deliver milk to customers. However money was short and he had time on his hands. This was something he had never before experienced in the whole of his life. He therefore became more involved with other activities, such as the Farmers' Union and chapel affairs, taking over the outdated register of all the people who had been buried in its graveyard, matching them up with the corresponding graves. He spent many hours daily, fascinated by checking all the names in the register, ensuring that those mentioned in the book were the identical names of those on the headstones. When relatives from away enquired where their relation was buried in order that they too could be buried in the same grave when they passed on, Daniel was immediately able to show them, because he now had everyone logged. He enjoyed this voluntary position and, in all fairness, Martha felt very proud when chapelgoers congratulated her on her brother's achievements.

"Your brother is doing a fantastic job of the graveyard register, giving so much of his time to it," they told her.

One evening, when darkness fell, Daniel called at Aelybryn, parking his car hidden away in the dairy area, refusing to tell Martha where he was going or what he was doing. She noticed he had on his feet his wellington boots, and in his hand a bag containing a change of clothing. He instructed her not to divulge the fact she had seen him or that his car had been parked there. He also asked her if he could borrow the large spade Evan had used to dig the garden. Martha told him it was still up in the old dairy where Evan had left it when he was alive

"Wherever are you going with it? What do you need it for?" Martha enquired anxiously, but when she saw the expression on her brother's face, a familiar smile she still recognised, signifying he was in some sort of trouble, she knew she would not get a truthful answer.

"I could do with your big torch as well. You know, the one you use to go up to the dairy at night," he told Martha.

"It's in the kitchen," she replied.

"I shall be gone more than a couple of hours," he told her slamming her front door behind him and setting off in the direction of the cutting which was a short lane to the chapel and graveyard. There was little point in any further interrogation of Daniel; it was obvious he had no intention of telling her anything, but Martha was still naturally concerned. She waited and waited for his return until the early hours of the morning. She thought she heard a car drive off at 2 a.m.but she did not go to the window to see if it was Daniel.

A few weeks later, when Martha was at the farm having a cup of tea, Daniel told her, "Don't forget to take back the spade I borrowed." She did not ask Beth anything about the incident but Beth confided to her, "I don't know where Daniel went that night. I was really worried. He didn't return until the early hours of the morning. I had been in bed hours. When I got up the following morning I found a heap of clothes in the outhouse, covered in earth, and very muddy. When I asked him how his clothes had got into such a state his reply was,

'Ask no questions and you'll be told no lies'."

Months passed before Beth learned what had happened that night. There had been a burial that afternoon in the graveyard and the relations from away had asked for their mother to be buried with their father but they were unsure of the grave. Daniel told them to leave the arrangements to him; he would ask the gravedigger the chapel employed to open the specified grave before the funeral and he would inform the undertaker concerned. Then the gravedigger would return after the burial service in order to fill in the earth over the coffin. It would be up to them to inform a stonemason to reinstate the headstone to its original position together with the added name of their mother.

Unfortunately, Daniel had misinformed the digger of the correct number grave. It was the third from the path, not the fourth.

There was nothing for it but for Daniel and the gravedigger to return to the graveyard during the night, dig out the coffin, open the correct grave, and place the mother in the correct one, hoping none of the family would notice when they returned to view the reinstated headstone.

"If they query it, I will tell them that in their grief they probably didn't realise which grave it was, but it certainly is the correct one," he told the gravedigger.

This procedure was of course against the law, to remove a body, but Daniel had risked breaking the law many times before and had got away with it. Yet again he had succeeded in doing so, but he waited until he was sure he had done so before admitting anything to Beth.

The following year Daniel had an offer he could not refuse. A large building company offered him a small fortune to purchase his farm in order for it to be used for the erection of houses. Within two years some six hundred were built on his land.

Mr Griffiths, from whom he had borrowed the money to purchase it in the first place, had died some years before. The debt had been passed on to a nephew, and Daniel still owed a few hundred pounds of the original sum. This was a mere drop in the ocean in comparison with what he had received for selling the land. However "There is no sentiment in business," Daniel would often be heard to say. He returned what was owed to the nephew. No more, no less. What a bargain that farm had proved to be. He still remembered one of the other bidders at the auction telling him he was a fool to pay so much for it, and must have often wondered if the man had been correct in his assumptions, having such a large millstone around his neck. But he had wanted it so badly that day at the auction to start his life with Beth and, as usual, the risk had certainly paid off. That was the story of Daniel's life.

Over the years, the village community that surrounded the farm had tried to acquire some land in the vicinity, to set up some sports facilities for the growing population coming to live in the area, but there was never any land available because the farm had once been in the green belt. The council had wanted to take part of it from Daniel by compulsory purchase in order to build some council houses in the area, but Daniel had objected because, although he was making very little money on the farm, compulsory purchase of ground by the council paid very little. He took his case to the National Farmers' Union, pleading that he did not want to lose his livelihood. They fought for him and once again Daniel won his case. He knew they would only take his best land anyway, leaving him poor ground to farm, and pay him a very nominal amount for compulsory purchase. However, planning regulations had now changed, and Daniel was forced to return to the Farmers' Union, cap in hand, to ask for the original objection to be rescinded. This large housing company had approached him to buy his farm, and were prepared to pay a very handsome amount of money for it. Small farms over the years had ceased to be profitable, and many farmers were continuing to go bankrupt. Daniel may well have ended up likewise, but he had been born under a lucky star and everything went his way. He designated a large area near the railway line which had now become a public footpath once the railway ceased to operate to be used for a sports facility for the village. He sold this area for a very nominal amount, so that two rugby pitches and a clubhouse could be erected. The whole village was delighted and very proud indeed of the new facility they had acquired for its residents. In fact, it is still flourishing there today.

Beth also had the fur coat she had often dreamed of, together with so many other luxuries. They moved to a large house near the coast, which had once been a farmhouse, now converted to private accommodation. Beth loved it. She made new friends and had new interests, joining in a floral arrangement class, and other new activities which she had never found time for when she and Daniel had the farm. But this happiness was unfortunately short-lived. Within a year, Martha received a distraught call on the telephone from Anne, Daniel's younger daughter. Beth had died suddenly of a pulmonary embolism. It was fortuitous that both her children happened to be with her at the time. They were both sitting with her when she suddenly collapsed. The doctor was sent for immediately, but by the time he arrived Beth was dead. There was nothing he could do.

Martha had now lost the two women closest to her. Customers commented that although she smiled through it all, her face had a sad look about it. Underneath that smile was heartache. She never discussed losing Beth with anyone or showed any outward signs of grief. Life, Martha believed, was for the living, and she continued to run the business and the house alone, ever since Evan and Mary had gone. Everyone was convinced Martha missed Beth more than she was ever prepared to admit. She had often made it known that Beth had been a wonderful sister-in-law, but that she and Mary had regarded her more like a sister to them and had taken to her from the very beginning when Daniel had brought her to their home for tea all those years before. They both loved her very much. She had never had anything worldly until she married Daniel, and then she had worked extremely hard for every penny they earned. Life had never been easy for Beth, no one knew her brother better than Martha did. He had been so fortunate to see her on the gate, all those years ago and she had made him a wonderful wife. Sadly, as soon as Daniel and Beth were wealthy and could enjoy more free time together with all the holidays and luxuries they now could afford, she had been taken away suddenly when she had so much to live for.

Daniel had never been on his own in his life. He had always had all the attention from his mother and sisters, and then when he bought the farm, Beth had seen to his every need, in every way possible. He had never done any household duties, made any food for himself, and literally could not boil himself an egg. He did not even have to find his clothes in the wardrobe or cupboards; Beth would lay them all out ready for him on the bed. He only had to dress himself. He had often called Beth from upstairs, so that she could turn off the kettle, or put his sugar into his tea. She had always been at his command. He had certainly continued in his marriage in the same way to which he had been accustomed all his childhood years.

Catherine and Anne decided there was no way he could manage alone, now that their mother had gone. They decided to advertise for some help in the local newspaper. As always, Daniel fell on his feet and a local domestic science teacher, living in the same village, applied for the post of housekeeper, without living in. She was able to remain in her own home across the village green, cooking, cleaning and washing for Daniel. What a superb cook she was, and very capable of running the home for him. Having two small children, it was easy for her to take them with her, and Daniel certainly had no objection to her bringing them along, letting them stay in the house, while she cooked, cleaned and washed for him. The arrangement worked perfectly. She came in every morning to prepare Daniel's meals and clear away afterwards. She left him plenty of food for the weekend when one of his daughters arrived to take over. The family were pleased that this arrangement was working so well and Daniel seemed very happy with it. Martha called to see him again one afternoon, about three weeks later, only to find him out. The next-door neighbour saw her and called out across the garden.

"Daniel went off early this morning as usual, but he should be back soon. I expect you know he has a new woman in his life?"

Martha was quite stunned by this remark.

"Oh no, my niece has arranged for a lady to come in and help him daily, since Beth died. He has never been on his own, you see, and as a farmer he has never been used to any domestic chores."

"Oh, this lady comes here about three times a week. He fetches her in the morning and they go off together in the car. They come back here about six, then he takes her back again to her home, in the evenings about ten o'clock. Very smart she is too. Haven't you noticed a woman's touch around the house again?"

Martha was shocked to hear this news. Beth had been only gone six weeks and when she had seen flowers in a vase and a woman's touch around the home when she called previously, she had assumed the paid helper did it from the village. She thought, at the time, how fortunate her brother had been to have such a thoughtful person around the home. She now wondered how the children would feel about this new development? It had never occurred to them that their father would find another woman and so soon, especially now he had someone to look after him. He did not have to do anything in the house, the helper was so efficient, seeing to his every need, but of course the helper did not share his bed.

Martha wondered what people's reaction be when they discovered her brother had found a replacement for dear Beth so soon. Martha was undoubtedly upset.

"What age would you say this lady is who comes three times a week?"

"Well, it's difficult to say, but I'd say just a few years younger than your brother. Very sociable lady she is. I have seen her arrive and she always smiles and waves to me when I see her, and she'll politely pass the time of day. I notice she has a very strong Welsh accent exactly the same as Beth had. I believe she must be from the same area. The trouble is we were so fond of Beth, you see. Such a kind and thoughtful neighbour. She is hardly cold in her grave when he has found someone else to replace her, nice as she is."

That was exactly what was in Martha's mind too, but Martha made no comment. She always kept her thoughts to herself.

She had to admit she was relieved to hear that he was not seeing some young bimbo, a young hussy who would obviously only be after his money, although he was still very handsome and distinguished-looking with his now greying hair. However Martha was anxious how this would affect his children's inheritance. Beth had worked so hard all her life, and so had the children for that matter. Surely it was just companionship Daniel was looking for and it was nothing serious at all. There was little need for any concern. Marriage wouldn't be an option.

Daniel returned soon afterwards alone, but with that well known wicked half smile on his face, a smile Martha recognised so well when he had something to hide. Martha knew then what the neighbour had told her was no doubt correct. He already had found another woman.

"I'm hoping to get married within the next six months," he told her.

"Oh, Daniel, that's a bit soon. Can't you wait a year for the sake of the children?"

"What children? Catherine and Anne have their own lives, and anyway we don't want to wait."

He told the girls the following weekend when they visited him, that they would soon be having a stepmother. Catherine did not appear to be as devastated as Anne. The latter did not want anyone in her mother's house, using her utensils and furnishings etc, especially so soon. They were still grieving and missing their mother so much. Also, Anne could not bear to think of anyone sharing her father's bed with him. That place was only for her mother and she had gone.

Within the year Daniel had remarried. He was quite right in saying that both his children now had families of their own, but they still found it difficult to come to terms with his marriage, when their mother had only been dead such a short time. Martha accepted everything fate dealt her and she tried hard to encourage Daniel's children to do the same. She endeavoured to take the place of their mother whenever they returned to the area and frequently rang them for a chat which their mother did so often when Daniel had been out.

One weekend, Anne had returned to visit her father and his new wife, and had recalled to Martha how they had all retired to bed.

"We were all in bed when I heard this regular tapping noise almost like a knocking sound but unsure of the source. I ventured out on to the landing and was about to call out, when I realised it was coming from my father and stepmother's bedroom. It was obviously the headboard of the bed, knocking the wall behind, with a rhythmic movement. A movement I then recognised only too well. They were having sex. How could he be? And with someone else so soon? And at their age too."

"You must be mistaken, Anne. Your father only wants a companion, because he misses your mother so much."

"Companion, my foot," retorted Anne with disgust.

But Martha was also somewhat surprised by her brother's behaviour, especially when they could be heard. Whatever was he thinking of? Well only of himself, as usual.

After that incident Martha made up food parcels for Beth's children, showering them with goodies whenever they came to visit. She made sure they never left her home empty-handed. They both adored their aunt, and she gave them all the love and comfort she could possibly offer them, not knowing what it was like to have children of her own. But these were as good as hers and she had to admit she felt very sorry for them. Beth's children appreciated what their dear Aunt Martha was trying to do for them in their grief, but the trouble was no one could take the place of their mother. Martha understood that only too well. It seemed almost like yesterday when she and Mary had vowed to look after each other forever when their own mother had died. They both had kept that promise to each other, despite the great sacrifices each of them must have made in order to do so.

Chapter 22

After Beth's death, Martha was now very much alone, but did not appear to be lonely. If she was then she would never have shown it or admitted it to anyone. She no longer had Beth to call on or talk to as she had done over the years. At least Martha had the satisfaction of knowing Beth had always been there if she ever needed her. She had seen very little of her brother over the latter years. Having the farm, he always seemed to be so busy. Now he had plenty of time with plenty of money so he was off enjoying himself with his wife who seemed to be the new love of his life. When she did see him, he tended to speak to her rather curtly. But because Martha loved him, she took no notice and always made excuses for him. Catharine and Anne had noticed this too

"I do wish Dad wouldn't speak to you so abruptly," Anne told her.

"Oh, he doesn't mean it. I know him of old. We all spoiled him you see, always giving him his own way."

Beth had been the go-between as far as the children and their father was concerned. If he was gruff, or short-tempered with them, she would try and console them, making different excuses for his behaviour and his actions, saying he loved them all very much but was unable to show what he felt. But then no one ever expected Martha or Beth to say anything derogatory about Daniel. They could not see any wrong in him. In fact both of them could always find some excuse or other for all other folk's poor behaviour. That was in their nature.

Martha was always grateful that Daniel had been blessed in his life to have herself and Mary when he lived at home and then followed not one but two very good wives. They all would do anything for him despite his often dictatorial and domineering disposition, especially in his adulthood. He had Martha's smile, but unlike her, even from a child he had often smiled when things went wrong. That was how he reacted if he was in trouble, which often happened when he was a child. His smile would often give him away, and this continued into maturity. His new wife, it transpired, was a cousin of Beth's, and a very thoughtful and caring lady called Esther who tried very hard to fit in with Daniel's family. He was indeed such a very fortunate man. For some, happiness in marriage only comes once in a lifetime, and for others, it never comes at all. For Daniel, he had found great happiness in his two marriages.

Martha decided it was best to continue setting her alarm to go off at 4.30 a.m. every morning, which as usual was seven days a week, rain or shine, just as when Evan was alive. She now really appreciated Prince whom she spoke to as if the dog was a human being. He followed her everywhere, running behind the van all day, up and down each street, until they returned to the dairy when her deliveries were completed. If she was out visiting, then he would wait patiently for her return, giving her such a welcome, jumping up, almost knocking her over with delight and excitement, and wagging his tail.

"If you wag that tail much more, it will drop off," she told him frequently. He was tremendous company for her, now she lived completely on her own. She treated herself to a brand new Renault van, which gave her enormous satisfaction, although it was not as easy to fill with her crates of milk. The open-sided one she had had for many years previously was more serviceable business-wise, but she could use this vehicle for pleasure too as her old car had been towed away for scrap. The van was mainly bought for the business, but because of the seat in the front, she could always offer to take a passenger with her whenever necessary. Her van could be seen around the village delivering the milk, visiting the sick, going to the services on Sunday, and collecting her hard-earned cash from her customers on Saturdays. Everyone also recognised Prince. Wherever Martha was, the dog was too, waiting for her outside shops and houses she visited. Once again she continued with her life, delivering over six hundred pints of milk, and climbing nearly one thousand steps daily. When her brother retired, she decided she would take over some of his milk rounds, having nothing to rush home for. Now, however, she became her customers' friend, agony aunt and confidante. Delivering the milk took her all day by the time she had listened to the gossip, their troubles, and good or bad news from all those whom she saw during her daily visits. Some would, of course, leave a note with the amount of bottles they required, and it was just as well they did so, saving her even more time listening to them when they talked to her.

Once she returned home, she would then commence the housework, never having any assistance. She maintained there was only herself to make it untidy and she now had only her own washing to do. She would play the piano during the evenings and attend some of the chapel activities during the week. She began knitting again, which she had not done since

Anne and Catharine lived with them during the war. She made lots of tea cosies, mittens, and hot-water bottle covers She loved crocheting too, and made various sizes and colours of doilies and collars for dresses. Although she was seventy-three, she joined a local class to try her hand at basketwork, making many items consisting of some branch of basketwork. She made trays, potholders, baskets varying in sizes, and the like. All her handiwork went for Christmas gifts for family, friends and customers. Some told her in jest, after receiving a number of her home-made gifts, she reminded them of the aunt in Dylan Thomas's book called "A child's Christmas in Wales". This aunt always made useful presents, including "engulfing mufflers of the old coach days, mittens made for giant sloths, and blinding tam-o-shanters like tea cosies". Martha was indeed like her when it came to "wearing wool next to the skin, and a rasping vest that made one wonder how she had any skin left at all". Both sisters were often "moustached" and periodically Martha would smell strongly of hair remover.

During the last years of Mary's life, Martha would say to her when all was quiet and nearly ready for bed. "Come on, Mary, we can't look like Father Christmas with white moustaches and beards." Then, with a chuckle, she would commence the hair-removing process. This became a ritual every six weeks or so, when the hair grew on their chins and above the top lips which became noticeable. Martha did not try her hand at crochet nosebags, which the aunt in the book had done, but over the Christmas period, she would enjoy a glass of sherry, home-made parsnip wine or port as she went from house to house. She could often be heard singing "Cherry ripe" to herself on her deliveries, but certainly could not be compared with the aunt of Dylan Thomas, who sang like a big-bosomed thrush. Martha's bosom had now completely shrunk. Daniel of course was never amused when he heard about her singing and the comparison with the aunt in the book by Dylan Thomas, even though he was now famous and had lived only a few miles from their family.

"That's no compliment, Martha. How dare you sing in the street after drinking alcohol. You aren't fit to go to chapel if you do that." But she took no notice; neither did she take any offence by it. Everyone said it was always a pleasure to meet her, no matter where or what time of day, Martha was always the same. Her broad smile lighting up her face and the sound of her usual chuckle. She gave everybody the impression she was always so very happy.

"I've been fortunate enough to have had everything in life that I could wish for," she would tell everyone, when in fact many felt she had absolutely nothing, nothing at all, and never had done. Perhaps it was for this reason many of her customers gave her their cast-off clothing, shoes and hats. She had enough of them to wear a different outfit every Sunday to chapel for six months. She would squeeze her feet into shoes that did not fit, and Daniel would be mortified some Sunday evenings when he and his wife, sitting in their seats in the front row of the chapel dressed in new expensive clothes, would have to witness Martha's arrival dressed in something that was either tight-fitting and far too small or an outfit that was like a tent on her, far too large and also well worn. She was usually last to arrive and instead of slipping in quietly and unobtrusively to her seat, she would smile and look around at everyone as if on the stage. She sometimes gave a small curtsy to those she recognised, even "whispering" aloud across rows of members' seats, enquiring about the welfare of their family. Afterwards Daniel would berate her.

"Martha, you are an embarrassment to the family."

But Martha took no notice, never letting anything bother her and continued to do exactly the same the following Sunday. Daniel eventually gave up.

When Martha had worked for over sixty years after her father had first bought her a can to go down the road, serving a few houses with their milk, the customers contacted the local newspaper and radio station. She was then seventy-three and still had no intention of retiring. What a wonderful time she had, being in the limelight. A reporter came from the BBC to interview her, recording it all on a tape, but once he began to ask her about her life, he had great difficulty in stopping her. She told him what a wonderful life she had been blessed with, telling him of the good and happy times, but never of the sad ones. She did not mention Rhys, nor anything of her sister's breakdown, which had at the time caused her great pain. That was typical of Martha. Sad things she kept to herself.

"Whatever have I done to deserve such special attention?" she asked the reporter modestly.

"Well, many people feel you are very special and want the fact recognised."

In the Herald of Wales newspaper that week, there was a full-page spread of Martha with her van loading up her crates before the morning delivery. There were many comments printed in the paper from her grateful customers writing on behalf of them all.

"She is a truly wonderful person. She carries all the problems and worries of people who wish to unburden them upon her. She always has a happy face to go with her pleasing nature."

Martha read it all with pride.

She could not listen to the recording on the radio, as it was on "Good morning, Wales". At that time she was already on

249

the road delivering, but many people recorded it for her. So many, in fact, that she had dozens of recordings which she distributed proudly to all her friends and family. She would always remember that week with great delight. It was, she said, the highlight of her life. Little did she know then what the future still held for her.

Chapter 23

After Martha celebrated her seventy-fifth birthday, she felt that she was taking so much longer to accomplish the tasks before her. She wondered whether she should now think of retiring. She hated that word "retire" but perhaps the time had now come for her to seriously consider this prospect.

It was by sheer coincidence that the company from whom she had bought her ready-bottled milk asked her if she would be interested in selling her business to them. They were keen to expand and wanted to purchase milk rounds in a reasonably affluent area. Suddenly she did not have to give the decision any agonising thought. They had made her mind up for her and it was an offer she was not going to refuse.

The director of the company and his manager called on her by appointment the following week. Martha felt very important indeed having these two well-dressed men in navy pinstriped suits, with their smart shirts, calling on her at a previously arranged time. They discussed the necessary financial agreement followed by a request to see all her milk books, scrutinising the customers' payments and bad debts. There were of course some who never paid her at all, leaving the area still owing her money. However, in the main, she had very reliable customers who paid their bills regularly. Mary was the one who had always balanced the books, but when her health failed this task became the responsibility of Martha. She was so busy delivering, she devoted less time to sorting out the bad debts. The trouble was that Martha always trusted everyone, believing that keeping to your word was of paramount importance. She always was heard to say, "Your word is your bond."

When the contract was signed with the company and there was no going back, Martha thoroughly enjoyed telling everyone her good news. Needless to say her customers did not welcome it as being good news. They all wanted her to continue, at least until perhaps her health failed. They could see no reason for her to give up something she could still do efficiently and still enjoyed. But she had certainly come to realise that she was getting much slower.

"It would be too late if I became ill," she told them. "Now it will be all organised and you will be well looked after by this new company," trying to persuade them into accepting her decision with a little more enthusiasm and to be pleased for her.

When the day came for her final delivery, as the bottles of milk in her van decreased so the bouquets of flowers increased. Soon the vehicle was full of colourful floral tributes and parting gifts. She was quite overwhelmed. She only wished that dear old Evan and Mary or Beth were still alive to share this happiness with her, witnessing all this generosity shown to her. Almost every customer tried to make sure they were at home to bid her farewell on that last time they would see her at their door. Indeed, many were in tears. She spent the whole day on the road, from dawn until dusk.

"Now, now, Mrs Jones," she would say, or to "Mrs Evans" or "Mrs Whoever" trying to comfort them, "I have not died. Well not yet, and from now on you can come to my door, instead of me coming to yours. I'll have all day to myself and plenty of time to see everyone. Also you will still see my van around the village visiting the sick and doing my shopping. Prince will be with me everywhere I go, so you will see him and know that I am somewhere around. I will be free now to go to chapel on Sundays to the morning service as well as the evening one. I cannot believe all the things I will be able to do from now on."

When she arrived back at Aelybryn she had so many flowers she was short of vases in which to place them, so flowers were put into jugs off the old dresser and some had to go in milk bottles. Each room had flowers in them. Her bedroom and even Evan's old room had a few jugs, filled with beautiful blooms. She therefore decided she would take some to the mental hospital where Mary had been taken all those years before. She drove up the winding road and parked in the same place she had done when she had driven there that last final visit, bringing her beloved sister home at last.

The staff were delighted with the flowers. "What a lovely thought, but unfortunately we do not remember your sister here. It was before our time," they confessed.

"Well, after all, it was a long time ago," Martha told them.

"Yes, I'm afraid staff soon change and move on." But to Martha it was like yesterday.

That night she was far too excited for supper, and when she eventually got into bed and put out the light, she could not sleep. So many thoughts were going through her mind. She heard Rhys saying to her, "But, Martha, so you should have all this acclaim and adoration. You deserved it." But it was never good to dwell on things that were past and not to be. She decided that now would be a good time to give more effort to her craftwork, and she would begin by going into the town the following day and purchasing some wool to make

Daniel a pullover for his birthday. With that thought in her mind, wondering what design he would prefer and what would be a suitable colour for him, she fell soundly to sleep.

It was strange when she awoke the next morning just before five, and realised there was no reason to get up that early any more, so she turned over and went back to sleep. She could not believe that when she did awake the second time and looked at the clock, it was nearly nine. The sun was already up, and beckoning her to start moving to see what the day would bring. Also poor Prince was still waiting to be let out for his early constitution. However when she went downstairs, Prince was not as eager as usual to go outside. She should have realised then that something was wrong, but she was deep in thought about her own future. That first morning, she needed to make herself some sort of new routine, but soon the doorbell rang. Family and friends continued to call all day, and the house seemed to be full with well-wishers. In fact it seemed to continue all the week. Chapelgoers joined in with the celebration of her final retirement. Cards arrived each day by post, and she enjoyed putting them all around the house with delight. She read the verses over and over, and moved them all around from room to room. She played the piano far more now she had more time, and she found that the days were so full of enjoyment and visiting. She hardly had time for cleaning and housework, but she liked her home to be neat and tidy. But Prince's health was deteriorating. He chose to remain at home instead of following her everywhere, and within a couple of weeks he stopped eating his food which he had always enjoyed. She tried to coax him with all sorts of treats but it was no use. Tomorrow she would have to ring Daniel and ask him who the best vet was to take him to be looked at and find out what was wrong with her dear old Prince. She hoped it was nothing serious, and perhaps some tablets would soon put him right. Hopefully he would soon be bounding around as usual and wagging his tail.

The following morning she awoke early and crept downstairs. Prince was still fast asleep in front of the hearth on his rug. But she realised when she opened the door to let him out, Prince did not stir. She went over to him and could see he must have died during the night. She immediately rang Daniel. Esther answered.

"Prince died in the night, Esther. Do you think Daniel could come over as soon as possible to bury him in the back garden."

"Oh, I am sorry, Martha. You really will miss him, won't you? I'll tell Daniel to come straightaway."

He arrived within an hour or so. When he went into the living room, he saw Martha bending over the dog and for the first time he could see tears in her eyes.

"It's only a dog, Martha, for goodness sake."

"Yes, I know. I am being very silly, but he was all I had."

With that, she wiped the tear away with the back of her hand and stood up.

"I'll put the kettle on for a cup of tea, ready for when you have finished digging the hole and buried him," she said bravely.

Daniel picked up the dog as if it was a sack of potatoes and carried him up to the back garden. When he returned, he sat down with his cup of tea exclaiming, "Well, that's another job done. Anything else you want doing now I'm here?"

"No, that's fine. It was just you would dig a hole quicker than me and Prince was too heavy to lift by myself."

"In that case, I'll be off. I want to call in the chemist for some laxatives." With that he slammed the back door and was gone.

But Martha had lost her last companion and would miss his company so much. Daniel had always dealt with farm animals all his life, together with the death of them. He was not used to them as pets so he could not possibly understand what she was feeling deep down inside. Her mind went back to when Anne had lost her pet Seren and how she had cried when the pony had died after giving birth. Now, after all these years, she realised how Anne had felt. An empty sickly feeling inside your stomach, but fortunately Anne had been lucky enough to have something left to help her over the loss. She had been left a foal which she was allowed to keep and that had certainly alleviated her feeling of loss.

About one month after she lost the dog, one of her customers, a Mr Watson, called on her. He often did odd jobs around the house which she now failed to do. He wondered if there were any repairs to be done or handles to be replaced anywhere. Her electric fire, which she bought long before Prince died, had fused the previous week so she asked him if he could have a look at it. She found the electric fire very useful in the evenings when it was cooler having given up lighting coal fires. While checking the electrical wires, he mentioned that his wife had not bought a gift for her on her retirement.

"But, Mr Watson, you are always doing things for me and I certainly don't want your wife to buy me anything. I have everything here I need, far too much in fact, but it was good of you to think about me."

"Well actually, we thought as you had so many gifts, it would be a better idea to take you out for supper the week after next."

Martha thought this was a very kind gesture and although she was not very keen to go it was something she had never done before, having a meal out. Anyway, it would be not only ungrateful, but also rude to refuse the kind offer made to her.

"Oh, are you sure, Mr Watson? It sounds great, but where will we go?"

"Ah, now my wife and I will find somewhere. We'll give you a bit of a surprise where we'll be taking you."

"Well, please don't book anywhere expensive, as my stomach has not been too good lately, probably not eating meals regularly when I was on my milk rounds. Somewhere simple will be fine."

He wondered whether it was to do with losing the dog that had taken her appetite away. He knew how much the animal had meant to her, but Martha never showed or said what she felt. That was the one thing everyone had learned about her over the years, but now she seemed quite excited about the supper out with the Watsons. They were such a lovely couple and good company too. She had more than a week to decide what to wear, so spoke to Daniel's wife Esther about it and told her what had been planned for her.

This would certainly take her mind off the dog, Esther thought to herself, not daring to mention Prince to Daniel. He didn't seem to understand.

"A pity they didn't tell you where they were taking you, but if I were you I'd go to the shops and buy yourself a new dress," Esther suggested tactfully. "You know how Daniel berates you if he feels you do not look dressed properly for the occasion, even if he can't see you."

"Oh no, there's really no need at all to buy anything new. I have plenty of clothes," Martha quickly explained. "I have already told them to find somewhere not too posh, as I can't eat very much. It would be a waste of money for them. I'll enjoy their treat and their company without going to the expense of buying a new outfit. My wardrobes are full, even if they aren't my own and none of my customers who have given them all to me will see me in them."

Martha had never been taken out for a meal in her life and was now quite excited at the prospect. Saturday could not come quickly enough. She was to be picked up at 6.30 p.m. by the Watsons in their new car so she made sure she was dressed all ready in plenty of time, so as not to keep them waiting. She decided to wear an outfit one of her customers had given her for Anne's wedding and had not worn it since. Fashions came and went and no doubt the outfit, although now probably old-fashioned, would soon be back in fashion again. If it weren't, then she would start a new trend with it.

The doorbell rang at 6.30 p.m. prompt and Mr Watson escorted her into the awaiting car where Mrs Watson sat in the back.

"In the front you go, Martha, you must have the privilege of sitting in the front with the driver." Martha turned around to look at Mrs Watson who she felt was somewhat overdressed for the occasion, but as usual she kept her thoughts to herself. She wore a flimsy dress trimmed with silver sequins and black strap shoes.

"Well," Martha said to herself, "I would never have any use for those sort of clothes again. I'm far more comfortable in this old-fashioned suit." It was the one Mrs Winterbottom had given it to her when she had failed to stretch it to fit herself following the birth of her last baby. She thought it would be ideal for Anne's wedding. Martha now had lost some weight since then, not eating so much, and it was on the big side, but that was always a good fault, she thought.

When they had travelled out of the town and had been in the car for almost half an hour, Martha looked concerned.

"Where are we going? It's quite a way to this place. I haven't been out here before, where are we?"

"Well no, this is why we thought it would be a treat for you, but we are nearly there now," Mr Watson replied smiling.

They pulled into a large depot, where there were all lorries, bottles and empty crates, behind which was a large white building.

"This looks like the company who bought my milk rounds. Do they own a café as well?" Martha asked seeing a large green and orange poster denoting the company's name in large letters. Soon a sign indicated the way to the offices and to the "canteen". She had suggested somewhere ordinary, but did not imagine that a works canteen was quite the place for the treat. Never mind, she was very grateful to them for taking her out, no matter if it was the work's canteen. She wondered what kind of food they would produce at this time of the day, as surely the offices were now closed and the employees would have all gone home, even the cooks.

"Well, it is a sort of café. You'll see it soon," Mr Watson replied hesitantly, feeling somewhat embarrassed by the question.

Martha got out of the car as instructed when they parked in a large car park packed with other cars. A man appeared at the front door and held it open for the three of them to enter. It seemed so quiet with no one else around. Martha thought to herself what a strange place to come, with no one about. They walked through a corridor, reaching another door, whereby the same man opened it and said, "Step inside here, madam" but when Martha stepped inside, the room was in darkness, and she could not see where she was going. It was so quiet you could hear a pin drop.

"Just a moment. Someone has switched all the lights off. I'll have to put them on," he told Martha who was quite relieved. At last he switched on the lights. She could not believe what she saw in front of her. There was a huge room, filled with people and bright lights. The first person whom she recognised was Daniel. He was standing right in the front with Esther who wore a big smile on her face. Then she saw all her nieces and their families, her nephew and so many of her customers, she could not count them. It looked as if they must all be present. She was speechless. There were surely three hundred or more people there all singing "For she's a jolly good fellow, and so say all of us" ending up all clapping until their hands were hurting.

What a memorable night it was. The Watsons had obtained a list of as many of her customers as possible and invited them with all Martha's family to attend a farewell supper all prepared and paid for by the company who had bought her business. There had been a collection too which enabled Mr Watson to purchase a Parker Knoll chair. She could relax in this at home, in front of the fire, now she was retired. It was presented to her together with a bouquet of flowers so big she could hardly be seen behind them. It may have been just as well for behind the flowers a few tears may have been detected, tears of happiness. There were speeches by lots of her customers paying tribute to her wonderful achievement of delivering all those bottles of milk to them, day in day out, in all weathers. How she always found the time to listen to all their troubles and worries giving advice and what she thought was the best answer to their problems. She had always greeted them with a happy face every day, despite the fact they knew she must have felt very sad at times.

The local newspaper was there again to report the event and take pictures, all of which appeared in the daily paper a day or two later. Daniel however had not been too happy at her choice of dress for that special evening. She could tell that by the look on his face as she arrived, when his beady eye glanced at her from head to toe. But Martha had taken no notice, and had smiled at everyone in front of her. She knew exactly what he was thinking but he said nothing. She worried not what people thought. She had had the most wonderful night of her life, and no one could take that away from her whatever clothes she wore. Not even Daniel. He did not mention the fact to her afterwards; no doubt his good and thoughtful wife Esther had seen to that, but she knew that look of disapproval only too well. She gave a chuckle to herself and smiled again with amusement. She climbed contentedly into bed, thanking God for yet another night she was allowed to live to enjoy and cherish. But sleep did not come easily. She was mentally exhausted.

Chapter 24

They say time flies when you are enjoying yourself and Martha's was no exception. Life still continued to offer her so much. She had often thought perhaps she should have made some enquiries at the dogs' home about obtaining another dog. Losing Prince was not easy and, she had to admit, the dog had been such good company around the house. It was lovely to have him greet her on her return from being out. She missed the welcome he always gave her.

Daniel had once suggested she should have one of the pups from his farming friend, but after Prince she could not face the work of training such a young dog when she was out and about so much. She certainly still had the patience, but Prince had not been a pup. He had certainly been a good housedog barking when anyone strange came to the door, but now only people she knew called, unlike when she had the business. She decided there and then it was not worth all the fuss and bother of having another animal, despite the fact they made good companions and were good company. She often wondered afterwards what had made her think about a dog again on that night in particular. It was when she was undressing in front of the electric fire, and climbing into bed, the dog had come into her mind. Putting off the light without doing any reading, she fell asleep. It was a habit of hers that she always put her slightly deaf ear on to the pillow, so that her good ear would hear the telephone if it rang. But for some reason, that night, she had omitted to do so. She awoke from a dream and realised when turning over, that her good ear was on the pillow and could hear nothing, so she immediately turned her head so that her deaf ear was now on it instead. As she did so, she thought she saw a light being shone across the landing, as if the headlights of a car were shining through the window. Or was it the light from a torch that was being used to see the way up the stairs? She jumped out of bed and peeped through the crack in her bedroom door. She was right. A thickset, large man dressed all in black with a balaclava covering his head, was disappearing into Evan's room flashing the torch to see his way. She decided the best thing to do was to get back into bed quickly, pull the blankets over her head, and pretend she was fast asleep. She just hoped that she would not begin to shake with fright and cause this intruder to discover she was awake, with any possibility she could describe his appearance to the police. Then she thought she could hear his footsteps outside Rhys's room. He was obviously trying the door to see if he could open it. Of course it was locked, so she heard him coming closer and closer to her room. She squeezed her eyes tightly closed and tried to pretend she was as good as dead. She sensed he was now near the bed. She tried hard not to swallow. Then she felt light from the torch shining on her face, but she still did not move. She remembered she had hidden about £100 in a bag of sugar downstairs in the cupboard, and another £100 at the bottom of the biscuit barrel. Perhaps she should tell him immediately where the money was, so that he would leave her unharmed? He could take it immediately without looking any further. But once he discovered she was awake, he could still harm her and still take the money. She had to think quickly. She decided to do as she first thought, remain perfectly still and calm. The torch was then directed towards the chest of drawers on the other side of the room, so she opened one of her eyes just enough to have a quick peep. She saw him quietly open each drawer, pulling out everything on to the floor. When he did not find what he was looking for, he shone the torch again back on her face. Obviously he decided she was still fast asleep, allowing him continue his search. He then opened the wardrobe door and looked inside. There was nothing in there, only old clothes of Mary's, which she had intended to dispose of but never got around to doing after she had died. Fumbling around in the wardrobe for a moment, he found the old shoebox. He removed it quietly, and emptied the contents on to the floor. It contained handkerchiefs of Mary's, given to her by her customers years before together with some newspaper cuttings she had collected. Suddenly she could see in her mind the picture of the battered old lady in a recent newspaper. The poor thing had been mugged for a very nominal amount and required hospitalisation with stitches across her face. It was then she could almost feel the weight of a blunt instrument striking her on her head. She could barely breathe. Was she really living this? Or was she having a dream again? She kept very still, for what seemed like an eternity. She did not move an eyelid. Then the intruder thankfully decided to go out of her room without harming her in any way. She heard his footsteps going down the stairs, and saw his torchlight slowly disappearing out of sight into the darkness. He slammed the front door behind him as he left. She remained there for some moments saying a quick prayer to herself, thanking God for her safety, before going immediately downstairs to the telephone. She felt her way along the landing, not wanting to put on a light, for fear of the burglar returning if he thought she was now awake. When she reached the telephone she picked up the receiver, but there was no dialling tone. It was completely dead. The wires had been severed.

Still in her nightdress, with a hairnet over her head, she ran out into the street. As she did so, luckily the headlights of a car shone brightly towards her, coming down the hill. There seemed no sign of the burglar. She waved her hands frantically and stepped out on to the road in front of the oncoming car. It was a police car. God was still looking after her, she thought. The occupants immediately spotted her as she stepped into the road. The car stopped abruptly and a policeman got out.

"I've been burgled, officer," Martha blurted out.

"What have they taken?"

"Nothing at all, officer."

But the policemen obviously did not believe she had been burgled because they immediately encouraged her to get into their car.

"We'll look after you, dearie," said one.

"Don't worry, lady, we'll soon have you back where you belong," said the other encouragingly, while the driver promptly turned the car around quickly and started off up the hill.

"Where are you taking me?" she demanded "I live back there. I'm not dressed for the police station. I just want to phone my brother, but my phone has been cut."

But they took no notice and continued to calm her, driving towards the hospital at the top of the hill. She knew this road very well. She recognised the entrance from years before but she failed to convince them that she did not belong there. She heard the policemen whisper to the driver.

"Same thing happened last year, one tried to go home in

the middle of the night, and she was found wondering in the park."

Martha was mortified. They parked the car right outside the main door as if expecting trouble and gently pulled her out.

"Come on, lady, we'll have you sorted out in no time at all," and still smiling, he headed for the main entrance to the mental hospital building.

There was nothing for it but to comply with their demands. They escorted her in through the main doors one either side of her, holding her arms. Obviously the sister in charge did not recognise her, but asked her name. She obtained a list of the patients and her name seemed to be omitted. After some consultation again with the doctor on duty and more questions, eventually they realised they had made a dreadful mistake. This old woman really had been telling the truth, but strange they had not seen anyone running away from the scene. There was nobody on the road at all at that time of the morning. They had immediately thought she had escaped from the mental hospital.

Obviously they were full of apologies, and felt very guilty indeed. When they returned to Aelybryn they immediately saw a forced entry through the kitchen window, there was glass everywhere. They were surprised she had not heard the noise of the glass smashing. Then she explained that her hearing in one ear was impaired, and the business about her head on the pillow. She noticed they smiled at each other, while telling her to get herself dressed before they telephoned her brother. They would take her there for the rest of the night because she could not be left alone in the house.

"Oh there's no need now, officer, I can sleep here by myself. That old burglar won't be back again for sure; there was nothing here for him although he looked everywhere."

They insisted she had company for the night as they were convinced she would suffer from shock later. Besides, the window could not be secured until the morning. They could hardly believe how lucky she had been to be left unharmed. Many others had not been so fortunate in that very same position. They wondered how on earth had she been so brave too? Even now after two ordeals in one night, she seemed to be prepared to go back to her own bed, all alone and almost immediately. But they didn't know Martha. They were heard to say, "She's a tough old bird."

In actual fact, they convinced her it would be far more sensible to stay at her brother's home for a few nights, and immediately they drove her to the coast. Daniel insisted she remain with them for at least three nights until the broken window was replaced and the front door secured. While Daniel was organising the work, he looked through the rooms to check for any other damage but found none, except that he failed to get into Rhys's room. For some reason he could not open the door. It seemed jammed.

"I can't open one of the bedroom doors upstairs, Martha. It's as if the door is locked," he told her when he returned from his visit to Aelybryn.

"Oh, there's no need to go in that bedroom, there's hardly anything in it now. Anyway I checked it over before leaving while the police were still with me. The door is swollen with the damp. The police had difficulty too."

After that incident, she made sure that she always put her deaf ear onto the pillow. She had no more unwelcome guests call at Aelybryn day or night for the remainder of her life. In fact, she never gave her unpleasant experience or the burglar another thought.

Chapter 25

In February 1981 there was great excitement throughout the country. The Prince of Wales proposed to Lady Diana Spencer. Martha watched with great interest as she remembered so well what had happened to the previous Prince of Wales years before, when he had given up the throne to marry Wallis Simpson. But this relationship looked perfect in every way. Diana was beautiful, a virgin, and her physical fitness to become the mother of heirs to the throne was commented on greatly at the time. The whole country was ecstatic about its future, and Lady Diana Spencer was sure to make an excellent queen when the time came. Martha watched the television with great interest and enjoyed seeing all the coverage in the newspapers. The wedding was to take place on July 29th, and everywhere Martha went and the people she met seemed to think of nothing else but the wedding. She was invited to spend this eventful day with Mr and Mrs Watson who had organised her retirement party. They were inviting friends and neighbours to witness the whole event on a large screen, and had gone to great lengths to organise food for everyone. Martha had a wonderful day. The royal couple looked so happy together.

"Have you ever been to London?" one of the group asked Martha while they had tea.

"Good heavens, no," Martha replied. "Much too far for me."

The newspapers were continually featuring photographs of the Prince and Princess of Wales, and again there was great excitement when their son and heir was born in June 1982. Martha had always loved children and often thought how lucky she and Mary had been to have her brother's children on loan for almost two years during those awful years of wartime. What happiness they had brought them. Daniel of course had never had his heir, but his two girls had been a credit to him, staying very close to their family and had never given him or Beth any worries.

The farthest Martha had ever been in her life was Porthcawl, when she had owned a car. She had taken Mary and Daniel's two children there to watch a firework display after the war was over. This year she would be 80. It was a bit too late for her to be thinking of travelling any farther than the village now. Besides, she had been very happy doing all the things she had done, in and around the principality. But that did not mean to say she would not like to have seen the Palace. She had seen it so many times on the television. But to actually see it in reality would have entailed travelling to London, and London to her was like another country. She knew her niece now lived there, and when she came back to the area and called on Martha, she talked so much about the Royals, the Palace, Westminster Abbey, the Houses of Parliament and all other places and buildings of interest in London. Talking about them seemed to bring them that much closer. But Martha never looked back. It was too late now.

On one of her frequent visits to her aunt, Catherine had asked her "Where would you like to go for your eightieth birthday, Aunt Martha?" meaning a trip out to the coast and possibly having tea there with the rest of the family. Or perhaps she would prefer to go down memory lane, and revisit Porthcawl?

"Buckingham Palace!" she replied with a wicked twinkle in her eye, and her usual chuckle.

"Are you serious, Aunt Martha?" her niece asked her, shocked at this reply.

"No, of course not. I would have liked to have seen it but it is too late. I'm too old for all that travelling."

"But we could arrange it for you; leave it to me."

"Impossible, love, much too far for me to travel now. It was wishful thinking. I was only teasing you, really I was."

However the seed had been sown, and arrangements were immediately put into action for a trip to London. Martha was to know nothing of it until nearer the time. It was to be a big surprise for her eightieth birthday.

During the weeks that followed, Martha again experienced discomfort in her stomach not wanting to eat. Once again she put it down to the fact that she had never had regular meals all the years she was delivering the milk. Now her poor stomach was being bombarded with all sorts of rich foods, kindly made for her by friends and family inviting her to meals, saving her from cooking and eating alone. Her stomach probably was trying to tell her to take it easy and eat less. But as the weeks went by, she began to have more feelings of nausea, followed by bouts of sickness. Everyone noticed that she had lost quite a considerable amount of weight.

"You must go and see your doctor, Martha," Esther told her kindly.

Eventually she was persuaded to do so. He immediately organised tests to be run in the hospital in order to find out the cause. Martha felt she was wasting their valuable time on her instead of giving the attention to really sick people. She knew what was wrong with her stomach, so why the fuss?

The family were devastated to learn that she had cancer of the intestine and would have to be taken into hospital urgently to remove a tumour. Martha was told that it was quite a simple procedure, omitting to tell her the true diagnosis.

The week before her eightieth birthday, Martha went into hospital and the surgeon removed a large part of her intestine.

"Well," said Martha to the nurses cheerfully, "I was hoping to see Buckingham Palace for my eightieth birthday, but it looks as if the Queen will just have to wait a bit longer now before I visit her."

The nurses thoroughly enjoyed having her in their ward. She was always so cheerful and grateful for everything they did for her. When they had to place a tube down her throat, apologising for the discomfort it may cause her, she chuckled, "I'm more sorry for the poor tube, being bent and twisted to get down my old throat."

She would make the other patients laugh with some of her experiences delivering her milk bottles, and when her eightieth birthday arrived, while she was still in hospital, she had the most wonderful day. The family provided a huge cake with candles, all of which Martha blew out with gusto and all the nurses had a slice of cake, the remainder of which was shared with all the other patients in the ward. She had so many cards sent to her and so many flowers she told everyone, "It's just like my retirement all over again."

The nurses had to string all the cards around the ward, on all the window ledges, and jokingly teased her, "Christmas has come early this year to the hospital, Martha."

When the surgeon came to visit her on his rounds, he gave her his observations. "The operation has been very success-ful, Martha, and soon you will be able to return home.

However, I couldn't help but notice the bad state of your feet. I thought that while you are in here you might be happy for me to remove some of your toes. That will make walking a great deal easier for you. They have obviously been squashed into shoes that were too small for you over a long period of time, causing corns and blisters which have turned septic. The only solution is amputation in order to give you more comfort. I really do not understand how you could possibly walk with feet like that. They must be very painful."

Martha looked him straight in the eye.

"You have already taken some of my intestines and now you want my toes. No thank you very much. I've only got ten, and I'd like to keep all of them if you don't mind. You've taken enough of me."

The surgeon laughed, and thought to himself, I really have a character here.

"Then before you leave, Martha, promise me you will agree to be fitted with shoes made to measure. You can no longer wear shoes readymade from shoe shops. We will measure your feet here in the hospital, and they will be ready for you by the time you leave."

Seeing the look on her face, and thinking she was short of money, he added, "You will not have to pay for them, don't worry."

He had also noticed her old toilet bag on the bedside cabinet, as well as her well-worn nightdress, when she had been admitted. Now, both had been exchanged for brand new ones, after her birthday. Little did he know that Martha could have had the best of everything had she not given so much of her hard-earned money away to others.

When she eventually left the hospital, she was told she had made an excellent recovery and hopefully would be free of her stomach problems. They also gave her two pairs of "made-to-measure" soft leather shoes free of charge, because the National Health Service paid for them. She was absolutely thrilled. She simply loved to receive anything that was free. She looked like Minnie Mouse in them, as they were built up very high, in order to prevent their touching her crippled toes and rubbing on the leather, which before had obviously caused the blisters and corns.

"Thank you very much for my stay, I've really enjoyed it," she told the nurses, before leaving. They were quite sad when she was discharged, although delighted to know that the prognosis for her recovery was so good.

"Just think how lucky I am," she boasted when she left.

"I'm taking home less in my stomach, but more on my feet."

The whole ward was sorry to say goodbye to such a remarkable old woman.

Martha's recovery was exceptional. Because she wanted to go straight from hospital to her own home, she was kept in the ward longer than was normal. She had made up her mind she never wanted to be a burden on any of the family, despite the fact they had all almost quarrelled with each other, deciding who was to have the honour of attending to Aunt Martha's convalescence when she returned from hospital. They all wanted at least to feel they had tried to repay her for some of the never-ending generosity and love she had always given to them. But not one of them was able to do so. She returned to her own home alone but happy.

Soon Martha was to be seen around the village once again in her old van, shopping, visiting and doing all the things she had enjoyed before her operation.

On September 15th 1984 the Princess of Wales gave birth to another son, Prince Harry. Martha watched the television coverage with great interest as usual. London seemed to be in the news continuously, and little did she know then that during the following week she would be told that she would be going there herself. All the children had returned to school by then and transport would be less congested. Martha was taken by train, from the local station, on the 10.30 a.m. to Paddington by Anne, Daniel's younger daughter.

"Now it is our turn to be taking you for a special trip," she told her, remembering the happy times they had spent while living with their two aunts, going to Porthcawl years before. How excited she and Catherine, her sister, had been when she took them off somewhere in the car, after school was over giving them a surprise. She could almost feel Martha's stomach turning over with excitement. So often she and her sister had experienced that same feeling when they were children living with them.

Catherine met them at Paddington Station where a taxi was waiting to take them around the sights of London. She saw Westminster Abbey, where all the royal marriages and funerals took place and which she had seen so many times previously on television. Now this was the real thing, and she could hardly believe it. She saw and fed the pigeons at Trafalgar Square, saw Piccalilli Circus, (as she called it), and the Houses of Parliament. Snapshots were taken of her outside each place, to commemorate her long-awaited visit. She was mesmerised by the amount of traffic in London.

"Why don't they all bump into each other, going so fast and so many of them going in different directions?" she enquired.

She had to admit that the noise of taxis sounding their horns, cars retaliating, and buses pulling out in front of them quite frightened her. It took her back to the day she had fetched Mary out of the mental hospital after she had spent two years there, never having been outside its walls. How frightened she had looked that first time on the road when traffic passing by must have seemed to her so busy, noisy and frightening. Now she understood exactly how she must have felt when one is not accustomed to this volume of traffic. It was indeed quite alarming.

Knowing that the trip would be tiring for Martha, the children had decided it would be sensible for her to stay the night with Catherine and her husband in London. She was thrilled to see their much talked about home, especially the bedroom. Martha felt it was far too luxurious for her, with beautifully decorated lemon and blue wallpaper and matching bedlinen. A far cry from her Aelybryn, which is now badly in need of decorating and repairs.

On returning later to ensure that she was comfortably asleep, they found her sitting in the chair alongside the bed.

"I am far too excited to go to sleep yet. You both leave me and go to sleep yourselves; I'll be fine. I always see myself to bed, remember." So off they went to bed as she requested.

The following morning they took her breakfast, thinking to give her a treat, but when they opened the door, she was still sitting in the same chair. Her eyes were wide open.

"I knew I wouldn't sleep, even if I climbed into bed. Anyway it would be a shame to use these lovely sheets," she announced. "Besides, I wanted to stay awake to go over in my mind all the places I had seen today. It seemed such a waste to go to sleep and not think about them, so I stayed here all night." Obviously she had been to sleep at some point, although they knew she needed very little of it, not ever being used to sleeping for more than a few hours all her life.

After breakfast, Catherine's husband drove them in his car to see Buckingham Palace while being fortunate enough to also witness the changing of the guards. They also took her inside St Paul's Cathedral. She visited Madame Tussauds, which she found unbelievably exciting, seeing famous and not so famous people.

"They must be real people," she had insisted wanting to have snapshots taken with all the famous men and women she had seen on the television and had so admired.

Soon the time came to return to Paddington and catch the train back home. What a trip she had had, and the memories of it remained with her for the rest of her life. Often she would sit in front of her electric fire at night and relive everywhere she had been. Then she would find the snapshots that had been taken in London, and smile to herself when she saw the one with a pigeon on her head in Trafalgar Square. She never stopped talking and thinking about it.

Aelybryn remained the attractive prominent detached house at the top of the now extended road, which had also been renamed. Traffic was so much heavier nowadays, but not nearly as busy as all that traffic Martha had seen in London. Because Aelybryn was at the junction of a now busy crossroads, it was not surprising that a number of accidents occurred outside Martha's home. The house almost became a first-aid post when there was a crash outside. Cars or lorries speeding down the hill, would often crash into each other, not heeding the "Stop" signs. There would be a loud noise, a bang, or the sound of skidding tyres. Martha would be prepared for a knock on her door and an injured person would be carried into her home and placed on her settee, until help came. She would often be asked if her telephone could be used to contact emergency services. Martha was glad that her home could serve some useful purpose to others in distress.

After returning from London, she thought it was time she

changed the will she and Mary had made years before, leaving everything to the surviving sister absolute. Now she wanted everything to be left to her nieces and nephew. She had chatted to Anne, Beth's youngest daughter, on the journey from London, and had told her what her intentions were. When they looked at the documents of the property, which she kept with other important papers in her little wooden box, they realised that her father had bought leasehold ground on which to build Aelybryn before she was born. Now that lease was running out. When enquiries were made to buy it, the cost was prohibitive. If they failed to find the money, the current landlord would reclaim the house. She would not only have nothing to leave, but no roof over her head. No home of her own, after all those years. Whatever would she do now? She could not sleep with worry. She simply had to remain in Aelybryn until she died, so she would have to find the money somehow. The family understood, no doubt having been born there and spent all her life there, it was natural she would never want to live elsewhere. Every room had its own memories for her. Some of her old customers had gone into an old people's home in the area which she visited regularly. Unlike them, she could still look after herself and she hated the thought of being restricted to mealtimes and anything else that took one's independence away. Her nieces told her there was only one solution for her. She would have to ask their father for the money. She hated the idea of asking Daniel for anything, let alone money. She knew he often felt she should have saved hers, instead of generously giving it away as she had done all her life. But her motto had always been "When my days of giving cease, my days of living cease".

Anne told her it was the only way out if she wanted to remain in Aelybryn. The family could not find the money;

therefore Martha took their advice and decided she would ask Daniel. As Anne had said, he now had plenty to buy it for her, but if it was necessary, the loan could be easily repaid when Aelybryn was sold after her days. The children tried to reassure her that, as their father had so much, it was unlikely that he would ever ask for it to be returned. Beth had always told her children how wonderful Mary and Martha had been when Daniel had bought the farm, giving him all they had at that time. They had never asked for the money to be returned because they never needed it. Beth had asked her children to always look after their aunts if she was not around to do so. Now they felt it was their father's turn to help his own sister out of a tricky situation and Beth was not there to ask him to do so. Martha was delighted at the prospect of having the money as a gift and not having to get her nieces and nephew to return the loan, so she eventually approached her brother who looked at her in disbelief.

"You've made a mistake, Martha. Our father bought freehold ground on which to build Aelybryn. There is no way he would buy leasehold ground. Let me see the papers."

"But I pay someone £4 a year for the rent. I always have done," she told him, producing the documents.

Martha was right. He had no choice but to help her. "You should have noticed before, woman. Now it will cost us so much more by your stupidity, but I can easily buy it for you. You are lucky I have plenty of money. I shan't miss it."

By 1986 Daniel had duly paid the exorbitant amount for the lease, so that the house was hers and in her name. She had a home once again, with a roof over her head and something to leave to her family. She was now so relieved and happy. All her worries were over, and each night she could sleep contentedly once again in her warm bed.

On October 4th 1989, just three years later, Daniel suffered a massive heart attack whilst digging the garden. Esther was waiting for the potatoes he was fetching in order for her to prepare the dinner. He died before the ambulance could reach the hospital.

Chapter 26

Martha was obviously shocked to receive the phone call from Esther to tell her the sad news that Daniel had died that afternoon. However she was always very philosophical about death and told herself that he had reached a good age and was so lucky to have had two good wives and two lovely children, even though they had been girls, not boys for the farm. The good news was that now the children would both inherit his estate and a very substantial amount of money which she knew both her nieces would welcome. She also knew Anne was longing to give up her job but had to continue because her husband's health had failed and he had been forced to take early retirement. She hoped that Daniel would have made some sort of provision for Esther of course, because she had been a very good wife to him after Beth had died and he had so much money he could ensure they were all happy.

"We have been left nothing, Aunt Martha," Anne told her angrily. "We both have to wait until Esther dies before we can touch anything. We both worked hard on the farm when we were young, and Mum worked so hard all those years, never having a holiday, and neither did we. Esther has enjoyed everything without having to work for any of it," she told Martha after the funeral was over. "I know she has been very kind and thoughtful towards us as a stepmother and has been a caring and loving wife to Daddy but that is not the point."

"Well, there is nothing we can do about it. We just have to make the best of it," Catherine continued with less anger in her voice. There was nothing Martha could do about it either. Daniel had always made up his own mind in life and he was obviously determined to do so, even in death. He had always had his own way since the day he was born, but she was sad to learn that even his car and eventually the house he had shared with Beth would have to be sold when Esther could no longer look after herself. If she had to go into a home for the aged, the proceeds from the estate and the interest would go towards keeping her there for the rest of her days. And for how long would that be?

Martha felt sad. She had loved Beth and knew that, without her, Daniel would never have been as successful as he had been on the farm. And where was Beth's share? Working so hard had counted for nothing. Also their children had not been able to enjoy privileges that many other children were able to enjoy when they were young. Martha was so glad they had been able to have them to live with them until the war was over. They were cherished years for all of them, when they could give them love and attention without having to earn it, and do things with them when their parents couldn't spare the time. Yes, Martha certainly felt somewhat sad at this time but kept her thoughts and feelings to herself.

"What a pity I am living so long," she told Anne. "Then you could sell Aelybryn and the ground and have some money now when you need it while it would be of greater use to you."

"No money could ever replace you, Aunt Martha. Because we have lost Mum, we want to keep you as long as we possibly can," she told her, putting both arms around her and hugging her.

Anne still felt very bitter about the whole thing. The estate money belonged to her mother as well as her father, but she had died with but ten shillings in her purse. The amount she possibly would have been worth when she had married their father all those years ago.

"Your mother often said money is of no value unless you have your health and your happiness," Martha told them, trying to comfort them. "And she was never happier than when she was on the farm with you children and working hard with her beloved Daniel. She adored your father too."

"Yes, but she would be very sad if she knew what he has done to us now. It could take years and years for us to have a penny, and it's not right that we should need to wait for such a lovely kind woman as Esther to die for us to have what we are entitled," Anne replied. Martha knew they were right of course to feel as they did, but she said no more on the subject. Nothing could change the situation or the will.

Within a year Martha began to have her old bouts of nausea returning, but she seemed to be so busy she had little time to worry about it. But after the summer of 1990 she had bouts of vomiting and began to lose weight. She was never hungry and lacked energy. The family realised there was something seriously wrong.

"You really must go and see the doctor," they told her, but she wouldn't hear of it. However in November, the vomiting continued day after day and Martha had to agree to let them send for the doctor.

"You will have to be admitted to hospital immediately," he told her.

"Oh don't take me to hospital. If I am going to die, I want to stay in Aelybryn and die here," she begged. But the doctor feared the cancer had now returned with a vengeance and eventually the pain would be unbearable if she remained at home. Drugs to alleviate it could be more easily administered and controlled if she was in hospital.

"It's only a temporary measure, Aunt Martha. As before, you will soon be home again," Anne lied comfortingly.

"Well, I must do what you think best."

Martha was admitted to hospital that same day. During one of the visiting times Martha slid a key into Anne's hand.

"It's the key to Rhys's bedroom. If I am to remain here for a while, I want you to keep it safe for me until I can go home again, and make sure no one touches my little wooden box either. It's all my private papers."

On Wednesday, November 28th 1990, within two weeks, Martha died peacefully at the age of eighty-seven years.

Chapter 27

After the death of her aunt, Anne drove immediately to Aelybryn from the hospital. She could not help thinking what the nurse had said to her on her last visit before her aunt had gone into a coma. Obviously she knew Martha was a spinster, it had said so on her notes. But the nurse had heard Martha whisper the name Rhys quite distinctly, and mentioned the fact to Anne.

"Was it the name of one of her brothers perhaps?"

"No," replied Anne, "her brothers were Daniel and John, both of whom are now dead."

Anne knew who Rhys was. He had lived in Aelybryn, and although they had called him "uncle", he had not been any relation to them. Anne often wondered where exactly he fitted in to the enigma of Aelybryn. She remembered being told that her Uncle John had brought him home with him, when the 1914-1918 war was over, because he did not have a home to go to. He had remained there until, she seemed to remember, he had committed suicide up in the dairy. It was all very mystifying and was never talked about by any of the family. Perhaps the key to his door had been on Martha's mind if she felt she would never return to Aelybryn. Anyway hopefully she was reunited with the rest of her family and all those she loved. That was what she deserved.

Anne quietly opened the front door of Aelybryn, as if Martha was still there asleep and she was afraid of waking her. It was such a strange feeling, entering the empty house. Soon she realised that Martha would never return. They would never have her back with them again. It was then she felt quite cold and a slight smell of mildew surrounded her, obviously caused by there being no central heating ever installed in Aelybryn and no electric fires switched on since Martha had gone into hospital. Her living room was always kept so warm, neat, clean and sparkling; she would often be seen polishing and dusting her furniture with pride. She simply loved her home and everything inside it.

"I have wonderful memories in every room in this house. That's why I never want to leave it," she had said emphatically. "I can go into each one, sit in a chair and daydream about all the happy times I had in each. When I look at the clock a whole hour may have passed. It is far more interesting than any book I could read."

But what of upstairs? No one had been up to the bedrooms for at least a year or so. Martha had slept downstairs for the latter part of her days at Aelybryn, in the parlour, which was situated directly underneath her own bedroom. Anne then ventured upstairs. Evan's room was almost bare but spotlessly clean, with just his iron bedstead remaining, having been cleared of any bedclothes. His old chair in which he used to sit, passing many hours up in the dairy, was alongside his bed. The wardrobe had been cleared and was empty, as was his chest of drawers. In the bathroom, clothes needing washing were in the bath. Martha had obviously struggled these past few months, but gave everyone the impression she was fine and was coping. The next room she went into was Martha's own bedroom. The bed was made and everything was neat and tidy as if she had only just popped out for a while. Anne walked back across the landing, fumbling in her handbag as she did so for the key that Martha had slipped into her hand, more than two weeks before. When she had called at Aelybryn the previous week, being in a hurry, she had only picked up the wooden box from under the stairs, which Martha had instructed her to collect in order that no one else laid their hands on it. She could not help but wonder why on earth it had been so important to her aunt, that she should look after the key to Rhys's bedroom? She looked back down the stairs at the carpet, now almost threadbare. It was the same carpet as when she and her sister had lived there during the war. But the colours were so bright then: red, orange and green. She saw those colours again now, so vividly in her mind, with the stair rods of brass, so brightly polished, you could almost see your reflection in them as you climbed the stairs. Now they were all tarnished, with some clips missing, and the regularly brown painted wood on either side of the runner now peeling away like the curls of wood shavings from a carpenter's plane. The colours in the carpet too were badly faded, as if covered by an artist's wash. She walked slowly towards Rhys's bedroom door with the key in her hand. Then she placed it carefully in the lock. She tried to turn it, but it was very stiff, as if the lock was completely rusted. After trying again a few times, she eventually went downstairs to find some oil which could possibly help. Yes, now she managed to turn the key. But the door still appeared to be jammed. It just would not move. She put all her weight behind it and pushed hard. At last she was able to force it open to peer inside. She gasped with horror at the sight before her. What was that awful smell that immediately seemed to attack her nostrils? She realised that nothing in that room had been touched for over thirty-eight years. In fact, she doubted Martha had ever been into it, since possibly locking it immediately after Rhys had committed suicide in 1952. The bed was just as he had left it. His pyjamas were still folded on the top of the faded counterpane, and everything was covered in thick dust. The bedclothes had rotted with age in such conditions, because the internal walls were wet with condensation and now droplets of water slowly trickled down over them. She supposed it could have been due to missing slates in the roof which her father had been anxious to have replaced but failed to get Martha to heed his advice at the time. Eventually the roof had been left for years without repair. During the past months there had been heavy rain, but what of the past thirty-seven years, with no form of heating and no ventilation in that room? The wallpaper on the walls dropped down over the bed forming drapes, like those found around a four-poster bed. On the other walls, the paper dropped to the floorboards in sheets, almost as if they were waiting to be pasted and rehung. The room smelt heavily of mildew and everything she touched felt cold and damp. But Anne could also smell this rank, unhealthy odour which she could not identify. As she ventured inside a little farther, her foot went through the rotten floorboards beneath, which were full of woodworm and quite unsafe to tread. She looked across at the window that was covered by a wooden slatted venetian blind, tilted so as to let in the minimal amount of light. It was covered in thick layers of dust. Dead flies crusted the windowsill and moths began to fly around her. Woodlice ran from the skirting boards as if checking who was disrupting this quiet and undisturbed abode of theirs. She ventured across the rotten floorboards very carefully. She noticed a drawstring hanging down from the blind, pulling on it so as to let in some light. As she did so, the cord snapped, and the whole blind fell crashing to the floor with a loud bang, frightening her out of her wits. The curtains were completely faded and were rotten, falling on top of her as she tried to draw them across. She had hardly touched them. Now she was covered in dust as if she had been caught in a sandstorm. Cobwebs hung everywhere like Christmas decorations, from the central light fitting to the corners of the ceiling. Spiders ran to and fro, as if they too did not like being disturbed. This had been such a peaceful environment for them for so long.

It was obviously quite dangerous to tread anywhere. There was a small kidney shaped dressing table, under which lay tiny piles of fine yellowish powder, the work of the woodworm beetles as they burrowed their way through the wood. She surely had to be dreaming? This could not possibly be real. It was the sort of thing one read about in books. Then she noticed a table, alongside the wardrobe, both of which were thickly covered with dust. There was a pile of leather-bound books, neatly stacked on the table. The complete works of Charles Dickens. Her eyes caught sight of the one on top of the pile, which was entitled "Great Expectations". Her mind went back to her schooldays, when she had read it. She immediately realised this room was just how she would have imagined Miss Haversham's to have been. Now she realised how Pip must have felt, going into a room that had been left untouched for years and years. But that was fiction. This was 1990, and what she was seeing was fact, real, though almost unbelievable.

Thank God there was no food in this room to attract mice. Miss Haversham's wedding cake, she remembered reading, had mice running through it. But when she looked towards the hearth, where the fireplace stood, she saw the carcasses of two dead birds. They had obviously come down the chimney, heaven knows when, and could not get out. They must have tried hard to find an exit, and had flown around, hitting the blinds of the window and the walls, with their beaks, and had left bloodstains, long since dried, forming dark red spots. Eventually they would have starved to death and rotted there.

When she opened the wardrobe door, the plywood of which was riddled with woodworm holes, she could see, hanging up inside, Rhys's army uniform and overcoat from the 1914-1918 war. The moths had fed on them for all those years and they looked more like fabric colanders. The brass buttons, which no doubt many years before when he had been discharged from the Army, had been brightly polished and stood out like bulging frog's eyes, were now all tarnished, some hanging on by a single thread; others were missing altogether. She then realised they must have been hanging there for seventy years. Why had no one ever thrown them out, or disposed of them during all those years? Anne could not remain there any longer. She carefully carried the Dickens books out of the bedroom, although the covers were spotted with mildew and all the pages looked as though they had stuck together with the damp. She remembered Rhys talking to her aunts about them during their stay with them at Aelybryn before the end of the Second World War. She remembered Martha telling Rhys it had been a fascinating book to read. Anne knew then she wanted to keep these books. She would take them home with her, because it was a part of Martha's past. When she reached the car which was parked outside she looked up at the bare window where the blind had once been, hiding light from the room and everything that lay beyond it. Often people stopped and looked up at Aelybryn, admiring that unique, dressed stone, detached house built at the top of the hill. Passers-by could never have imagined what an extraordinary scene lay behind that ordinary-looking window. But no one would ever see inside that room again. She put all the books on to the back seat, returning immediately to the house. She quickly marched upstairs, carefully relocked the door and put the key safely into her handbag. She vowed that door would never be opened again. She would make certain of that.

The house was immediately condemned and certified as unfit for human habitation, eventually being completely demolished. Bulldozers crushed its structure to the ground and all that remained was rubble, but nothing could crush or obliterate all the memories that Aelybryn left behind.

Epilogue

2006

It had stopped snowing outside and the light was now fading. All that remained of the fire was a heap of embers and white ash. The logs looked like layers of burnt wafer biscuits, giving off little warmth. I had allowed the fire to burn out while I was being carried away by the past. The fire would now have to be relit once again for my evening's comfort, as the temperature outside was below zero.

The Dickens books were still there on the shelf in front of me, and the faces in the two brass frames, those of Mary and Martha, continued to gaze lovingly down at me. I was still sitting comfortably in the old Parker Knoll chair which Martha had been given on her retirement and which I had inherited. Why had the old grandfather clock from Aelybryn not chimed? Then I realised that I had forgotten to rewind it the night before. Had I remembered to do so, its loud chimes would have disturbed my daydreaming and immediately brought me back to the present.

After Martha's death, a brown envelope was handed to the family from her bank. It had been retained by them until after her death. It was an IOU from her brother Daniel who had died twelve months before her. The money he had given her to purchase her freehold, such a generous gesture we all thought, in order for his sister to own her own home once again was to be returned after her death. It carried with it the demand for a high interest rate on the borrowed amount, to be paid into his estate which would benefit Esther, for her lifetime. The family were all so grateful that Martha died thinking the money had been a gift from her brother after all as he had not mentioned the loan in his will when he died. She had been so thrilled about that outcome.

Esther lived in a home for the aged for another eight years after Daniel's death, and where she died peacefully in 1999. She proved to be a very caring and humble lady, thoughtful and unselfish. Even if she had known what Daniel intended to do in his will, she could never have persuaded him to act differently. Daniel did what he wanted to do and always had done. He was a law unto himself and continually had all his own way. I was his younger daughter Anne, and no one knew him better than I.

The estate money was eventually released after Esther's death and at last this cottage, for which I had waited so long, was purchased with the proceeds.

To write this story I have used the contents of Martha's wooden box from her home which contained many old and interesting documents dating back to 1889, helping me to piece together a number of unexplained details and true facts. Also inside the box were carefully kept wills, records of births, marriages and deaths of all the family, but I could not find Rhys's death certificate. There were a number of old postcards from him. These had been sent from different parts of the country, when he had left Aelybryn to learn his trade. They had all been carefully wrapped in brown paper. There was also an official photograph of Martha and Rhys, at the bottom of the box. They were smiling and both looked so happy. Underneath was another small brown envelope. Inside was the last letter Rhys had written to Martha before he had taken his own life.

The story I have written is based on Martha's life, partly how I imagined it to be and partly using my own personal experiences. It all happened a long time ago, therefore some of the facts may have been distorted during the retelling of them to me. The names of some of the characters have also been changed, but my family look back on Martha's life, not with sadness but with humble gratitude, because she taught us so much. She was like the sun; she gave us so much of her warmth. She steadfastly held on to what she believed in, no matter what the cost. She set us all an example, but she was someone none of us could hope to emulate. No one ever knew what Martha really felt. She kept her thoughts and feelings to herself. Despite everything that I was told, I am always convinced that she truly loved Rhys Hopkins very deeply during her lifetime, but that duty and a promise had come before all else. Her life could so easily have been very different, but that was how she had chosen it to be.

After Aelybryn was totally demolished, Aelybryn Court, a block of flats for the elderly, was erected in its place. Martha would have been very proud of that. The block still stands there today.

Acknowledgements

I am greatly indebted to the late Bryan Thompson who was my friend and critic, and who chose the title for me. He read the last draft from his hospital bed, but unfortunately did not live to see the book published. To Penny Vincenzi whom I met in Gower and who encouraged me to begin writing a book. I would like to thank Barbara Williams originally from Swansea, for all her support and encouragement over the years. To Hilary Williams of Llanishen Golf Club, Cardiff, who put me in touch with Wild Cherry Press. To all the Ladies Section of the Golf Club, who encouraged me weekly during my highs and lows, an inevitability when writing a book. To the Cardiff General Library who allowed me hours of browsing through old newspapers. To the late Dylan Thomas , author of "A Child's First Christmas" who had aunts similar to my own. To the Wild Cherry Press team. To my family, especially Sara, who dealt with and sent all my e-mails and to my husband Alan, who always believed I could write a book and made me endless cups of coffee when I was burning the midnight oil trying to finish it. Last but not least to all my friends in Swansea who have kept closely involved with me during this frustrating time of getting my book into print.